Scarborough Fair

MARGARITA MORRIS

This novel is a work of fiction and, except in the case of historical fact, any resemblance to actual persons, living or dead, is purely coincidental.

Margarita Morris asserts the moral right to be identified as the author of this work.

Published by Margarita Morris at CreateSpace.

Cover design by L1graphics at 99designs.com

http://margaritamorris.com

ISBN: **1530046432**
ISBN-13: **978-1530046430**

For Thomas and Oliver

CONTENTS

Every man is the architect of his own fortune.
Early 16th century. (Oxford Dictionary of Quotations)

~~~

Men at some time are masters of their fates:
The fault, dear Brutus, is not in our stars,
But in ourselves, that we are underlings.
Shakespeare: Julius Caesar; Act 1, Scene 2.

~~~

Are you going to Scarborough Fair?
Parsley, sage, rosemary and thyme.
Remember me to one who lives there,
She once was a true love of mine.
Traditional English ballad..

PROLOGUE

19th August, 1899

I am not insane. I was brought here under false pretences. Henry told Dr Collins that I am delusional, that I had tried to harm myself. He showed Dr Collins the wound on my arm, saying that it was self-inflicted and that I would have done worse if he, Henry, had not been there to prevent it. He always likes to portray himself as the hero, a knight in shining armour, when in truth he is nothing but a deadly serpent, full of lies and rotten to the core. I tried to protest but was too shocked, and weak from the loss of blood and I fear I may have come across as confused and incoherent which did not help my case.

"You have done the right thing in bringing her to us," said Dr Collins to Henry in what seemed to me a conspiratorial manner. The doctor, a balding man with a pointed nose and penetrating eyes, regarded me with curiosity as if I were a specimen in a museum. "We will see that she receives the very best medical care. However, the mind is a delicate organ and I should warn you that her treatment may take some time."

"Take as long as you need," said Henry. "My only wish

is that she should be returned to me in full health and in possession of her wits."

Doctor Collins started explaining to Henry the latest techniques that he would use in my treatment. I understood little of what he said. It was the words "returned to me" that struck a note of dread in my heart. I was Henry's possession and he would have me back once I had been brought to heel. My own wishes were of no consequence.

Doctor Collins picked up a little brass bell from his desk and rang it vigorously. Moments later two stout-looking women in nurses' uniforms entered the room. Fishwives, the pair of them, they both had strong arms, rough hands and unsmiling faces.

"Nurse Barrett, Nurse Cooper," said Dr Collins, addressing each of them in turn. "Please admit Miss Hawthorne to the women's ward."

As the nurses approached, I roused myself from my stupor. "You can't do this to me!" I shouted at Henry, but my voice came out more like a whimper.

"It's for your own good, Alice," he said, turning his back on me and staring out of the window.

The nurses took hold of my upper arms, one on each side of me. The wound on my left arm throbbed painfully at Nurse Cooper's tight grip. They pulled me to my feet. I tried to resist but they were too strong for me.

"I hate you," I hissed at Henry as the nurses dragged me away. Henry refused to turn around or even acknowledge that he had heard me.

The nurses led me down the corridor and up a flight of stairs to the bathroom, a cold, tiled room with a row of sinks along one wall and three bath tubs lined up on the opposite side. I had never before seen a bathroom more lacking in privacy.

"Ge' yer togs off," said Nurse Barrett. She spoke in an abrupt Yorkshire dialect and when I looked at her questioningly she pulled at my clothes so that I understood she expected me to undress. Shocked by this request, I hesitated. She clucked her tongue in impatience and went to unfasten the buttons on the back of my dress.

I recoiled from her touch, but Nurse Cooper held me firm by the shoulders. "I've 'eld down lasses bigger'n you," she said, "so you can stop yer faffin'." I stared at her in fright.

Nurse Barrett yanked at the buttons of my gown, not caring if she tore the fabric. One of the buttons popped off and rolled away into a corner. Between them they pulled the black dress over my head and tossed it on the floor.

"Ooh, ge' a gander a' that," said Nurse Cooper, fingering the jet necklace that hung around my neck. It had been hidden under my gown so not even Henry had noticed it. *Especially not him.* "'Ow much di' tha' cost yer? From a fancy man, were it?" I tried to swat her hand away from my neck, but she grabbed hold of my wrists, gripping them so hard that I winced. "Take it off," she said to Nurse Barrett. Nurse Barrett undid the clasp and dropped the necklace onto the floor next to the dress. I suppressed a sob. I didn't want these women to know how much that necklace meant to me.

With my dress off, the wound on my upper arm was now revealed in all its goriness. The blood had spread onto my chemise and stained the white cotton a deep red colour. "We'll 'ave to burn this shimmy," said Nurse Barrett, pulling the fabric off the wound where it had stuck and causing a fresh trickle of blood to run down my arm. Neither nurse was concerned to tend to the wound itself.

Nurse Cooper went to the nearest bath tub and turned on the taps. There was a sharp sound of metal grinding against metal and then water spluttered into the tub with a deep-throated gurgling noise as if it was being drawn from the belly of the building.

"Ge' yer kegs off," commanded Nurse Barrett, folding her arms across her ample chest. This time I understood her only too well. She expected me to remove my underclothes. "What?" she scoffed. "Y'ain't shy are yer?"

I glanced at the door, which they'd left ajar. For a brief moment I saw myself making a run for it, but where could I go dressed in nothing but my drawers, corset and chemise?

"Flippin' 'eck," said Nurse Barrett, losing patience. She untied my corset, dragged the chemise over my head, and ripped off my bloomers and stockings. I was shaking more from shock and humiliation than from the cold. I hung my head, covering my face with my hands.

"Get in't tub," said Nurse Cooper.

I stepped gingerly into the water. I needn't have worried about it being too hot. It was barely lukewarm. I gasped in surprise as Nurse Cooper's rough hands pushed me down into the water. "Righ' under," she said, forcing me down beneath the surface. I struggled against her hands, thinking she meant to drown me, but she let go immediately and I came up spluttering and choking.

"On yer feet," ordered Nurse Cooper. I stood, shivering, and she handed me a thin bar of rock-hard carbolic soap. "Cover thissen in that."

I rubbed the soap in my hands, trying in vain to produce a decent lather. My hands shook so badly that more than once I dropped the soap and had to fish for it in the rapidly cooling water. My only thought was, the sooner I get this bath over, the better. When I was covered in a thin lather from my shoulders to my knees, Nurse Cooper picked up a long-handled brush and scrubbed me as if she were spring cleaning the pantry. I winced as the brush skimmed over the torn flesh of my arm. She pushed me under the water one more time to rinse off, but this time I was ready for her, holding my breath and squeezing my eyes tight shut.

"That weren't so bad, were it?" said Nurse Barrett, as I stepped, dripping, onto the cold, tiled floor. I could have sworn she was laughing at me. She rubbed me dry with a threadbare towel, then went over to a row of lockers and came back with a pile of clothing.

"I'm not wearing that," I said, staring aghast at the coarsely woven, blue smock dress that she held in her hands.

"Ooh, 'oity-toity," said Nurse Cooper. "Yeh'll wear wha' yer given and stop yer mitherin'." She handed me a pair of greying bloomers from the pile. "Or yeh can go round in yer birthday suit. Tha'll give the male patients summat to talk 'bout." They both laughed at her cruel joke and I felt myself colouring. All the clothes were too big for me but that didn't seem to matter to the nurses. Nurse Cooper pulled the shapeless, woollen dress over my head and handed me a pair of black boots to wear. Then they each took hold of an elbow and walked me up another flight of stairs and down a corridor, unlocking and locking doors behind them as we went.

We came to a large room with a dozen beds in it, six along one wall and six along the opposite side. The room was full of women, all wearing identical clothes to the ones I had been given. Some were sitting on their beds, not doing anything; one was marching up and down the centre of the room, talking to herself. When she saw me being brought in she shouted at the top of her voice, "Ooh, a new lady. Looks like she thinks she's the Queen of Sheba!" A few of the women sitting on the beds lifted their heads to look at me, but most of them just ignored her.

"Tha's yer bed," said Nurse Barrett, pointing to an empty bed in the corner of the room. They exchanged a few words with the nurse in charge of the dormitory, then they left me there. The woman who was talking to herself came over and prodded me on the shoulder. "What's wrong with you?" she asked.

"Nothing," I said.

"That's what they all say," she said. She laughed in a high-pitched cackle before resuming her pacing.

I curled up on the bed and turned my back on them all.

This is where I am now. I must escape from this place by whatever means. Or die trying.

CHAPTER ONE

Present Day

Rose stretched and yawned, staring out of the car window at the miles of endless countryside spread out under an ominously grey sky. It was just her and her mum in the car and topics of conversation, mostly to do with school and what her friends were doing this summer, had dried up barely twenty minutes into the journey, before they were even out of London and on the motorway.

Rose had no wish to be reminded of her friends' holiday plans, it only made the prospect of her own summer seem even more dismal. Kate would be sunning herself on the gloriously hot Amalfi coast and attracting oodles of attention from gorgeous Romeo types eager to lavish her with platefuls of Italian food. Holly would be zooming around New York in one of those yellow taxis, eating bagels and taking selfies from the top of the Empire State Building. As for Joe, well at least he was getting to stay in London and could hang out and have a good time. Go to a club, hear a gig.

Meet other girls.

Stop it, she told herself. Just because their last date had been a bit tense, didn't mean it was over between them, did it? They'd been going out for six months and during that time had had a lot of fun together. It was only in the last couple of weeks that Rose had detected a coolness which she had put down to the pressure of exams. She had assumed it would disappear once the exams were out of the way, but it hadn't and that worried her. For what must be the hundredth time that journey she tapped the screen of her phone to see if she still had a signal. She did. So why hadn't he replied to any of her last three texts? Was he just busy or was he deliberately ignoring her? A knot of anxiety tightened in the pit of her stomach.

At the roundabout, take the first turning on the left.

The calm tones of the female SatNav voice jolted Rose back to the present. They'd been on the same road for absolutely ages, stuck behind a tractor for the last five miles. Andrea, her mother, was the sort of driver who never risked overtaking on country roads even though other vehicles had overtaken them *and* the tractor. It drove Rose mad and had accounted in large part for the silence that had descended. It was saying something when the SatNav was the chattiest person in the car.

"Nearly there," said her mum. She sounded like she was trying hard to be upbeat, but Rose could hear the tiredness in her voice. Well, that was hardly surprising after all this driving. Over five hours so far, due to endless roadworks on the motorway and slow-moving farm vehicles on the country roads. A quick glance at the SatNav perched on the dashboard told Rose they still had another forty minutes to go. Hardly *nearly there.*

They had *escaped* London - her mum always talked of *escaping* London as if it was a prison and not one of the most exciting cities in the world - at eight o'clock that morning after loading the car with enough stuff to see them through the whole summer in Scarborough, some two hundred and fifty miles away on the North Yorkshire coast. Andrea had wanted to set off early so she could "take her time" with the driving. "Now that your father isn't here..." she'd said, her voice still tinged with bitterness.

Rose had noticed that ever since the divorce, Dad had become *your father* as if Rose was somehow responsible for what he got up to. Not that he was showing many signs of being responsible for *her*. By now he'd be somewhere in the south of France with Shona, his new girlfriend. The invitation for Rose to join them (from Shona) had been so half-hearted that Rose had declined it without hesitation. So here she was with her mum on their way to her gran's house, the option of Rose staying behind in London being, in her mum's words, *unthinkable*.

"First one to see the sea!" said her mother in her best jolly aren't-we-having-fun voice.

"Mu-um! For goodness sake, I'm *sixteen*, not six."

"Sorry," said her mother, making Rose feel bad that she wasn't more enthusiastic about this holiday. As a little girl, going to her gran's house at the seaside had been the best thing ever: building sandcastles with a bright red bucket and spade; donkey rides; humongous amounts of ice cream; paddling in the sea. And, was it just her rose-tinted memory, but hadn't the weather always been hot and sunny when she was little?

They arrived in the town just as it started to drizzle, a thin grey rain that looked like the harbinger of something more serious. *Marvellous,* thought Rose, regarding her shorts, bare legs and flip-flops. *Welcome to the great British summer!* In the rain, the red-brick Victorian terraces and corner shops looked even more drab and worn than Rose remembered them. They passed a laundromat and a grimy-looking tattoo parlour offering a *two for the price of one* sale on body piercings. The cinema was showing a film that Rose had seen in London two months ago. What on earth was she going to do for six whole weeks here?

In the past Gran had come down to London in the summer and looked after Rose whilst her mother went out to work at the solicitor's where she was the secretary and indispensable chief organiser. But this year Andrea was taking the whole summer off whilst the offices were being refurbished and had insisted that they spend the time in Scarborough. Rose loved her grandmother dearly and was looking forward to seeing her, but having Gran visit them in London meant she could still see her friends and get on with her life.

Still no text from Joe.

"Now, Gran isn't going to be up to much," said her mother as if she was talking to an unruly child. "So don't go wearing her out."

"Of course not," said Rose.

"She had a nasty fall last month. She was lucky she didn't break anything. I'm going to try to persuade her to come and live with us in London. At her age she needs keeping an eye on and I can't do that very well when she's all the way up here."

"Do you think she'll agree?" asked Rose. Her grandmother knew her own mind and wasn't afraid to make her opinions known. That was one of the things Rose loved best about her.

"We shall see," said her mother through gritted teeth.

Uh-oh, thought Rose, *I sense a battle coming.*

They turned into Tollergate. It was a peculiarity in these parts that *gate* meant *street.* Tollergate was a steeply descending street of small terraced houses, a short distance from the headland. Her grandmother had lived here for the past sixty years, and Rose's mother had grown up here. Rose liked the quaintness of Tollergate with its narrow pavement, cobbled road and old houses, painted in pastel shades of pink and cream, but Andrea frowned. "These streets were not built for cars," she said, shifting down to first gear in order to negotiate the steep descent.

Andrea parked the car round the back and turned off the engine. "Well, here we are," she said. A seagull landed on the bonnet of the car and screeched its noisy welcome before lurching off into the storm-filled skies.

~~~

Heads…Right again!

He must be psychic or something. He should have set himself up on the sea-front as a fortune teller. He'd be raking it in by now instead of being stuck here in the booth at his dad's amusement arcade being paid less than the minimum wage. *You're family*, his dad had said, as if that made all the difference. On the other hand, thought Dan, maybe being a fortune teller was not such a great idea. He didn't think the hooped earrings would suit him.

For the last half hour he'd been idly spinning coins to see if he could guess which way they would fall. Heads or tails. Fifty-fifty chance of getting it right or wrong. So far he was right about sixty percent of the time, so he was beating the odds, which was more than those poor sods at the fruit machines were doing. Every few minutes one of them would feed more pound coins into the machines that dispensed change so they could have another go, convinced that if they kept at it they would eventually strike lucky and hit the jackpot. Didn't they realise those machines were rigged?

A little kid who'd won a batch of yellow tickets in the penny drop machine came up to the counter with his dad to claim his prize. He had his eye on one of the teddy bears lined up against the back wall of the booth, but he didn't have enough points for one of those and had to choose between a crummy plastic keyring or four chocolate mice. He chose the chocolate mice. A sensible decision in Dan's opinion.

It was depressing working here. Growing up, his mates had envied him. Taken in by the pounding music and the flashing lights, the amusement arcade had seemed to them like a place of glamour and excitement, somewhere fortunes were made, a tiny bit of Las Vegas on the
~~~

otherwise dull and slightly tacky sea-front of this faded Victorian resort. And Dan had loved it too once, when he was too young to know better. But then he'd learnt to recognise the signs of gambling addiction, the way some people compulsively thrust coin after coin into the slot machines until they had nothing left. Plus his dad had let him in on the secret of how the machines were designed to pay out much less than they took in. He'd realised people were living in a fool's paradise if they thought the arcade was a place they might get rich and that had taken the shine off it. This year his mates were off camping in Scotland whilst he was stuck here. He still had two years of school left, but next summer he intended to go backpacking once he'd saved up enough money. For now he had no choice but to do this job and lump it.

A shadow fell across the booth and Dan looked up. Two men were leaning against the counter in a way that put Dan on his guard. There was something quietly threatening in their attitude. They looked to be in their twenties, maybe early thirties. One of them was short and thick-set with a neck like a bulldog and a nose that looked like it had been broken on numerous occasions. The other was tall and thin with a spider tattoo that covered the left side of his neck and extended up to his jawline. Both of them had close-cropped hair and about three days' worth of stubble. If this was a raid then they were going to be disappointed; they didn't keep that much cash behind the counter, unless it was chocolate mice they were after. If it was money these guys wanted they'd be better off trying to nick one of the slot machines. The short bloke looked like he could lift one of the newer machines on his own.

"Can I help you?" asked Dan, trying to keep his voice level. *They're probably just holidaymakers,* he told himself although somehow he didn't believe it.

"We're looking for Ryan," said the man with the tattoo. He spoke with a distinct Geordie accent, marking him out as coming from Newcastle. It sounded more like *Luke-ing for Ryan.*

Ryan was Dan's dad and Dan didn't have a clue where he was right now. He certainly wasn't in the amusement arcade, that was for sure, having left Dan to man the fort two hours ago. His dad was getting increasingly good at these disappearing acts. But even if he knew where his dad was, he didn't think he'd be inclined to tell these two. He wasn't normally one to judge by appearances but if these two were just regular dudes then he was the Dalai Lama.

"He's not here at the moment," said Dan, trying to sound authoritative and, to his ears, failing miserably.

The men scowled.

"Shall I tell him you called?"

"Aye, do that," said the fat bloke. Another Geordie.

"What are your names?"

"Just tell him Max wants to see him. He'll know who that is," said the guy with the tattoo.

"Got it."

Dan watched the retreating backs of the pair as they sauntered out of the arcade. *God, what a couple of jerks.* Dan didn't know anyone called Max, but then his dad's business activities were a mystery to him most of the time. He picked up a pen and wrote a big red "M" on the back of his hand as a reminder. Then he went back to spinning coins.

~~~

"Hello, Gran," said Rose, hugging her grandmother tight. Rose loved the way her grandmother always smelt of lavender and Pears soap.

"Goodness, you've grown," said her grandmother. It was true. She'd shot up in the last year and was now towering over the old lady. "Still as skinny as a rake though! We'll have to get some fish and chips inside you."

Andrea ran inside with the last of the bags from the car and added them to the pile that had accumulated on the
~~~

floor in the back room.

"Goodness," said Rose's grandmother. "It looks like you're staying for good."

"Well you never know what the weather's going to be like here," said Andrea, shaking the rain from her hair as if to prove a point.

"I'll put the kettle on. You look like you need a cuppa."

"No, you sit down. I'll do it."

"I'm perfectly capable of making a cup of tea, Andrea. It's just a light sprain, that's all."

Rose looked at the bandage around her grandmother's right wrist. She was also sporting a real shiner on her right eye. "Why don't I do it?" said Rose, stepping around the bags and moving into the kitchen that overlooked the small backyard. Anything to get away from her mother and grandmother if they were going to start bickering.

By the time Rose took three mugs of strong Yorkshire tea into the tiny front room, her mother was already saying how the steep staircase in the cottage was no good for someone her gran's age and she should really think about coming to live with them in London where they could keep an eye on her. They hadn't been there five minutes and already her mother was lecturing Gran on taking better care of herself. *Gran will give as good as she gets though,* thought Rose, *that's for sure.*

"Thank you dear," said her grandmother, taking the offered mug of tea and giving Rose a wink that Andrea couldn't see. Rose suppressed a laugh. The trouble with Andrea was that she was such a worrier. Rose felt a strong solidarity with her grandmother. They would have to stand united against her mother's constant onslaught of concern. She sat down cross-legged on the floor by her grandmother's feet, sipped her tea and tried to tune out the conversation that had suddenly turned into a blow-by-blow account of the roadworks on the motorway.

By the time Rose had finished her tea the rain had stopped and a weak, watery sunlight was filtering through the window.

"I think I'll go for a walk," she said, jumping to her feet. "If you don't need me right now?"

"Well..." said her mother.

"I think that's a super idea," said her grandmother, interrupting whatever objection her daughter was going to come up with. "In Scarborough you have to make the most of it when the sun comes out. You don't want to be cooped up in here all the time."

"Thanks Gran," said Rose. "I won't be long."

"Take as long as you like."

Rose kissed her grandmother on the cheek and stepped outside. The cobbles still glistened from the rain but the sun was warm on her face.

She set off down the hill, pulling her mobile phone from her back pocket as she went. Still nothing from Joe. Why wasn't he getting in touch? She couldn't very well send him a *fourth* text without making herself look pathetic and needy and she didn't want to do that. Maybe she'd overdone it already with three texts. But the first two had just been chatty, *Hi, how's it going?* type of texts. Only the last one had had a hint of resentment (*So where are you?*) about it.

She passed a shop called *Krystal's Charms* that had dreamcatchers hanging in the doorway. The precious gemstones in the window were accompanied by handwritten notices promising *Inner Calm* and *Powerful Healing*. Next door was a traditional sweet shop piled high with pink sticks of rock, the shouts of small children clamouring for sweets detracting from the *Inner Calm* on sale next door. On the other side of the street was a joke shop painted in primary colours with the words *Jokes, Wigs, Magic and Toys* picked out in 3-D capitals. *This place is such a time warp,* thought Rose. *Bet they still sell Kiss-me-Quick hats.*

She turned the corner onto the sea-front which was chock-a-block with shops selling buckets and spades, postcards, wind-breakers, dinghies and inflatable dolphins.

What she really needed to find was a café with Internet access where she'd be able to use her laptop. If one thing was going to make six weeks in Scarborough tolerable, it would be access to the Internet.

~~~

Dan handed over to Dave, the bloke who did the evening shift at the arcade. He was glad to be out of there. It was in the evening that things could get rowdy. He was just pulling on his jacket when he heard the roar of an engine outside. His dad had come to pick him up. In the Ferrari.

"Enjoy the ride," said Dave, waving him off.

"If only," said Dan.

Ryan strode into the building, mirrored shades reflecting the flashing lights of the slot machines. *Why does Dad have to dress like an ageing rocker?* Ryan had on a too-tight pair of black jeans and a leather jacket with the collar turned up. He'd let his hair grow and had recently started experimenting with a goatee. *Is he having a mid-life crisis or what?*

"All right, son?" said Ryan, slapping Dan on the upper arm in an attempt at *cool* but which just felt awkward. "How was business today?"

"Same as always."

"Lots of punters?"

"I guess." Dan hadn't been counting.

"Right, come on then," said Ryan. "Need to get going. Lots of stuff to do."

Outside, a crowd of chip-munching holidaymakers had gathered to admire the sleek lines, shiny red bodywork and plush leather interior of the Ferrari 458 Spider which was parked half on the road and half on the pavement despite the double-yellow lines.

"Excuse me," said Dan, shouldering his way through the crowd of spectators and climbing into the passenger
~~~

seat. Of course, Ryan had to have the roof down, so now everyone was staring at Dan as he sat there. He fastened his seat belt and tried to ignore the stares by checking for messages on his mobile phone. Ryan climbed into the driver's seat, adjusted his shades and pulled sharply away from the curb in a thunderous roar of 570 horsepower.

"Oh, by the way Dad, two men came looking for you today. A couple of Geordies. They said someone called Max wants to see you."

The effect on his dad's driving was immediate. At the mention of Max's name, Ryan gripped the steering wheel so that the whites of his knuckles showed and pressed his foot down hard on the accelerator, over-revving the engine. They spun round the corner, tyres burning. Dan was thrown backwards and to the side by the force of the acceleration. Something about Newton's Laws of Motion from school physics lessons flashed through his mind.

"Watch out!" shouted Dan. A girl, eyes glued to her mobile phone, was just about to step off the pavement. She jumped back in the nick of time, eyes wide with shock, and shouted something rude. *Bloody hell,* thought Dan, *that was close.* All his friends thought the Ferrari was super-cool, but sometimes Dan wished his dad just drove a regular hatchback like ordinary people.

"So who's Max?" ventured Dan when the car had slowed to a speed that was only one and a half times the speed limit instead of two and a half times.

"No one you need to worry about." Ryan jumped a red light. It was beyond Dan how his dad still managed to own a driving licence.

"Those guys looked quite rough to me."

No response.

Whatever, thought Dan. He hated it when his father still treated him like a child, cutting him out of things. Dan figured that if he was old enough to work in the arcade then he was old enough to be treated like an adult.

They drove the rest of the way in silence, Ryan taking

the bends up Oliver's Mount as if he was on the circuit at Le Mans. Dan clutched the door handle and shut his eyes. The face of that girl, the one they'd nearly killed, flashed before his eyes. He'd only glimpsed her for a split second, but when someone looks as if they're about to die, it kind of makes an impression on you. She'd been pretty, despite the look of terror in her eyes: slim, dark hair in a loose pony-tail. He'd recognise her if he saw her again and if he did he'd apologise for his dad's crappy driving.

Ryan swung the car into the gravel driveway and pulled up sharply in front of the Victorian villa, making the tyres screech. He crunched the handbrake as he yanked it upwards. Dan opened his eyes and breathed out. He was still in one piece. His dad must have ninety-nine lives or something, never having had an accident and never getting caught by the police for his numerous violations of the Highway Code. Some people were just lucky, Dan supposed.

Ryan was already out of the car, leaping up the front steps two at a time. Dan had never seen him so agitated. He followed his father into the house just in time to see Ryan disappearing into his office, slamming the door behind him.

Dan wandered into the kitchen and helped himself to a can of Coke from the fridge. He was starving but his mother was nowhere to be seen and there was no sign of anything cooking for tea. She was probably at the health club again, getting herself pampered. It was all she ever did these days, that and redecorate the house. If she wasn't at the health spa improving herself, she was hiring teams of builders to improve their sprawling Victorian villa, never satisfied with the décor, as if happiness were to be found in a subtler shade of paint or a new kitchen counter. But what was the point of having a flashy kitchen if you never cooked in it? Dan wished now he'd bought some fish and chips when he was in town. He pulled open the freezer door and hunted for a pizza.

~~~

Rose bought herself the biggest ice cream she could find (chocolate chip with a chocolate flake) and took it down to the beach. She reckoned she deserved a treat after that near-miss with *Death*. Her heart was still pounding five minutes after she'd almost been mown down by that crazy idiot of a driver. She needed some chocolate to calm her nerves, the more the better. That car was pretty easy to spot so if she saw it around again she'd give the driver one hell of a mouthful and it wouldn't be pretty to listen to.

She licked the ice cream and sighed. She didn't want to be here; Joe still hadn't texted her; she'd nearly been killed by a lunatic driver; her mother was clearly going to get on everyone's nerves; and a seagull was making aggressive moves to steal her chocolate flake. Things couldn't get much worse.
~~~

CHAPTER TWO

Grand Hotel,
Scarborough,
7pm, 12th August, 1899

Dearest Susan,

We have arrived safely at our destination and are comfortably installed in Scarborough's Grand Hotel. I wish you could have joined us, dear sister, but I understand you have a duty to your husband and must remain in London. However, I am grateful to have Mary with me and I feel we shall be more like friends on this trip than mistress and maid.

Doctor Bradshaw was very wise to recommend a spell at the seaside. Already I feel easier in my mind and I breathed more calmly with every mile that the train carried me away from London. No doubt the oppression and anxiety that have plagued me of late are nothing more than pre-wedding nerves. I do not mind admitting to you, sister, that recently I have been suffering from terrible nightmares and waking in the middle of the night with a thumping heart. As I say, pre-wedding nerves, no doubt, which the sea air will hopefully dispel. I hope Henry will understand, although I fear he does not look kindly on what he calls "feminine foibles."

But enough of my troubles. Let me tell you about Scarborough. We took a carriage from the railway station to the Grand Hotel and as we rounded a corner there was the sea, an endless stretch of glittering blue. I thought my heart would explode! How I would love to board a ship and sail far away to some distant land. But I am becoming fanciful, something which Henry deplores! I will have to suppress these urges when I am married, but for now I hope I may be permitted a little day-dreaming. I promise you that I will collect some postcards for my scrapbook so that you can see what a delightful place Scarborough is.

The hotel is built on such a grand scale that the sight of it truly took my breath away. If I had imagined that we would be staying in some small, provincial hotel then I was mistaken. The coachman who drove us from the station was proud to inform us that the hotel has twelve floors, one for each month of the year, four towers for the seasons, fifty-two chimneys and three hundred and sixty-five bedrooms. What is more, the building is constructed in the shape of a "V" in honour of our dear queen. I love the idea that a building should be designed with such ingenuity. The interior is very fine with marble pillars and a grand, sweeping staircase leading to a gallery that overlooks the foyer. My room is most comfortable with its own bathroom and the bath even has an extra tap so that I may choose to bathe in fresh water or sea water. How innovative! Everything is new and modern and the plumbing works like a dream.

I have a splendid view of the sea and the ruined castle on the headland and am looking out over the bay now as I write these words to you. Tomorrow, Mary and I will explore this charming town and I will write and tell you all about it.

Your ever loving sister,

Alice.

~~~

Grand Hotel,
Scarborough,
7pm, 12th, August 1899
~~~

Dear Ma,

Well we got here at last, no thanks to the steam engine that broke down outside of Peterborough. We had to wait for a new engine to arrive which delayed us over an hour so we missed our connection in York. Changing trains at York was a right palaver what with all the bags and everything. Alice has packed enough clothes for the rest of the year! Goodness knows how long she intends to stay here.

The hotel is very grand although a bit gaudy in places. Alice has a nice room with a sea view but mine is rather cramped and looks out onto the inner courtyard where the kitchen staff sit gossiping. Anyway, mustn't complain. At least I've got a room to myself for once and won't have to share with the scullery maid whilst we're here.

I expect you're wanting to hear what the sea is like. Well we haven't seen much of it yet, but it looked pretty cold and wet to me. And the gulls! Blimey, they don't half make a racket. You never heard such a screeching in all your life. One of them tried to peck at my bonnet when we arrived at the hotel, but I gave it a whack with the handle of my umbrella and sent it off. Ruddy birds!

Between you and me, though, I do think Alice looks a bit perkier already and we've only been here an hour or so. I'm glad for her sake that Dr Bradshaw advised a trip to the seaside. It'll give her time to think about her engagement to that Henry Blackwood. If she's got any sense she'll break it off. I've never trusted him. I reckon he's a gold digger and only wants to marry her for her inheritance. Best keep that to yourself, though. I don't want to get into trouble!

You look after yourself Ma. I'll write each day to let you know what we're doing.

Love,

Mary.

~~~

The man calling himself Jackson alighted from the last train of the night onto the platform at Scarborough. A solitary figure dressed in plain black trousers, black jacket and a bowler hat that had seen better days, he carried one
~~~

small suitcase. When the porter came forward to assist him, Jackson dismissed the man with a wave of his hand and, head down, strode briskly towards the exit.

Outside the station, there was one horse and carriage still waiting. The driver greeted Jackson with a cheery *Evening Sir,* obviously keen to earn one last fare before retiring for the night, but Jackson turned his collar up and walked past the horse and carriage without so much as a sideways glance. He wasn't in the mood for the inevitable conversation about why he was here and would he be visiting the spa during his stay? In his experience carriage drivers were all too keen to ingratiate themselves with visitors in the hope of receiving more business. Jackson wasn't here to provide the locals with a living.

As he walked down the hill towards the town, Jackson reflected on the rather curious job he had been given which had resulted in his purchasing a last-minute ticket from the station at King's Cross and boarding the northbound train. His master, the formidable Sir Henry Blackwood, had called him into his club at St James's and given him his instructions. Jackson had served as valet and general dogsbody to Sir Henry for the last two years after Henry had seen him win a boxing fight in Shoreditch and had offered him a position in his household. If Jackson had thought that being valet to Sir Henry would mean just starching collars and dressing him for dinner, then he was quickly disabused of that idea. The work was much more varied and suited to Jackson's particular skill set. If Henry desired the services of a lady at any time of the day or night, Jackson would procure the said lady (although ladies were definitely not what Jackson would have called them.) If Henry required opium, a drug to which he was increasingly addicted, Jackson knew a particular corner of East London where it could be had for half the going rate if you knew how to negotiate. If Henry got into debt, which he frequently did through gambling, Jackson would dust off his boxing skills to ensure that the creditor stopped demanding his money back and never bothered them again. Oh yes, being valet to Sir Henry was an interesting and varied business.

By contrast to the usual jobs he undertook for his master, this assignment would be laughably genteel. He was to keep an eye on Henry's future bride, the charming Miss Alice Hawthorne, and report back to Henry on all her comings and goings. "Keep a close watch on her," Henry had demanded. "I don't like the idea of her going off on her own like this, but Doctor Bradshaw insists it is necessary for her health. Poppycock! I want you to report to me daily on her activities and bring her back to London if I tell you to."

Jackson was happy to oblige. He had started to grow tired of Henry's ever-increasing demands for whores and opium. A week or two by the seaside spying on a lady and her maid would make a pleasant change and give him time to reflect on his own future. He'd almost saved enough to make a clean break and set himself up in business. But he mustn't fail in his duty to Sir Henry or Henry would see to it that all Jackson's plans came to nothing.

He found a boarding house with a sign in the window advertising vacancies. It was located conveniently close to the Grand Hotel, in a row of four-storey brick terraces. The sign above the door read *Sea-View Villa* even though the sea was nowhere in sight. Jackson straightened his hat, marched up to the front door and knocked. A few moments later the door was opened by a stout landlady who looked him up and down before admitting him into the hallway. She demanded a week's rent in advance and then showed him to his room at the top of the house, making it clear in no uncertain terms that she would not tolerate the entertaining of young ladies on her premises.

"Of course not, Madam," said Jackson, bowing slightly and offering her his best gentlemanly smile. The landlady, softening at once, asked if she could bring him anything, a slice of pie perhaps or a mug of ale? Jackson declined politely.

He waited until the house was quiet and then he crept down the stairs and out into the night. It was not quite ten thirty. He would find an inn where they served good beer and pies. Then he would go and see what entertainment and female company were to be had at the theatre. He intended to enjoy himself on this job. After all, Sir Henry was footing the bill so he might as well make the most of it. In the morning he would begin spying on Alice and Mary.

~~~

The boy I love is up in the gallery,
The boy I love is looking now at me,
There he is, can't you see, waving his handkerchief,
As merry as a robin that sings on a tree.

The audience erupted into a frenzy of clapping and cheering. That song, or at least the way Kitty sang it, always brought the house down. She smiled and curtsied, lifting up her skirt to reveal just enough ankle so that the male members of the audience would clap even harder. Enthusiastic punters threw roses onto the stage and Kitty bent down to pick them up, making a show of holding each one to her nose and breathing in its musky scent. Cries of "Kiss me" were shouted from the gallery. Kitty blew a stream of kisses to her admirers in the audience, causing another wave of excitement to ripple through the audience, then she skipped off the stage. Always leave them wanting more, that was what she had learnt. Then they would come back the next night and the night after that, and she would keep her job. She went back to her dressing room and shut the door.

She laid the roses on her dressing table beside the faded blooms of the previous night, sat down in front of the mirror and started to unpin her hair. She frowned. Was
~~~

that a grey hair amid her rich, auburn locks? Surely not. She was only twenty-three. She pulled the offending hair out and let it fall to the floor. If she lost her looks the theatre manager would sack her on the spot and hire in a younger, prettier girl to take her place. Someone more suited to singing about boys in the gallery.

Kitty sighed. If only there really was a boy, or better still a man, in the gallery that she loved and who loved her, but there never was. Most of the men she met at the show had wives tucked up in bed at the Grand Hotel. They were looking for a quick fling, nothing more. If only someone more serious would show up for a change, then she might be interested. He didn't have to be perfect, she wasn't that fussy. Heaven knows, Kitty herself hadn't got this far in life without making the occasional compromise with a man capable of furthering her career. But she wanted someone whose heart was in the right place.

There was a knock at the door. Three short raps followed by a final, decisive knock.

"Yes?" called Kitty.

The door opened and Alfie, the young lad employed by the theatre to run errands and do odd jobs, stood on the threshold, a card in his grubby fingers.

"Please Miss, sorry to bother you Miss, but a gentleman left this for you."

Kitty sighed and took the proffered card from Alfie.

"Who's it from?" asked Kitty. "Anyone you've seen before?"

Alfie shook his head. "He was new, Miss. I ain't seen 'im before."

"And where is he now?"

"He didn't stay, Miss."

That's strange, thought Kitty. Normally gentlemen insisted on waiting for her by the stage door. She turned the card over and read the hastily scribbled note. In spite of herself, she couldn't help wondering about the identity of the man who had sent her this communication.

Very much enjoyed your show tonight. Will return tomorrow evening. I would be honoured if Madam would accompany me on the promenade one day.

The card was signed with a single letter "J."

CHAPTER THREE

Rose lay in bed in the converted loft room at the top of her gran's house and listened to the screeching of the seagulls. It was only eight o'clock and normally she wouldn't even be awake at this time in the holidays, but the birds had woken her an hour ago and it was impossible to get back to sleep with that racket going on. Through the sky-light she could see the birds circling overhead. *Like vultures,* she thought. One of them landed on the roof and started pecking at the glass. Rose groaned. At least the previous day's rain had cleared and the sky was a bright, startling blue. Would it be warm enough for sunbathing? Just about. What about swimming in the sea? You had to be pretty brave to try that, but Rose thought she might give it a go.

The smell of frying bacon wafted its way up to her bedroom. That did it. She pushed back the covers and swung her legs out of bed. If the gulls hadn't persuaded her to get up, the smell of bacon was too much to resist.

Downstairs her mother had commandeered the tiny kitchen and was in mass-catering mode. Her grandmother was sitting at the dining table eating toast and drinking coffee.

"I've been banned from my own kitchen," she said as Rose sat down at the table.

"Not banned," called Andrea from the stove. "I just think you should take it easy whilst you're still recovering."

Her grandmother rolled her eyes at Rose. "Your mother thinks I don't eat enough," she said conspiratorially. "She's determined to get a cooked breakfast down me."

"She's the same at home," said Rose in a whisper.

Andrea bustled into the room carrying a plate of bacon and fried eggs and started to serve everyone with generous helpings. "I'm taking Gran to the optician's this morning," she said to Rose, "and then this afternoon I've made an appointment with the solicitor to go through her will."

"She thinks I'm about to drop dead," said her grandmother, winking at Rose.

"Mum, honestly!" Andrea glared at her mother. "It just makes sense to do these things whilst I've got the car here and can drive you around."

"I'm perfectly capable of getting the bus."

"You were hurrying for the bus when you tripped and fell," countered Andrea. She turned to Rose. "Do you think you can entertain yourself today? I'll give you some money for fish and chips."

"Sure," said Rose. She had no idea what she was going to do on her own all day, but anything was better than listening to her mum going on all the time.

~~~

Dan pulled his bicycle out of the shed and checked the tyres. He'd decided this morning to cycle into town, partly because he preferred the independence and partly in the interests of self-preservation. The way his dad was driving these days, Dan didn't rate his chances of survival very highly. Plus he'd just about had enough of his dad's odd behaviour. Ryan had been in a funny mood all yesterday
~~~

evening, hardly talking to anyone at the dinner table and snapping at Fiona, Dan's mum, when she brought out her latest batch of home improvement magazines and suggested that what they really needed in their lives was a new kitchen. The discussion at the dinner table had rapidly descended into a slanging match about the *ludicrous expense of granite worktops* (Ryan) and the *folly of owning a Ferrari* (Fiona.) Dan had retreated to his room and played his favourite music very loudly to drown out the increasingly hysterical voices.

Free-wheeling down the hill with the sun on his face and the wind in his hair felt good. He sped under Spa Bridge and turned onto the sea-front. It was low-tide and the bay was a vast stretch of golden sand, not yet packed with holidaymakers. On days like this the North Yorkshire coast beat the Mediterranean hands down in his opinion. He still had half an hour before the amusement arcade opened, so he decided to supplement his hasty breakfast with an ice cream from one of the vendors along the front. Biting into a chocolate flake, he pushed his bike in the direction of the harbour.

Lobster cages and fishing nets were piled high along the water's edge, giving off a stale fishy smell. Docked alongside the fishing boats, its Jolly Roger fluttering in the breeze, was the pirate ship, the *Hispaniola.* It was one of Scarborough's most popular tourist attractions, taking holidaymakers on trips around the South Bay. Dan walked down to the water's edge to get a better look. It really was a fine ship, a replica of an eighteenth-century galleon complete with sails and rigging. He had loved going for trips on that boat when he was a little kid, feeling the surge of the waves beneath the hull and imagining that he was Captain Jack Sparrow. He should have tried to get a summer job on board the boat. It would have been more fun than being stuck in a booth at the amusement arcade all day.

Next to the pirate ship was a sleek, white yacht that

looked like it should have been moored in St Tropez but had drifted off course and wound up here by mistake. It was the water-borne equivalent of a luxury sports car, with its elongated prow and dark-tinted windows.

A door on the yacht opened and two figures appeared on deck. Dan did a double-take. It was the two men who'd come into the amusement arcade yesterday asking for his dad. Bulldog and Tattoo-face was how Dan thought of them. What on earth were they up to now? He squinted into the sun to try and see what they were doing. They appeared to be carrying boxes out of the hold and onto the deck, piling them up in neat rows. It was broad daylight so presumably they were engaged in legitimate business, but there was something about those two that made Dan think of pirates. *Oh well, as long as they don't pay another visit to the arcade,* he thought as he started pushing his bike back towards the centre of town.

~~~

By a quarter to nine, Rose was on the sea-front, this time with her laptop in her backpack. Yesterday, just before being almost run over, she'd spotted a café with Internet access next to the amusement arcade. Crossing the road with extra care *(who'd have thought that Scarborough was more dangerous than central London?)* she went into the café, ordered a large hot chocolate with cream and settled herself in a window seat.

Ten minutes later Rose had *liked* dozens of holiday photos, sent loads of LOLs and smiley faces and was feeling utterly miserable. Kate was looking tanned and happy in Italy, eating *gelato* with a guy called Angelo; Holly had indeed posted a selfie from the top of the Empire State Building and had been shopping in Madison Avenue; and Joe was having a *wicked* time in London, going to parties and live music events. No wonder he was too busy to send a text. Rose had *not* liked his posts. If he was
~~~

ignoring her, she wasn't going to bolster his ego by mindlessly clicking the *like* button. She considered updating her own status but couldn't think of anything remotely interesting or funny to say.

She warmed her hands on the mug of hot chocolate and stared out of the window. Across the street, the deckchair attendant was pulling the tarpaulins off the stacks of blue and white striped deckchairs; a queue was already forming at the ice cream vendor; families with little children were making their way down to the beach, laden with buckets, spades, picnic cool boxes, wind breakers, beach mats and enough survival equipment for a week of camping. Rose sipped her chocolate and, not for the first time, wondered how on earth she was going to fill six whole weeks here. She was gazing out of the window when a teenage boy pushing a bicycle along the pavement suddenly stopped, walked back a few paces and stared at her through the window. Rose shifted uncomfortably in her seat. Why was he staring at her like that? Did he think she was someone else? She turned back to her laptop and started scrolling up and down her news feed without properly seeing anything.

Go away, she thought.

He was still there, though, she could see him out of the corner of her eye. She stared back at him, giving him her best *what's-your-problem* stare. That usually got rid of unwanted attention. Unbelievably he smiled at her, propped his bicycle against the café window and came inside.

"Hi," he said, pushing a strand of blond hair out of his eyes. "I thought it was you."

"I'm sorry?"

"Yesterday. The girl with the phone."

Rose frowned at him. "Look, I don't know who you think I am but…"

"My dad nearly killed you," he blurted out.

A hush fell on the café as people stopped talking and

looked up from their cappuccinos. Rose felt herself colouring. "Well, as you can see, I'm alive and well," she said, shutting her laptop and standing up. Who was this guy?

He took a step towards her. The other customers, obviously deciding that he wasn't a threat, went back to their phones and tablets. "I'm sorry," he said, "you obviously don't know what I'm talking about."

"Well, you're not exactly making yourself clear."

"It was my dad driving the red Ferrari yesterday, the one that nearly got you killed."

Ah, so that was it. "You mean that idiot who was burning rubber like he thought he was on *Top Gear* or something?" She had a vague recollection of seeing someone in the passenger seat but registering his features hadn't been paramount in her priorities.

"Yeah, that would be him," said the boy. "He can get a bit crazy behind the wheel."

"Well, tell him from me that he's a bloody menace and shouldn't be allowed on the road."

He looked like she'd slapped him, and Rose immediately regretted her harsh words. After all, this boy hadn't been the one driving and here she was taking out all her frustration on him. At least he'd had the decency to apologise.

"Sorry," she said. "I didn't mean to snap. It wasn't your fault your dad drives like an idiot. Thank you for apologising." She put her laptop into her backpack and headed towards the door.

"You're welcome," he said, following her outside. "I'm Dan by the way. And you are?"

"Rose."

He hesitated for a moment then said, "I haven't seen you around before. Are you on holiday?"

She nodded. If you could call it a *holiday*.

"Well," he said, biting his lower lip, "I don't know if you'd like to, I mean you've probably got other plans or something, but if you're not doing anything tomorrow night, there's a fair coming to town. We could go together. If you want to, that is?"

Rose looked at him and considered his offer. He was really nice looking, with dark brown eyes and a serious, intelligent expression. And more than that, she appreciated the way he'd come into the café to apologise to her about something that wasn't even his fault. She decided there and then that Joe was a lost cause and she wasn't going to waste any more time on him.

"Yes, I'd love to go to the fair," she said, "but on one condition."

"What's that?"

"Your dad's not driving us there."

~~~

Dan tossed a coin into the air and caught it deftly on the back of his left hand. *Heads*, he guessed. Yes, he was right again. His luck really had taken a turn for the better. If he hadn't cycled into town today he wouldn't have been walking past the café when Rose just happened to be sitting in the window. And he wouldn't have cycled if his dad hadn't driven like a maniac yesterday. It was funny how things turned out. Dan wouldn't have said he believed in *Fate*, but it was almost as if he and Rose had been meant to meet. *Fatalistic*, he thought. But hopefully not *fatal*. That was something else entirely.

He'd recognised her straight away, the dark brown hair tied up in a loose ponytail, her slightly upturned nose and those big brown eyes of hers that had stared at him through the window. He'd seen that face yesterday in a state of terror as its owner had almost been killed. He wasn't going to forget it in a hurry.

She'd looked a lot prettier today, although admittedly not exactly pleased to see him at first. Probably thought he was some kind of weirdo, staring at her through the
~~~

window like that. Still, he was glad he'd had the nerve to go and speak to her and she'd agreed to go to the fair with him, so it didn't look like she was the sort to hold grudges. He hadn't initially intended to ask her out — *had he asked her out on a date, or were they just going to the fair as friends?* — but apologising for his dad's driving hadn't seemed like quite enough and there was something about her, something that really drew him to her, and the words had come out before he'd had time to think through the consequences.

There weren't many people in the amusement arcade yet. They'd get more customers this afternoon when the tide came in and forced people off the beach. A guy in an *I Love Scarborough* T-shirt came to the counter and exchanged a five pound note for a bag of twenty pence pieces.

"Good luck," said Dan because he was in a cheerful mood, even though he secretly thought the guy would be better off digging for buried treasure on the beach. But business was business as his dad always said. Ryan maintained that people didn't mind losing a bit of money because they were on holiday and having fun was all that mattered. But last year they'd had to ban a local man from the arcade because he was so addicted to the slot machines he'd bankrupted himself and would then turn up drunk and cause a nuisance, frightening the ordinary punters, especially those with kids. After that Dan was always on the lookout for any signs of trouble whenever he was manning the fort.

Oh God, not those two again. Dan swore under his breath as the two guys from yesterday, Bulldog and Tattoo-face, walked into the arcade. Bulldog was carrying a large cardboard box sealed with brown packing tape and Dan was reminded of the boxes on the yacht. He braced himself as they approached the counter.

"Where's Ryan?" asked Tattoo-face in his strident Newcastle accent. He was leaning so close that his breath misted the security glass.

"He's not here right now," said Dan.

"We've got a delivery for him."

Dan glanced at the box. It was about eighteen inches square and gave no clues as to its contents. They were due a delivery of skeleton key-rings, but somehow he didn't think these guys worked for a bona fide parcel delivery company.

The men glanced at each other and seemed to come to some sort of agreement.

"We'll leave this here for him," said the bulldog.

"OK then," said Dan, not sure what else to suggest.

He didn't like opening the door to the booth with those two around. He had an image of them charging at him as soon as the door was open, knocking him over the head and running off with all the cash in the till. But the bulldog handed the box over without any fuss. Dan kicked the door shut with his foot and deposited the box under the counter, out of view of the customers.

"I'll tell him there's a parcel for him," said Dan.

"Aye, you do that," said the guy with the tattoo. "He'll know what to do with it."

Dan watched them leave. They each lit a cigarette as soon as they were outside the arcade, then they headed off towards the harbour. Dan had no idea what was in the box and didn't want to know. Whatever business his dad had with those two jerks was his own. He pulled his mobile phone out of his back pocket and sent his dad a text.

CHAPTER FOUR

Grand Hotel,
Scarborough,
2pm, 13th August, 1899

Dearest Susan,

I passed a wonderfully comfortable night at the hotel. I really think the sea air must be conducive to a good night's sleep. This morning when I rose, feeling more refreshed than I have done in a long time, a sea mist like a silver-grey veil had rolled in, shrouding the coastline so that the castle on the headland was barely visible but had a dreamlike quality to it that made it look even more romantic than it had the previous evening. The girl who brought me my breakfast assured me that the sun would break through by the afternoon.

On account of the mist, I resolved that Mary and I would spend the morning taking tea in the hotel's lounge. I thought it would be a splendid opportunity for us to meet some of the other guests and I was not disappointed. We made the acquaintance of a charming old lady called Mrs Goodly who comes here every year and swears by the sea air for keeping her rheumatism at bay. She asked if we were planning to go to the fair which will arrive in the next day or so. I thought that would be a rather fun thing to do. She then invited us to join her for lunch and by the time we had finished our fish (they have the freshest fish here you could possibly imagine!) the sun had indeed broken through the veil of mist and I informed Mary that we would make the most of the afternoon by taking an invigorating walk up to the castle.

I realise as I write these lines that I have not given one thought to Henry and our impending marriage. It is as if the ties that bind us grow weaker with every minute I spend away from his presence. Oh, what should I do Susan? We have been betrothed for such a long time now that I am unable to imagine any other future except as Henry's wife. I know it is what Mother and Father wish for me and Henry is the type of man of which society approves, with his family connections and his promising political career. But I seriously doubt I could ever love him.

Ah, that is Mary knocking at my door. It is time for our walk to the castle. I will write again this evening and tell you all about it.

Your ever loving sister,

Alice.

~~~

Grand Hotel,
Scarborough,
2pm, 13th August, 1899

Dear Ma,

Hope you're well. Those wretched gulls kept me awake half the night. I tell you, if I had to live here I'd take a gun and shoot the whole ruddy lot of them.

A right pea-souper of a fog had come in this morning, so you couldn't even see the sea. There could have been murdering bands of pirates out there for all we knew. Still, it meant we got to stay indoors and have a nice cup of tea in the hotel lounge which is ever so posh! We chatted to a lady called Mrs Goodly who was friendly enough, but she went on and on about her ailments. It was rheumatism this, and lumbago that… Honestly, I started to wonder if we were staying
~~~

in a hotel or a hospital. Still, I mustn't complain. She invited us to have lunch with her and it was the tastiest fish I'd ever eaten. If I find a handsome fisherman around here I might have to marry him. Only joking!

Anyway, the fog has cleared now and Alice is determined that we are going to walk up the hill to the castle, although it looks like a bit of a ruin to me. But I'm pleased to see she's looking more like her old self. The fresh sea air might help her get her thoughts straight. With any luck she'll see sense and send that Henry Blackwood packing.

I'll tell you all about the castle in my next letter. Look after yourself.

Love,

Mary.

~~~

Jackson loitered outside the Grand Hotel, doing his best to appear inconspicuous amongst the cab drivers, crossing sweepers and other riff-raff who made their living from tending to the needs of the wealthy. He kept his hat pulled down low and wore a scarf around his mouth and nose. The fog was chilly, but the scarf helped to conceal his appearance. If the ladies saw him they would recognise him at once and know that Henry had sent him to spy on them. He'd have to do his best to stay incognito.

He found himself humming a tune from last night. *The boy I love is up in the gallery.* A silly little ditty, but with a catchy tune that was difficult to get out of your head. The girl who'd sung it was a bit of a stunner though. Lovely auburn hair falling over her shoulders and those lips! Perfect rosebuds. *Kitty,* the programme said her name was. She probably had men queueing up by the dozen. Still, he wasn't bad looking himself and he had the advantage of being unattached. Most of the men in the audience had displayed the self-satisfied air of married men. He'd given a note to the odd-job boy and told him to take it to Kitty, hoping to rouse her interest by maintaining a sense of
~~~

mystery, at least for the next twenty-four hours. He planned to go back to the theatre tonight and take his chances with the rest of them. He'd take some flowers and wait for her by the stage door. If he could persuade her to accompany him on his spying trips, he'd be less conspicuous, at least that was the plan.

A dark-suited figure appeared in the doorway of the hotel, paused for a moment, then strode purposefully in Jackson's direction. From the highly polished shoes to the impeccably trimmed moustache, Jackson recognised the type immediately. Hotel managers were the same the world over: obnoxious and obsequious in equal measure, fawning over their wealthier guests and disdaining the common man.

The manager stopped in front of Jackson and dispensed with any formal greeting. "What is your business here?" he demanded. "You have been loitering outside the hotel for upwards of half an hour. You are creating a bad impression. If you have no business here then I must ask you to leave."

Officious little toad, thought Jackson, eyeing the man with instant dislike. He was a puny figure and Jackson could have floored him in an instant with a sharp right hook to the jaw. The man took a step closer, evidently over-confident in his position of authority. On the streets of Whitechapel, faced with a more formidable opponent, Jackson would have had no hesitation in reaching for the small but lethal knife he always carried in an inside breast pocket of his jacket, but here in the genteel environs of Scarborough, the need for a weapon seemed like overkill.

"I asked you what business you had standing outside the hotel," repeated the manager.

Jackson considered his options. Whilst it was tempting to give this trumped-up official a bloody nose, it would achieve nothing and would most likely jeopardise his mission. The fog was showing no signs of lifting and it was unlikely that Alice and Mary would emerge in this miserable weather. There was no point hanging around.

"My business is no concern of yours," he said. The manager shrank back under the intensity of Jackson's gaze and Jackson experienced the satisfaction of winning a small, but significant, victory. Then he turned and started walking towards the inn he'd found last night - *The Three Mariners.* They did a very tasty steak and kidney pie. He'd return to the hotel this afternoon if the weather cleared and no jumped-up little manager was going to stand in his way.

CHAPTER FIVE

Rose woke to a thick sea-mist that had rolled in overnight. Not beach weather, that was for sure. She didn't suppose Kate was having this problem in sun-drenched Italy. It was just as well her mother had insisted on packing warm clothes. Still, it wasn't all bad here she thought to herself, remembering her meeting with Dan yesterday at the café. She pictured his blond hair and the way it had flopped into his eyes, the way he had looked at her through the window. At first she'd taken his gaze the wrong way, thinking him impertinent, but it was just that there was an intensity to his eyes that was both attractive and slightly off-putting. She was really looking forward to going to the fair with him later on.

Rose showered and dressed, choosing jeans and a sweater, then went downstairs to breakfast. Her mother and grandmother were sitting at the table, Gran reading the local paper and sipping a cup of coffee, her mother making a list of jobs. *We're supposed to be on holiday,* thought Rose. *Doesn't she ever switch off?*

"I'll pick up your prescription this morning," said Andrea to her mother. "Then I'll go shopping. We're eating you out of house and home at the moment. Oh, morning Rose. I'll do you some bacon."

Rose sat down at the table as her mother disappeared into the kitchen.

"Morning Gran."

"Good morning, dear. Sleep well?"

"Yes thanks. The gulls didn't wake me up so early today."

Her grandmother laughed. "You get used to them. I don't hear them anymore and it's not because I've gone a bit deaf. Have you got any plans this morning?"

Rose shook her head. She'd arranged to meet Dan at seven o'clock in the evening outside the amusement arcade. He'd assured her that they'd catch a bus to the fair, not be driven there in the Ferrari which was a two-seater anyway.

"Well, in that case," continued her grandmother, "would you be able to help me do some clearing out? Your mother thinks I should sort out the cupboards." She dropped her voice and leaned closer to Rose. "I think she wants me to sell up and move into a nursing home."

"You don't need to go into a nursing home, Gran," said Rose, quite shocked at the idea.

Her grandmother pulled a face. "Well, at my age you have to be prepared." She didn't say for what.

"Of course I'll give you a hand Gran," said Rose.

"Wonderful. It'll just be the two of us this morning."

"Even better," whispered Rose.

"What are you two plotting?" asked Andrea, carrying a plateful of bacon into the dining room.

"Oh, nothing," said her grandmother with a wave of her hand.

An hour later the floor of the front room was covered in boxes that Rose had retrieved from the understairs cupboard. Rose knelt down, opened the flaps on the nearest box and pulled out a selection of books about fly fishing.

"Those were your grandfather's," said her

grandmother, wistfully. "We can give them to the charity shop, although goodness knows who'd want them."

Rose agreed. She replaced the books and put the box by the front door.

The next two boxes contained an assortment of old children's books, mostly Enid Blyton stories and girls' annuals.

"And these belonged to your mother." Her grandmother thumbed through a dog-eared copy of *Five Go To Smuggler's Top*. "She used to love these."

Rose picked up *Five on a Treasure Island.* The cover showed four children and a dog sailing a boat on the open sea. The next book, *Five Get Into Trouble,* depicted the foursome lurking in a moonlit clearing whilst a shady figure in the background went about some clandestine, and no doubt criminal, activity. Rose couldn't imagine her mother letting her have as much freedom as *The Famous Five* had enjoyed.

"The trouble with paperbacks," said her grandmother, wrinkling her nose, "is that the paper dries out and ends up smelling so musty." She put the book back in the box. "Charity shop?"

"I think so," said Rose.

She pulled a battered cardboard box towards her. It was so old it was almost falling apart. "What's in this one?" She pulled back the flaps, peered inside and pulled out a large book, about the size of a photo album. The faded green leather cover was embossed in gold leaf and had the words *Scrapbook* in fancy lettering on the front.

"Oh goodness." Her grandmother leaned over Rose's shoulder. "I'd forgotten about this. Now this really is a genuine antique."

"A scrapbook?"

"Yes. It's Victorian. It belonged to a lady."

"Who?"

"Someone called Alice. My grandmother worked for her."

"*Your* grandmother?" said Rose, trying to work out how long ago that must have been.

"Yes, her name was Mary and she would have been your great-great-grandmother."

"Wow," said Rose. "That's, like, really old! Can we have a look inside?"

"Of course." Her grandmother patted the space next to her on the sofa. "Come and sit here."

Rose sat down and carefully opened the leather cover which creaked with age. Inside, in faded brown ink, were the words *This scrapbook is the property of Miss Alice Hawthorne, Bedale House, Richmond, London.*

"So, if this belonged to someone called Alice," said Rose, "how did your grandmother come to have it? Mary, did you say her name was?"

"Yes, Mary. And that's a very good question," said her grandmother, "and something of a mystery."

"Go on." Rose was intrigued.

"Well, it seems that Alice and Mary came here on holiday, I think in 1899. Alice was from a wealthy family and Mary was her lady's maid. But something happened to Alice on that trip and she disappeared."

"What, just vanished?"

"Yes. I never understood exactly what had happened, but Mary ended up with Alice's scrapbook in her possession. She showed it to me once when I was a little girl and I've never forgotten it." For a moment there was a faraway look in her grandmother's eyes, as if she was lost in the past, then she said, "Mary always said the best thing about the trip was that she met and married a fisherman. That's how she came to be living in Scarborough."

"So you're saying my great-great-grandmother had a holiday romance and ended up getting married?"

"There's no need to sound so shocked. Contrary to popular belief, sex wasn't invented in the 1960s you know!"

Rose laughed, turning the first few pages of the

scrapbook. It was full of pictures of late Victorian fashions, ladies modelling silk gowns with bustles and wide-brimmed hats decorated with flowers and ostrich feathers. One double-page spread was filled with fliers from the London music halls advertising the singer Marie Lloyd. Over the page, a poster for Wombwell's Travelling Menagerie promised intrepid visitors the chance to see giraffes, lions, elephants and even a boa constrictor.

Rose turned the page. "There's the Grand Hotel," said her grandmother, pointing to a black and white postcard of Scarborough's most famous hotel. "Mary was always proud of the fact that she stayed in Scarborough's most luxurious hotel although she'd turn in her grave if she could see it now. It's gone rather downhill. I heard from a neighbour that they have slot machines in the lounge these days." Rose laughed. She didn't think the hotel was the most attractive building in the world. Each of the four corners was topped with a peculiar circular turret that resembled a Victorian diving bell.

There were more postcards of Scarborough: ladies in white dresses and gentlemen in black suits and bowler hats thronging the promenade; horse-drawn bathing machines; donkey rides on the sands and open-air concerts at the spa. The Victorians certainly knew how to enjoy themselves.

Rose turned the page and found a sepia photograph of two women standing side-by-side on the sea-front. The woman on the right was wearing a plain black dress and a bonnet tied under her chin with a neat bow. The other wore a lace-trimmed white gown with a wide-brimmed hat set at an angle and held a frilly parasol over her shoulder with a white-gloved hand. Clearly visible against the perfectly white dress, was a distinctive black necklace, an intricate design of loops and rosettes made out of black beads. Rose thought the woman in white had a dreamy look about her, but the woman in black was squinting into the sun, her mouth set in a grimace, looking as if she wished the photographer would hurry up and get a move on.

"Is that them?" asked Rose. "Alice and Mary?"

"Yes, that's Mary," said her grandmother, pointing at the woman in black. "The woman in white is Alice."

Rose studied the photograph. It was strange to think she was seeing her own great-great-grandmother from so long ago. Mary herself could have had no idea that one day her great-great-granddaughter would look at this picture. Rose peered closely at Mary's face. There was a firmness about the mouth that reminded her of her own mother. Mary didn't look as if she would stand for any nonsense. Alice, on the other hand, was more difficult to pin down. She seemed less solid, less anchored to the real world than other people, as if a gust of wind might catch her parasol and send her flying into the air.

At the top of the next page, in the same flowery handwriting as inside the front cover, were the words *Scarborough Fair*. There were fliers for a travelling fair featuring a host of bizarre attractions from *The Spectacular Bearded Lady* to *Pepper's Ghost* and *The Living Skeleton*. "Looks like they went to the fair whilst they were here," said Rose, thinking about her own plans for later that evening.

"I'm sure they did," said her grandmother. "But as you can see, fairs were rather different in those days."

The next page was entitled *A Day Trip to Whitby*. There was a postcard of Whitby Abbey standing dark and brooding on the cliff and another of the one-hundred and ninety-nine steps that led from the town to the Abbey.

The rest of the scrapbook was blank, but when Rose flicked through the pages to the end, a loose sheet of newspaper slipped out and floated to the floor. She bent to pick it up, its yellowed paper dry and brittle between her thumb and finger. At once, the headline caught her attention.

Lady Goes Missing, Feared Dead.

"Is this about Alice?" asked Rose.

"Ah, yes," said her grandmother, reaching for her reading glasses. "Mary must have cut this out and kept it."

Rose glanced quickly over the article which was printed in small, closely spaced type. On the nineteenth of August, 1899, Miss Alice Hawthorne had disappeared. A shawl that she had been wearing had been found covered in blood in St Mary's Church. Inspector Booth was actively following all lines of enquiry and was appealing for witnesses to come forward.

"Do you know what happened?" asked Rose.

Her grandmother shook her head. "No, I'm afraid I don't. I should have asked more questions when I was young, but people never do. Anyway, you should have the scrapbook now," she said, handing it to Rose. "It's a family heirloom."

"Oh, I'd love it, thank you."

Her grandmother delved into the box and pulled out a bundle of envelopes tied with a red ribbon. "You might as well have these too."

"What are they?"

"Mary was a great letter writer. People were in those days, when there was no email. These are the letters she wrote to her own mother in London. They came back to her when her mother passed away in the 1930s."

"Have you read them?" asked Rose, turning the bundle of letters over in her hands. Was it right to read someone else's correspondence?

"No," laughed her grandmother. "I dare say they're full of trivia, but they might be interesting. You never know."

CHAPTER SIX

Grand Hotel,
Scarborough,
9pm, 13th August, 1899

Dearest Susan,

Where to begin! We have had the most wonderful afternoon you could possibly imagine. Mary and I took the funicular railway, a most ingenious device, down to the sea-front and strolled along the promenade. The sand was a rich golden colour and the sea sparkled silver in the sun.

The promenade was bustling with society. There were finely dressed ladies and gentlemen, happily strolling and wishing each other good day. There were donkey rides on the sands for the children and deck chairs for hire. Down by the water's edge there was a row of horse-drawn bathing machines painted in red and cream stripes and gentlemen and ladies were actually bathing in the sea. They looked to be having so much fun! The men wore striped bathing suits and the ladies wore frilly knickerbockers and slips in colourful reds and blues. Oh Susan, how I longed to throw off my clothes and join them. I noticed where the bathing machines may be hired from and tomorrow, if the weather is fine, I will persuade Mary to come with me into the water.

Anyway, we proceeded on our planned route and took the path up to the top of the headland. The walk was just as invigorating as I had hoped it would be. We came first to St Mary's church which overlooks the South Bay. It seemed like the perfect place to stop for a short rest and I spent a few moments in contemplation beside the grave of Anne Brontë, that poor dear sister of Charlotte and Emily who died so tragically young (well they all did, I suppose.) Her grave is situated in the most beautiful spot overlooking the bay. If I were to die here, I too should like to be buried in this graveyard with a view of the sea so that I could spend eternity dreaming of far-off lands. Oh dear, I am becoming morbid and sentimental. Rest assured, I have no intention of dying here, rather this place fills me with life and vigour.

I am letting my words run away with me because I am putting off telling you what happened next. On the far edge of the graveyard, overlooking the bay, there was a painter, a handsome young man with shoulder-length fair hair and fine features. He was painting a view of the distant coastline, oil on canvas. I watched him at work from a short distance, not wishing to disturb him. But he must have sensed my presence for he turned, greeted me in a most gentlemanly manner and invited me to take a closer look at the painting if I so wished.

I was thrilled to do so and stepped up to the canvas. I told him how perfectly I thought he had captured the reflection of the sunlight on the water. He said that had been his intention but he wasn't sure if he had achieved it. I assured him that he had and he thanked me for my good opinion of his work. Henry has never asked me my opinion on anything. He then enquired whether I was keen on paintings and art and I told him that I love to wander around the rooms of the National Gallery when I am in London. He asked me if I had a favourite artist and I said I particularly like the landscapes of William Turner and he said that he, too, adores the work of Turner, the unique way in which he captures light and makes you want to fall into one of his paintings and bathe in its radiance, and I thought to myself, this man understands my feelings exactly. It was as if I had stumbled upon a kindred spirit. Susan, I can't tell you what it was like to converse with someone so sympathetic. Henry has no understanding or liking for art of any description. He regards artists as wastrels and spongers. He is a philistine who sees the monetary value of everything and the beauty of nothing.

I asked the painter if he lives in Scarborough. He told me that he normally resides in York but that he comes to Scarborough every summer to paint the changing coastline and that it is an endless source of fascination for him. I enquired how it could be that the coastline changes, for surely, I said, the land is solid, the ground under our feet is sure and firm. He didn't patronise me as Henry would have done but took my point seriously, explaining that, in fact, the land is forever changing and shifting. He told me how the sea erodes the cliffs and how a walk along the coastline always reveals something new: a fossil lain buried for thousands of years, a cave carved out by the waves. Sometimes whole sections of the cliff fall into the sea! His words had a profound effect on me for they revealed something which I had not before considered, namely that so often we build our lives on ideas that we believe are firm and fixed, but which could easily crumble beneath our feet.

I wanted to ask him to show me the cliffs and fossils about which he seemed so knowledgeable, but then Mary, who had been dozing on a bench by the church, joined us. I think she was alarmed to find me talking to a man and eyed him suspiciously, but he was not offended and greeted her warmly. He asked us if we would do him the honour of accompanying him around the castle, which I was only too happy to do. He was an excellent tour guide, telling us all about the castle's illustrious history and the damage it suffered during the Civil War. Afterwards, he walked us back to our hotel.

Oh Susan, even though I have only just met him, I feel as if I have known this man all my life. The painter's name is Mr George Hartright and I have taken the bold step of inviting him to take tea with us tomorrow afternoon at the hotel. I saw no harm in it, since I have Mary to act as chaperone, but I know Henry would not be pleased. Promise me you will burn this letter!

Your ever loving sister,
Alice.

~~~
~~~

Grand Hotel,
Scarborough,
9pm, 13th August, 1899

Dear Ma,

What an afternoon! I'm quite jiggered. We took the funicular railway down to the sea-front and goodness me, it descended so quickly and steeply I thought I was going to see the fish I'd had for lunch again. I was glad to get out and walk on the prom.

It's ever so busy here, like blooming Piccadilly Circus, and I thought we were coming to the seaside to get away from it all!

The beach was littered with bathing machines that look like horse boxes. And you should have seen what the gentlemen and ladies were wearing! The most ridiculous outfits you ever saw. It made me blush to see the men in those close-fitting bathing suits which leave nothing to the imagination. I bet the water was freezing too. You won't get me in the sea, that's for sure.

Now if they could build a funicular railway from the hotel down to the beach, you'd have thought they could build one up to the castle. It's one heck of a climb. We got as far as St Mary's church and thankfully Alice decided it was time for a rest. I parked myself on a bench hoping to shut my eyes for a moment or two whilst Alice went off to look for the grave of Anne Brontë. She's read all the novels by those Brontë sisters, although apparently Henry doesn't approve of ladies reading, saying it gives them "fanciful ideas."

Now, you'll probably tell me that I'm the one with fanciful ideas, but as I was sitting there having forty winks, I got this funny feeling that we were being watched. I couldn't tell you why, it was just something I felt. I counted to ten and then turned round pretty sharpish to try and catch them out, whoever it was, but there was no one there. Maybe I imagined it after all. All this sun and sea air must be addling my brain. Still, I just had this feeling, like someone had walked over my grave.

But then I noticed that Alice had started talking to a painter and I had to go over and join her because it isn't right for a young lady to be seen talking to a man on her own. They were chatting and laughing and I thought, she's behaving with this stranger as if she's known him all her life. I intended to say it was time to head back to the hotel, but the painter greeted me so pleasantly that I took quite a liking to him, although I thought he should get his hair cut. Mr Hartright his name is, and he took us round the castle, or at least what's left of it. He knew ever so much about the place, but I couldn't keep up with it all. By the time we'd finished my head was swimming with dates and battles. He has promised to call on us tomorrow at the hotel for afternoon tea. I'll write and tell you all about it tomorrow.

Love,
Mary.

~~~

Sea-View Villa,
Scarborough,
10pm, 13th August, 1899

Dear Sir Henry,

I spent the day observing the activities of Miss Alice Hawthorne and her maid, Mary, as per your instructions. This morning the weather was dismal and consequently the ladies stayed in their hotel. At a quarter past two they emerged from the hotel, took a walk along the promenade and proceeded up the hill to St Mary's Church where they stopped for a rest. I followed at a safe distance behind them.

In the graveyard of the church Miss Hawthorne fell into conversation with a young painter, a foppish sort of fellow with long hair. I was not close enough to hear their words, but from their mannerisms and expressions they appeared to be discussing his painting and the landscape. Mary, during this time, was snoozing on a bench and not carrying out her role as chaperone. Mary eventually woke up and noticed what was going on. The painter then took both of them round the castle and then walked them back to their hotel. He seems to have ingratiated himself with both of them in a remarkably short space of time. If you would like me to cause him to suffer a little accident or something, then just say the word.
~~~

The maid is somewhat fidgety and may prove to be a problem. She kept looking over her shoulder as if she suspected someone was following them, even though I kept well out of sight. After they returned to their hotel, I kept watch for an hour longer but they did not reappear. I will return to the hotel in the morning and send you further communication by the evening mail.

Your faithful servant,

Jackson.

~~~

As Kitty sat at her dressing room mirror, removing her stage make-up and reflecting that the audience had been even more enthusiastic than usual this evening. there came a knock at her door.

"Come in," called Kitty.

The door opened a fraction and Alfie poked his head in.

"It's all right," laughed Kitty. "I'm perfectly decent. You can come in."

Alfie blushed and entered the room, carefully stepping round a silk gown that Kitty had draped carelessly over a chair and which had such a voluminous skirt that it filled half the space in this cramped little room. Alfie was carrying a note like the one he had brought her yesterday evening. This time he also carried a single red rose.

"Is that for me?" asked Kitty, eyeing the rose with interest. Single blooms were always so much more appealing to her than lavish bouquets.

"Yes, Miss. It's from the gentleman what was here last night. He says to tell you he'd be honoured if you would meet with him."

"What sort of gentleman is he?" asked Kitty, fingering the rose and inhaling its sweet scent.

"Well," said Alfie, "to be honest I don't rightly know."

"What do you mean?"

Alfie frowned, trying to find the right words. "He's not
~~~

your regular gentleman, if you know what I mean."

Kitty laughed. "You mean those overweight, balding men who stay at the Grand Hotel and who all have matronly wives waiting for them?" Kitty was rather tired of *regular gentlemen.*

"Oh, he's nothing like that," said Alfie. "He's a bit of a dark horse is this one. He looks like he'd know how to defend himself in a fight, but he comes across as straightforward too. No messing with him. If you said you didn't want to meet him, he'd go away and not bother you again, Miss. You just say the word." Alfie sounded hopeful as if he wished she would just tell this mysterious stranger to go sling his hook. But Kitty was curious. The note said he would wait for her by the stage door. If she didn't appear by ten thirty he'd assume she wasn't coming and would leave. Kitty made up her mind. She wouldn't do anything foolish, but there was a respectable tavern nearby where they could go for a drink, nothing more.

"Give me ten minutes to get ready," she told Alfie. "Then you can introduce me to this man."

"Righto, Miss. I'll wait for you outside in the corridor."

Kitty quickly changed out of her costume and into the silk gown. She checked her appearance in the mirror one last time and then she went to meet the mysterious "J."

~~~

That afternoon, with her mother out at the supermarket, and her grandmother taking a nap, Rose found herself at a loose end. This was how it was going to be for much of the holiday, she supposed, so she might as well get used to it. She gathered together the scrapbook and the pile of letters and took them up to her room. She untied the ribbon that held the letters together and let them tumble onto the bed. There were dozens of them, the oldest bearing stamps with a profile of Queen Victoria. The later letters had stamps with kings on them, Rose
~~~

wasn't sure exactly who, her knowledge of early twentieth-century British history being somewhat vague. Each envelope had been carefully sliced open with a sharp object, probably a letter knife. Even though the writer of these letters was long dead, Rose hesitated to delve into someone else's private correspondence, wondering how she'd feel if, in years to come, a complete stranger read her emails and text messages. Mind you, they'd probably think her life was full of meaningless trivia. But judging from the thickness of some of these envelopes, Mary had had plenty to say for herself. Rose suddenly found herself curious to know what her great-great-grandmother had done and what she had thought of life. She selected one of the letters sent whilst Queen Victoria was still on the throne, slid the contents out of its envelope, unfolded the paper and started to read.

Grand Hotel,
Scarborough,
4pm, 14th August, 1899

Dear Ma,

You'll never guess what we did today! We went in the sea! It was a scorcher of a day, no more of that nasty grey fog, and Alice was determined we were going to bathe. Well, what could I do? I couldn't let her go in on her own. Mrs Goodly encouraged her by spouting some nonsense about sea water being good for the complexion and how she'd have joined us if her hip wasn't playing up. There's a convenient excuse, I thought.

So anyway, off we went to this little shop where they sell ladies' bathing costumes. You never saw anything so ridiculous in all your life. Frilly knickerbockers and mob caps - we looked like French tarts. My costume is blue and Alice's is red with white polka dots. What a sight!

Once we'd bought our outfits, we went down to the beach. There's this place where you can hire a bathing machine pulled by a horse.

We climbed into this contraption, which was painted in red and white stripes and looked like a fancy garden shed, and a young lad led the horse down to the sea. It was the most uncomfortable ride I've ever had in my life.

Then we had to change into our bathing costumes inside this shed on wheels. It was like taking your clothes off in public! There were peepholes in the side of the machine so we could look out but, thankfully, they were too high up for people outside to look in.

I helped Alice into her bathing costume and she helped me into mine, even though she's a lady, and when we were both changed she said, "There now, Mary. We look more like sisters than mistress and maid!"

I didn't know what to say to that so I said, "Oh, get away with you Miss. I'll never be a lady like you." And she laughed and said, "Being a lady isn't always fun you know."

I wondered what she meant by that, but there wasn't time to ask her because she opened the door of the bathing machine and started to make her way down the steps and I had to follow her whether I liked it or not.

She was already up to her knees in the water by the time I got down the steps, standing there with her arms outstretched and her face turned towards the sun. She came running back to me and said, "Oh, Mary, I have discovered for the first time in my life what it is like to be truly alive."

I was so shocked by the water lapping at my ankles that I just stared at her and said, "Well that's good Miss. I'm very pleased for you." Then she ran off into the sea, her arms wide, leaving me to paddle at the edge and wondering at her words. What this means, if anything, for her forthcoming marriage, I really can't say. But somehow, I don't think it looks good for Henry and that made me happy.

Now, I bet you're dying to know what the water was like. Well, it was wet. And none too warm! But it wasn't as freezing as I'd thought it would be and I went in all the way up to my knees! If you stand still in one place for too long your feet sink into the sand and you start to lose your balance! I saw quite a few ladies topple over.

Later on, we went back to the hotel and, as promised, Mr

Hartright joined us for afternoon tea. All that bathing had given me an appetite and I tucked into a plate of scones with cream and jam. Delicious! Anyway, Mr Hartright has invited us to go to the fair with him tomorrow. I can see Alice is very excited at the prospect. I think I might have my fortune told - see if there are any handsome fishermen looking for a wife! Well, I'm off to bed now. The sea air has knocked me for six!

Love to all,

Mary.

CHAPTER SEVEN

"But you've no idea who he is," said Rose's mother at tea time. They were having shop-bought lasagne and peas, Andrea having stocked the freezer with enough food for the next six months.

"His name's Dan and his dad owns the amusement arcade on the sea-front."

Andrea pulled a face as if *owning an amusement arcade* was a sure sign of social delinquency and criminal activity. "He could be *anyone.*"

"I've told you who he is."

"But what sort of a fair is it?"

"For God's sake Mum, it's just a travelling fair, you know, with rides and stuff?" Rose really couldn't see what the problem was. It was only a fair; there'd be loads of people around, and Dan was a really nice guy. She was sure her mother would agree if she actually met him. Meeting Dan had been the best thing to happen to her in a long time. The only thing Rose hadn't divulged to her mother was the circumstances of how she and Dan had actually met, namely that his dad was a maniacal Ferrari driver who had almost flattened her under the wheels of his car. Some things were best kept under wraps.

"But how are you getting there?" persisted Andrea.

"On the bus."

"What about getting home? Do the buses run that late?"

Rose shrugged. "It's only a couple of miles outside of town. I guess we can walk back if we have to."

"Along country roads? In the dark? With a boy you've only just met?" Andrea's voice rose in pitch with each succeeding question.

"Oh, for goodness' sake Mum," said Rose. "Stop being so Victorian!"

"It sounds fun to me," said her grandmother. "I'd love to go to the fair, but I'm a bit old for that sort of thing now."

Andrea rolled her eyes. "Well, just make sure you're not back late."

"Oh, don't worry," said her grandmother. "We can leave the door on the latch." Andrea shot her mother a furious look.

Rose checked her watch. "Well, now that we've sorted all that out, I'd better get going. I said I'd meet him at seven."

"Have a nice time dear," said her grandmother.

"Thanks Gran."

Rose walked quickly down the hill, worried that the interrogation from her mother was going to make her late. Her mum was such a nag, always looking for problems where there weren't any. Her grandmother still understood what it meant to be young, whereas her mother seemed to have completely forgotten. Well, she was going to enjoy herself tonight. She pushed thoughts of her mother from her mind and thought instead of Dan, his fair hair tumbling into his eyes, his lean but broad-shouldered figure. She turned the corner onto the sea-front and there he was, just as she'd imagined him, standing in the lights of the amusement arcade, hands thrust into the pockets of his skinny jeans. The wind ruffled his hair, giving him a tousled look that suited him. She called to him and his face broke into a smile of relief. He must have been worried she wouldn't show.

"Hi there," she said.

He pushed a lock of hair out of his eyes and grinned back. "You made it then."

"Of course."

He checked his watch. "There's a bus due in two minutes. We should catch it if we hurry."

"Great."

~~~

Alice took the hand that George offered and stepped down from the carriage.

"Thank you," she said, looking up into his face that glowed with health and vitality, the result, no doubt, of the many hours he spent outside, painting and walking. How different to Henry's pasty flesh, she thought, Henry who hardly ever left the confines of his club and whose eyes were often bloodshot with alcohol.

"My pleasure," said George. He helped Mary down too and then went to pay the coachman.

"I'm so glad we came to the fair," said Alice to Mary. "This is going to be so much fun." George had visited them again in the hotel earlier that afternoon and they had taken tea in the lounge with Mrs Goodly. They had talked about art and literature and music. They had so many shared pleasures and interests. Mrs Goodly had ordered more tea to help keep the conversation flowing and that dear old lady had all but given her blessing to the idea of them visiting the fair, saying that they were young and should enjoy themselves whilst they could. It seemed to Alice that here, in Scarborough, she was no longer tied to the social conventions which, back home in London, would have made a trip to the fair, with a man she had only just met, absolutely out of the question.
~~~

George reappeared at their side and offered his arm to Alice. "What would you like to see first?"

"Oh, I don't know," said Alice, looking around with a sense of awe and excitement. "There's so much to do. What do you suggest?"

"Let's take a walk around and see what takes our fancy," said George. Alice thought him wonderfully accommodating. Henry was never remotely interested in what she might like to do.

And so they wound their way amongst the stalls and entertainers, pausing to watch a marionette show and, further on, listen to an old man cranking out a tune on a hurdy-gurdy whilst a monkey in a scarlet waistcoat danced a jig. There were jugglers and acrobats and even a fire-eater but Alice couldn't bear to watch such a show, fearing that the man would burn himself to death, and so George moved them on. Everywhere they went, pedlars promoted their wares, dangling brightly coloured ribbons in their faces and trying to entice them with gaudy knick-knacks. *A blue velvet ribbon for the lady, to match your eyes! A piece of lace, Madam, to enhance your beautiful neckline.*

They passed a stall selling hot gingerbread, the smell sweet and succulent, and promised each other that they would buy some later when they had worked up an appetite. By now they had arrived at the show tents. Bare-footed children were running around handing out fliers advertising human grotesques, an Indian Snake Charmer, a Living Skeleton and a Flea Circus. Just as she was trying to make up her mind what they should do first, a little boy ran up and thrust a leaflet into Alice's hand.

"In there, Miss," said the boy, pointing towards a tent with red and white striped awning. "It's about to start." Alice looked down at the leaflet. It was an advertisement for *Pepper's Ghost and Other Amazing Magic Tricks*.

"Shall we?" said Alice, turning to her companions. She had never seen a real magic show before and was curious.

"Certainly, if you wish," said George. He paid the

entrance fee to the man at the doorway and escorted them into the tent.

~~~

"They went in there," said Kitty, pointing towards the large tent.

"Then we'd better go in too," said Jackson, rummaging in his waistcoat pocket for some coins. It hadn't been hard to persuade Kitty to accompany him to the fair. She had been delighted at the prospect of spending an afternoon doing something fun. And she had readily accepted what he'd told her, that he was here *to keep an eye on Alice* and that he *mustn't be seen.* He hadn't told her about Henry, but had rather given the impression that Alice was *a bit delicate* and her family (well Henry would be *family* soon enough) had charged him with making sure she didn't come to any harm whilst she was on holiday. He had managed to make his assignment sound more like a charitable venture instead of the underhand spying mission that it really was.

And it certainly made it easier for him to blend into polite society with a pretty woman on his arm. No one would challenge him now. They had followed Alice, Mary and George (Jackson had made enquiries in the local public houses and had eventually learnt the painter's name from the barman at *The Three Mariners*) around the fair without Mary ever once suspecting a thing.

But Kitty was proving to be more than just a useful accessory. She was fun company, with a lively sense of humour to boot. Jackson hadn't enjoyed himself so much in the presence of a woman for a long time.

"I love magic shows," said Kitty, clapping her hands together as they took up their positions at the rear of the tent. From here they had a good view of the audience as well as the stage.

"Just so long as Alice doesn't do a vanishing trick on us," said Jackson.
~~~

The last few customers entered the tent and the doors closed. The show was about to start.

~~~

Rose stuck close to Dan as they made their way through the crowds that had flocked to the fair. Around them, coloured lights flashed and loud music thumped from enormous speakers and the air pulsed with an energy that made Rose feel extra alive. The lorries, trailers and caravans belonging to the fairground travellers were parked on the far side of the field, leaving plenty of room for the stalls and rides, most of which looked pretty scary but thrilling all the same.

"Want to try that one?" asked Dan, pointing at a pendulum swing called *The Kamikaze*. The riders sat in two cages on the end of rotating arms which swung in opposite directions until they had built up enough momentum to swing a full three hundred and sixty degrees.

"Go on then," said Rose. She wouldn't normally have been keen, but somehow being here with Dan made her feel bold.

They joined the queue and climbed aboard the next time the ride came to a standstill. They strapped themselves in and Rose pulled out her mobile phone.

"I have to get a picture of me on this thing before it starts," she said, holding the phone out at arm's length. She was worried she might throw up that evening's lasagne afterwards and then all photo opportunities would be null and void.

"Smile!" she said, leaning in towards Dan. She snapped a picture of them and only just had time to stuff the phone back into her pocket before the ride started.

To begin with it was just a gentle swing, backwards and forwards, quite pleasant really. But then the arms of the pendulum gained speed, lifting the rows of riders higher and higher into the air. With every upward swing Rose felt
~~~

herself grow heavy as if she'd eaten a rock for dinner instead of a supermarket ready-meal, and then with every downward swing she weighed nothing as the carriage seemed to descend without her, her stomach following seconds later.

Rose clung on to the harness as the world started to tilt at an alarming angle and the screams of her fellow riders filled her ears. Before she realised it, she too was screaming from the sheer terror and exhilaration of being swung up to almost vertical. If the arms of the pendulum were the hands on a clock they would be up as far as one and eleven respectively by now.

Next time we're going to go over the top, thought Rose. *Hold on tight!*

They plummeted towards the ground and flew straight up in the opposite direction. As the world turned over, Rose clenched her stomach muscles as if they, and not the harness, were all that was preventing her from plunging to her death. They reached twelve on the imaginary clock face and for a heart-stopping moment seemed to hang upside down, suspended in air, then they were going over the top and Rose let out a scream that was half terror and half relief at having made it all the way round without throwing up. The pendulum did a couple more loop-the-loops and Rose closed her eyes and let herself relax, enjoying the feeling of freedom and motion. Then the ride started to slow and before long they were staggering off, shaking and laughing.

"Oh my God, that was awesome," said Rose. She took a step forwards and the ground seemed to disappear from under her feet.

Dan caught hold of her arms, and held her upright. "You OK there?"

Rose blinked as the world lurched from side-to-side and black spots danced in front of her eyes. "Sorry," she said. "Bit dizzy, that's all."

"Take a couple of deep breaths."

She did as she was told and gradually the world stopped moving.

"That ride was a bit much," he said. He was still standing in front of her, holding her by the arms. As her vision cleared Rose looked into his face. His deep brown eyes reflected the lights of the nearby rides. For a moment they stood there, looking at each other and it seemed to Rose as if the jostling crowds, the throbbing music and the sugary smells all faded into the background. It was just the two of them. Then some guy carrying a can of lager knocked into her with a slurred *Sorry, love,* and the spell was broken.

"Want to try *Shoot the Duck?*" asked Dan. "I used to love that as a kid."

Rose nodded. She'd be happy to keep her feet on the ground for the rest of the evening.

~~~

It was hot and dark inside the tent. Smells of tobacco, beer and sour milk mingled with gingerbread and toffee apples, making Alice feel quite lightheaded. George ushered them to a bench close to the front and Alice found herself squashed in between Mary and their host. Normally she didn't like confined spaces, but she took comfort from George's presence. He laid a hand gently on her arm and asked if she was all right.

"Quite all right," she said, thinking, *Quite all right with you here beside me.*

A gentleman in a black top hat and tails, the master of ceremonies, strode onto the stage and the audience fell silent. "Ladies and gentlemen!" he proclaimed, twirling his exceptionally long moustache between finger and thumb and fixing the audience with his dark eyes. "Welcome to Marvel's Magic Show! Today you will see the most astounding, the most amazing, the most astonishing, nay, the most awe-inspiring magic performed right before your
~~~

very eyes!" Loud gasps of anticipation issued from the audience. Alice felt her pulse quicken.

"And without further ado, I present to you, Pepper's Ghost!"

An eerie, haunting music played on violins and a flute started up from somewhere off the stage. Alice's spine tingled and the hairs on the back of her neck stood on end. Without thinking, she reached for George's hand and grasped it. He responded by taking her hand in his and giving it a gentle squeeze. He didn't let go and she left her hand where it was.

At that moment an ethereal figure, veiled from head to toe in a translucent robe, like a shroud that had unravelled, started to drift across the stage. There was a sharp intake of breath from the audience. The figure was there and yet not there at the same time, like an apparition one might expect to see in the dungeon of a deserted castle, or an uninhabited wing of a grand house fallen into ruin. It appeared to float across the stage, not flying exactly, but not making solid contact with the boards either. Then more ghostly figures appeared from the other side of the stage, like guests entering a ballroom. The figures wove around each other in a wraith-like dance, graceful and serene. From somewhere near the back of the audience there was a cry and a thud as a lady fainted and crashed to the floor. Alice was in no danger of fainting. She was far too engrossed in the show, mesmerised by its spectral beauty, and not wanting to miss whatever was about to happen next.

The ghost show came to a startling conclusion when a very real and solid man wearing tweed breeches and a hunting cap marched onto the stage, unsheathed a sword and, to the consternation of a number of female members of the audience, proceeded to stab the ghosts through their spectral bodies without any bloodshed. As each ghost was stabbed, it collapsed to the ground and vanished into thin air. When he had finished his ghostly murdering spree, the gentleman held his sword aloft and took a deep bow. The audience erupted into applause.

Alice let go of George's hand and clapped enthusiastically. She didn't care if the show was real or just a trick of the light, it was the most astonishing thing she had ever seen.

"Did you enjoy that?" asked George, leaning close and speaking into her ear.

"Absolutely," said Alice, smiling at him.

"Good, I'm glad."

~~~

"There's a trick to that," said Kitty to Jackson. She was applauding as much as anyone, but she leaned close and said, "It's all done with mirrors you know."

"I thought as much," said Jackson. It didn't surprise him. Smoke and mirrors, that's all these shows ever were: a means to entertain the masses who were easily fooled. And that ridiculous master of ceremonies was the biggest charlatan Jackson had ever seen.

"Still," said Kitty approvingly, "they did a good job of making the ghosts seem real."

"Hmm," said Jackson. He'd lost any interest in the show. What interested him more was the proximity with which Alice and George were sitting next to each other. Although they were some rows off, he could see them clearly. Was it really necessary for them to be so close to each other? *It looks as though Henry might have a rival on his hands,* thought Jackson. *And he won't like that at all.*

The master of ceremonies walked back onto the stage to announce the next act and Jackson braced himself for the next fraudulent piece of tomfoolery.

~~~

Dan guided her through the crowd, keeping his hand

on the small of her back. Rose was no longer dizzy but she didn't want him to take his hand away. She was acutely aware of the pressure of his fingers and felt a tingling sensation running up her spine. Maybe they could do a couple more things at the fair and then go for a walk, somewhere quiet, just the two of them. The evenings stayed lighter here much later than they did in London. Rose imagined them walking along the beach in the setting sun. And then…

"Here we are," said Dan, breaking into her thoughts. They had arrived at the *Shoot the Duck* stall and got into line behind a little boy of about six who was there with his dad. *He's not embarrassed about queueing up with the little kids,* thought Rose. Other boys she knew wouldn't have the balls to do that.

"Have you always lived in Scarborough?" she asked.

Dan nodded. "Yeah. People always think it must be wonderful to live by the seaside but that's because they only come here in the summer. You should see this place in the winter. The wind nearly blows people off the prom."

Rose laughed.

"And," he continued, "we never get to go away in the summer because of the amusement arcade. That's our busiest time of the year so we have to spend every summer at home."

"I hadn't really thought of that," admitted Rose.

The queue shuffled forwards. It was now the little boy's turn. He had to stand on tiptoe to reach the rifle. He aimed the gun at the line of metal ducks as they swam past and shouted *BANG* every time he pulled the trigger. Unfortunately he had more enthusiasm than accuracy and most of the ducks were still swimming.

"So you're a bit of a mean shot with the rifle, are you?" she asked Dan, wondering if the ducks were actually designed not to fall over. That poor kid was having no luck.

Dan didn't reply. He was staring fixedly over her shoulder at something or someone.

"What is it?" she asked, turning to see what he was looking at. There were groups of people milling around, some of them eating enormous pink swirls of candy floss, others munching on toffee apples; there were children with helium-filled, animal-shaped balloons; groups of laughing teenagers; young couples arm-in-arm; neon lights flashing on and off and the constant thump of loud music. Rose couldn't see anything out of the ordinary.

"Those men over there," said Dan. "By the Ghost Train."

"Which ones?"

"Those two, in the leather jackets."

Rose saw them. "So? Do you know them?"

"Not exactly," he said, "but they came into the amusement arcade yesterday asking for Dad and saying that someone called Max wanted to see him. When I told Dad about them, that was when he put his foot on the accelerator and nearly ran you over. He wouldn't say what those guys wanted, but I kind of get the impression they're trouble. And they came back today with a box."

Sensing Dan's unease, Rose looked more closely at the men. One was short and thick-set, almost as wide as he was tall. The other was tall and thin and even at this distance she could see the spider-web tattoo on the side of his neck. They were leaning against the side of the Ghost Train ride and the one with the tattoo was talking on a mobile phone. A man and a woman exited the Ghost Train. Laughing and fooling around, they accidentally brushed past the two men. The guy with the tattoo spun around and raised his fist in a burst of anger and shouted something that Rose couldn't hear. The couple looked stunned and put their hands up as if to say, *Cool it, man!* Then they walked on, shaking their heads in disbelief at this unprovoked display of aggression.

"Next, please," called the guy running the *Shoot the*

Duck stall.

"Hurry up, mate," said a man behind them whose young son was hopping up and down with impatience.

Dan seemed to make a snap decision and stepped out of the queue. "You go," he said to the man behind him. The little boy squealed with delight.

"What are you doing?" asked Rose.

"I'm going to follow them," said Dan. "I want to see what they're up to. Look, they're leaving now."

"Are you sure that's a good idea? I mean, they look pretty tough to me."

"You don't have to come with me," he said, then added, "unless you want to."

Well we came here together, thought Rose. *And now you're going off to spy on a couple of thugs.* Rose shook her head, she was starting to think like her mother and that had to stop. "No, I'm coming with you."

~~~

"And now, ladies and gentlemen," declared the master of ceremonies, "for your delectation and delight, I present to you the most daring, the most dazzling, nay, the most dumbfounding demonstration you have ever seen!" A collective "Ooh!" rose up from the audience.

George could sense Alice's excitement at the prospect of the next magic trick. Her face was rapt with attention, her eyes sparkled in the lights from the stage and a gentle smile played about her lips. From the moment he had encountered her in the graveyard of St Mary's Church, he felt as if he had been blessed by fortune. She had captivated him with her natural beauty, her intelligent, enquiring mind, and her easy-going manner. That evening he had gone back to his lodgings and drawn her face from memory, filling a whole sketchbook with her likeness, imagining her as the tragic Ophelia, the magical Titania or the wise and beautiful Portia.
~~~

"Ladies and gentlemen! I present to you, Marlo the Magician who will perform the Metamorphosis Magic Trick!"

Whilst the master of ceremonies had been talking, two assistants had placed a large wooden box in the centre of the stage. In front of the box they had lain a curtain on a pole. Marlo the Magician, clad all in black, appeared from the wings, accompanied by a young woman in a slim-fitting silk gown. The woman twirled around a few times as if to demonstrate that she was real flesh and blood, unlike Pepper's Ghosts of the previous show. Then the magician helped her to climb inside the box and the assistants fixed a lid on the top. The tension in the audience rose a notch.

The magician then climbed onto the top of the box and his assistants, each standing on a chair, hoisted up the curtain pole between them. Off-stage a drum roll sounded. The magician lifted his arms to the sky; the drum roll became louder and more intense; the audience held its breath; then the helpers lifted the curtain high, obscuring the audience's view of the magician; there was a loud bang on the drum and when the helpers lowered the curtain only moments later, the woman, who had been in the box, was now standing on top of it. Marlo had vanished.

"Ooh!" chimed the audience.

The helpers lifted the woman down from the box and, as she twirled off to the side of the stage, they removed the lid, and the magician jumped out. As the applause erupted, George heard Alice laugh with astonishment. The trick was truly amazing.

She turned to him. "Wasn't that fantastic? I'd love to know how they did that."

"Who knows?" he replied, pleased that she was enjoying herself so much. He would do anything to make her happy, anything at all.

~~~
~~~

Jackson joined in the clapping merely for form's sake. The trick was clever, to be sure, but there was obviously a logical explanation for it, not that he was interested in what it was. Beside him, Kitty was applauding enthusiastically. No doubt she would fill him in on how the trick was done later on. For now, Jackson kept his attention fixed firmly on Alice and George, still sitting in their places near the front of the audience. Unless Jackson was blind, they had moved even closer towards each other during that performance. Well, well, well. For his own part Jackson couldn't have cared less, but he knew Henry would care an inordinate amount if he found out and Henry was paying Jackson to make sure his future bride didn't stray. It was in Jackson's own interest to ensure this situation didn't progress, otherwise it would be Jackson who would ultimately pay the price.

~~~

Rose and Dan wound their way through the crowds, trying not to lose sight of the two men, but staying far enough back so the men wouldn't suspect they were being followed. They lost sight of them by the Dodgems but then Rose spotted them heading towards the lorries, trailers and caravans parked on the far side of the field. It was quiet over here, away from the crowds. Rose felt uneasy, like they were trespassing on private property, but Dan seemed intent on following the men.

Outside a battered, old caravan, a couple of bare-footed children, a boy and a girl, were playing with a ball, tossing it to each other in sullen silence. They paused in their game to stare at Dan and Rose as they walked past. They turned a corner and a black dog suddenly sprang at them out of the shadows, letting off a volley of vicious sounding barks.

"Bloody hell," cried Rose as she jumped back. The dog
~~~

was a monster and looked like some kind of cross between a Rottweiler and a Pitbull Terrier.

"It's OK," said Dan, taking her arm. "It's tied up. It can't hurt you."

Rose wasn't so sure. Weren't breeds like that supposed to be banned? The dog wore a studded collar around its thick neck. One end of a thin, fraying rope was tied to the collar, the other end was tied to a metal hook in a wooden post. It seemed like a totally inadequate means of restraint for such a vicious dog. And even if the animal didn't break free, its incessant barking was sooner or later going to attract attention and someone would come and ask what they were doing snooping around the homes of the fairground travellers. Or the men might realise they were being followed and come after them. She gave the animal a wide berth, not trusting the rope to keep it under control. The dog chased after them as far as it was able to, snarling and barking all the time. She was starting to regret her decision to accompany Dan on this foolhardy venture. What was he hoping to achieve anyway?

"Hold on," whispered Dan, once they were past the dog.

The two men had stopped beside a vehicle at the very edge of the field. This wasn't just an ordinary towing caravan like the others, but a much more substantial camper van, more like a small lorry, with a sleek, modern exterior, a luxury home on wheels. There was a light on inside and they could hear the beat of loud rock music. The men climbed the short flight of steps to a door in the camper van's side, knocked once, then disappeared inside.

"Come on," said Dan. "Let's go round the back."

Before Rose had a chance to protest, Dan was crouching low and running across the grass towards the camper van. *What is this,* thought Rose? *An action movie?* She didn't want to get any closer to the camper van, but neither did she want to go back on her own for fear of the dog. They'd come this far, so they might as well see the thing through, she supposed. She ran as lightly as she could across the grass and joined Dan round the back of the van.

"I can't see what's going on in there," whispered Dan. "The window's too high. Is there anything to stand on?"

"No," said Rose, looking around. She didn't *want* to find something to stand on. It sounded like a really bad idea.

"Over there," said Dan, pointing to a shabby caravan with a pile of empty packing crates outside on the ground. Dan ran over, grabbed the top crate and ran back with it, placing it directly under the rear window of the camper van. *Thank goodness for the loud music,* thought Rose, otherwise the occupants would surely have heard them moving about by now.

Dan climbed onto the crate, then held out a hand for Rose to join him. *Oh, what the hell,* she thought, climbing up beside him. She might as well take a peek now they'd gone to all this trouble. Keeping as low as possible, Rose peered inside.

Wow, thought Rose. To say the camper van was luxurious was an understatement. This was not your typical family caravan with tartan sofa, narrow bunk beds and Formica-topped table. The interior gleamed like something out of a glossy magazine. There were cream leather sofas on either side with minimalist white cabinets overhead. A high-tech kitchen area sparkled with chrome fittings. Rose noticed a well-stocked drinks cabinet and a huge flat-screen television. The men they had followed were seated on the sofas. There was a third man who occupied a swivel, leather armchair, the sort that would recline at the push of a button. They couldn't hear the conversation inside the caravan, but from the way the third man was gesticulating and pointing, it was clear that he was the boss. Everything about him, from his shaven head, his bronze tan, his expensive-looking linen suit and the gold medallion he wore around his neck made Rose think of a mafia boss. *Good grief*, she thought, *what movie set did he crawl out of?* He reached out a hand for a glass of whisky on the table beside him. On his knuckles, tattooed in bold capitals, was the name MAX.

"So that's him," muttered Dan under his breath.

Max stood up, opened one of the overhead cupboards, reached inside and brought down a black box. He put the box on the table next to his glass of whisky and opened the lid. From inside, he produced two small handguns. He gave one each to the two men who examined the weapons with an air of indifference, as if people gave them guns every other day. They put the guns in an inside pocket of their leather jackets.

Bloody hell, thought Rose, *this is getting serious.* She looked at Dan and saw that he was thinking the same thing too.

"What are you doing?"

Rose jumped out of her skin at the accusing, high-pitched voice behind her. She spun around, lost her balance and fell off the crate with a thud. She landed awkwardly on her hands and knees, her right knee hitting a stone.

"Ow!" she cried.

The two children they'd seen earlier were standing there, the little girl tossing the ball into the air and the boy staring at them with his fists clenched as if he might duff them up. It was the girl who had asked them the question.

The camper van door flew open and a Geordie voice shouted, "Who's there?"

"Run," hissed Dan, pulling Rose to her feet as the sound of footsteps thudded round the side of the vehicle.

~~~

Mary stepped outside the tent, fanning herself with a programme. It had got rather heated inside the tent with all those bodies pressed together in such a confined space. But what a show! That would be something to write and
~~~

tell her Ma about.

Even though she had been so engrossed in the performances, it had not escaped Mary's notice that Alice and George were becoming ever more friendly. *Well, good for her,* thought Mary. Mr Hartright is a much nicer chap than that bloated, old windbag, Henry Blackwood. Mary was a great believer in true love, and not simply marrying according to the dictates of social convention or the whims of one's parents. Mary judged that it wouldn't do any harm to leave Alice and George alone together for a little while whilst she went off in search of some hot gingerbread.

She picked her way through the crowds, trying to remember where they had seen the gingerbread stall.

"You look lost, dearie," said an old woman, standing outside a small, circular tent. She wore a scarf, wrapped turban-style, around her hair and large, hooped earrings dangled from fleshy lobes.

"I'm looking for the gingerbread stall," said Mary.

"Is that all you're looking for?" asked the old woman.

"I'm sorry?" Mary took a step towards her. The woman's bird-like face was deeply lined but her eyes were bright and alert.

"Would you like me to read your fortune?" she asked, laying a bony hand on Mary's arm.

Mary paused to regard the old woman more closely, the gingerbread temporarily forgotten. She'd joked in her last letter to her Ma that she might have her fortune told; see if there were any handsome fishermen out there. Well, why not? It would be a bit of a laugh if nothing else.

The old woman led Mary inside the tent. Persian rugs covered the floor and swathes of red and gold silk were draped around the walls. A single lantern hung from a wooden pole, casting a warm, flickering light. There was a circular wooden table with two chairs facing each other and in the centre of the table was a crystal ball. They sat down and Mary waited for the old woman to speak.

The old woman cradled the crystal ball in her bony hands and started to hum gently to herself as she gazed into its depths. Mary tried to peer into the ball but all she could see was the reflection of the light from the lantern.

"Ah," intoned the old woman in a faraway voice.

"What is it?" asked Mary.

"I think you are visiting Scarborough, is that right?"

"Yes, that's right," said Mary.

"And you are here…alone? Or maybe with a friend?"

"Well, with a lady I work for actually."

"Yes, of course, a lady. So you are a…"

"Lady's maid," supplied Mary.

"Yes, a lady's maid. I thought so. And the lady is kind to you, but you do not have anyone special in your life, no gentleman friend."

"That's right," admitted Mary.

"Oh, but wait, I see…I see a handsome stranger."

Mary giggled. *A handsome stranger?* The old woman had to be making this up. Still, it was nice to imagine a handsome stranger. A girl could but hope!

"My dear," said the old woman, looking up from the crystal ball. "You are soon going to meet the man of your dreams."

"When will that be?" asked Mary. If there was any truth in this she wanted to know whether she should look out for him in Scarborough or wait until they had returned to London.

"When you are least expecting it," said the old woman enigmatically.

Mary thanked her and paid her a penny. No doubt it was all nonsense, but it was fun all the same.

The old woman escorted her back outside. "The gingerbread stall is just over there," she said, pointing with a finger. And so it was! How could she have missed it? Mary pressed the old woman's hand and thanked her once again. Then she hurried over to the stall and bought three hot slices of the most aromatic gingerbread she had ever smelt in her life.

~~~

Right now, Rose would have given anything to be back on the Kamikaze ride, hanging upside down, stomach clenched, screaming with fear, instead of running from two men with guns. *This is what real fear feels like,* she thought, as she willed her legs to move faster. Her heart thumped against her ribcage and her breath came in short, ragged gasps. She skirted around the corner of a lorry, trying to keep up with Dan who was already way ahead of her.

"Hang on," she cried, forgetting about the tethered dog until she almost ran into it. It leapt into the air, barking and snarling at her. She swerved to the side and felt her feet slip from under her as she skidded on a patch of oily ground. Her ankle twisted painfully and she landed with a thump on her side.

The dog went berserk. It was only a foot away from her now, barking like a demented thing, pulling at the rope. The animal lunged at her, every muscle in its body straining to break free, saliva drooling from its mouth. And those teeth. Rose couldn't take her eyes off its yellow, pointed teeth which snapped together like a vice every time the dog closed its jaw.

There was a creak, the sound of splitting wood. The hook to which the rope was tied was going to break loose any second. Then the animal would be on her, sinking its teeth into her flesh. She had to get to her feet but she didn't know if her ankle would bear her weight. And what about the men with the guns? And where was Dan? She put a hand out onto the muddy ground, pushed herself onto her knees and started to crawl away as fast as she could.

"Where did they go?" shouted a Geordie voice from somewhere behind a lorry. *Shit!* It was them. In
~~~

desperation, Rose crawled behind a nearby trailer, wedging herself into the space between the trailer's rear bumper and the caravan parked behind. The dog strained to follow her. She crouched low, hoping to hide herself in the shadows, but she worried that even if the dog couldn't reach her, it would give away her hiding place. Then the men appeared and, to Rose's relief, the dog turned its attention to the newcomers. They stopped dead in their tracks at the sight of the animal barking its head off. If it had been angry before, now it really went bonkers, pulling and jerking at the rope. For a split second it sat back on its haunches, hackles bristling, then it leapt forward with such force that there was a cracking sound. The wooden pole splintered and the hook broke loose. Free at last, the animal went for the nearest target, the short man. In one swift movement it sprang into the air and knocked him to the ground.

"Arrgh! Gerroff me!" The man's shouts were drowned out by the incessant barking and the sound of the dog's jaws snapping shut every few seconds. He kicked at the animal with his legs whilst trying to protect his face and throat with his arms. *Oh my God,* thought Rose, *it's actually going to kill him!*

A gun shot split the air. And then there was silence.

Rose, cowering behind the trailer, hardly dared look.

For a while the man lay on the ground with the collapsed body of the dog on top of him. Rose couldn't tell if both of them were dead or just the dog. Then with a grunt of disgust, the man threw the lifeless body of the dog off him, jumped to his feet and turned on his companion. "What the hell man? You shot the fookin' dog man!"

"It was gonna kill yer, man!"

"What's the owner gonna say? He'll fookin' murder yer."

"Not if yer keep yer gob shut." He gave the dead dog a kick in the ribs. "Stupid mutt!"

The men had their backs to her now as they argued over the dead dog and what to do about it. Rose pushed herself to her feet, holding onto the side of the trailer for support. She needed to get away before they noticed her. And then Dan reappeared.

"Oh thank God," he said. "I heard the gun shot and I thought… I thought…"

"It's all right, they didn't shoot me," said Rose. "Just Fluffy over there." She nodded towards the men who had started to drag the canine corpse away from the scene of the crime and had apparently forgotten about pursuing Rose and Dan.

"Thank goodness you're safe," said Dan. "I'm sorry I got so far ahead of you. I didn't realise."

Rose gingerly put some weight on her ankle and winced.

"Here, let me help you." Dan put an arm around her waist. She put her arm over his shoulder and, with Dan's support, hobbled back into the crowded hustle and bustle of the fairground.

"Come here," said Dan, once they were back in the light. "You've got mud on your face." Very gently, he wiped her cheek with his thumb.

"Do I look a right sight?" she asked.

"You look lovely," he said.

She looked down at her mud-stained clothes. "Mum'll go nuts when she sees these jeans."

"That's mothers for you. How's the ankle?"

"It's easing up a bit." But she didn't take her arm away from his shoulder and he didn't let go of her waist.

"Want to see anything else?" asked Dan.

Rose shook her head. "Maybe we should head back."

"Yeah. That was probably enough excitement for one night."

"What do you think those guys are up to?" she asked, as they walked towards the bus stop.

"I don't know, but it's got to be some kind of criminal

activity. You don't carry guns around just for the fun of it."

"And did you see the inside of that camper van? It was palatial. It must have cost a fortune. Where does a fairground traveller get that sort of money from?"

"And it's not just the caravan," said Dan. "Yesterday I saw those two guys on the deck of a luxury yacht down in the harbour."

"So what are we going to do?" asked Rose. "Should we go to the police?"

"And tell them what? That we were snooping around the private caravans at the fair and a couple of men chased us?"

"But they had guns. They could have killed us."

Dan thought for a moment. "Let me talk to my dad first. If he's got some business with Max and we go to the police, then he could get into serious trouble too. I'll try and warn him to stay away from Max, make him understand what sort of man he's dealing with."

Rose was still in favour of going to the police, but then the bus arrived and they were not the only people on board so they had to drop the discussion about armed criminals. By the time they got off the bus on the sea-front it no longer felt like an appropriate topic of conversation.

"Do you want some fish and chips?" asked Dan.

Rose suddenly realised that she was starving. The adrenalin rush of the ride and the terror of being chased by two armed men had left her with a raging appetite.

"Sounds like a great idea."

They went to a takeaway and ordered two portions of battered haddock and chips, served with a generous sprinkling of salt and vinegar and wrapped in sheets of paper, the traditional way. They took the food down to the sea-front and sat on the prom to eat their supper. The chips were big and fat and utterly delicious. The fish was succulent and fresh and covered in a light golden batter that was gently crisped on the outside and soft inside.

"That was amazing." Rose licked her fingers, savouring the tangy salt and vinegar.

"Best fish and chips in the world here," said Dan without a hint of irony. Rose believed him.

A bright moon had risen over the sea. On the horizon a ship's light blinked. Rose would have liked to sit there for longer but she was aware it was getting late. She had to admit the evening had not gone exactly as planned. There was little hope now of a moonlit walk along the beach. Her ankle still throbbed and she was going to have to make up some story about why her clothes were covered in mud. Staying out any later would only confirm her mother's worst fears and make her more likely to put her foot down over future dates, assuming that Dan wanted to see her again.

"I better be getting back," said Rose tentatively, hoping Dan would catch the bait and ask her what she was doing tomorrow. "Mum'll throw a wobbly if I'm late."

"I'll walk you home," said Dan, then added, "got any plans for tomorrow?"

"No. But you can show me more of Scarborough's fun-filled attractions, if you like." *Just no more armed gangs, please,* she thought.

He laughed. "That won't take long, but OK. I finish work tomorrow at four o'clock. Why don't you come and find me at the amusement arcade?"

"OK."

They climbed the steep road to her gran's house and then paused outside the front door. A light was still on in the living room and Rose suspected her mother had waited up for her. There was going to be one hell of a row when she saw the state of Rose's clothes.

"Well, thanks for an… exciting evening," she said brightly.

"Sorry about how it ended."

"Oh, don't worry. It was all part of the fun."

"See you tomorrow then."

"Sure. Four o'clock. I'll be there."

He squeezed her hand and gave her a quick kiss on the cheek. Then he was off down the hill, hands thrust into his jeans pockets. Rose watched his retreating figure until he disappeared out of sight. She touched the spot on her cheek where he'd kissed her and smiled to herself. Now she'd deal with her mother.

~~~

Mary ate most of her gingerbread on the way back to the tent where they'd watched the magic shows. The sweet, spicy smell was irresistible and the cake melted in her mouth.

She looked for Alice and Mr Hartright and found them still sitting inside the tent where she had left them, seemingly oblivious of the fact that the rest of the audience had departed. As she approached she heard them discussing the paintings of the Pre-Raphaelites. Alice was especially fond of the works of Edward Burne Jones and Dante Gabriel Rossetti. Mary had once accompanied her to an exhibition in London but had been shocked at the brutality of the paintings by William Holman Hunt and had thought that *The Lady of Shalott* looked ill and needed someone to do her hair for her.

Mary coughed gently to announce her arrival, and Alice and George sprang apart as if caught in an illicit embrace. Mary pretended not to notice.

"I've brought you some gingerbread," she said. "It's delicious."

They thanked her and took the hot slices from her. When they had finished their cake, they stepped outside. The crowds had thinned now and the entertainers were starting to pack away their barrel organs and violins. George offered Alice his arm and they started to make their way towards the exit. Mary followed behind, wanting to let Alice and Mr Hartright have the last few minutes to
~~~

themselves.

As they approached the exit, Mary turned around for one last look at the fair. As she did so, something caught her attention. She could have sworn that a gentleman in a bowler hat, escorting a lady in a flouncy dress, had darted behind a stall the second she turned her head. She had the exact same feeling that she'd experienced up at St Mary's Church, as if someone had just walked over her grave. Was someone following them? But why would someone do such a thing?

And then the answer came to her, as if she had just looked into a crystal ball and seen it there, plain as day. *Henry Blackwood.* Well, obviously not Henry himself, he was far too grand to go tiptoeing around a fairground. But could he have sent someone to spy on them? The reasoning half of her brain argued that the idea was preposterous and she had no firm proof, but in her heart of hearts she knew it was precisely the sort of thing Henry *would* do.

She looked around for Alice and Mr Hartright and saw that they were already climbing into a waiting carriage. Mary pulled her shawl tighter around her shoulders and hurried after them. She'd keep her suspicions to herself for now, she didn't want to spoil the lovely evening they'd had. But she'd keep her eyes peeled from now on. If Henry had sent a man to follow them, Mary would make sure she found him out.

CHAPTER EIGHT

Rose woke with a start from a nightmare in which she was being chased by a whole pack of vicious, snarling dogs and armed men. Her heart pounded at the memory of last night's events. Never before in her whole life had she felt so scared. How close had she been to having her throat ripped out by that mad dog or being shot in the head by those lunatics? She was really regretting her and Dan's decision not to go straight to the police. But Dan had said he didn't want to get his dad into trouble and that he would speak to him about Max. She wanted to trust Dan, but was he making the right decision? Should she just go to the police on her own? But she didn't want to go behind Dan's back and, besides, her mother would go ballistic if she knew half of what had gone on last night. That thought alone made Rose hesitate about going to the authorities.

She decided to do nothing until she'd seen Dan later that day. Maybe by then he would have spoken to his dad and everything would be sorted out. Or he might change his mind about going to the police, in which case Rose would go along and support him.

She tried to push the frightening memories of last night

from her mind and concentrate instead on the good ones. Like the way Dan had caught her in his arms when she'd felt dizzy after the ride. Rose smiled to herself. She'd practically swooned just like the Victorian ladies Mary described in her letters about the fair. Not that Rose could blame her dizzy spell on too-tight a corset or the terror of seeing a ghost appear on the stage. But Dan had been the perfect gentleman, holding her steady, making sure she was all right. And then afterwards, when he'd escorted her from the fair, his arm around her waist, she had leaned into him enjoying the smell of his skin. When she closed her eyes Rose could feel the pressure of his fingers, gentle but firm. She couldn't wait till she saw him again.

Downstairs, her mother was clanking pots and pans in the kitchen. Rose couldn't face bacon and eggs right now. She could still taste the vinegar from the late-night fish and chips, and she didn't feel up to another volley of questions about last night.

When she let herself into the house at a quarter to midnight, she'd been dismayed to find her mother sitting up waiting for her. Andrea had put aside the book she was reading and said in a pointed tone, "I thought I told you not to stay out too late." And then she'd noticed the state of Rose's clothes, the mud and oil stains on her jeans and top. She jumped to her feet and said, "What on earth happened to you?"

"It was nothing Mum, I slipped and fell, that's all."

"Was it that boy? Was he rough with you?"

"No, Mum, not at all."

"Don't try to protect him. If he tried anything on…"

"Mum, I swear, it was nothing like that. I fell over and sprained my ankle." That much at least was true. "He helped bring me home actually." Andrea had looked sceptical but had let the matter drop. But one thing was sure. From now on her mother would be on high alert, looking out for any sign of trouble. Rose would have to take extra care not to land herself in any more sticky situations.

She sat up in bed. She didn't want to go downstairs whilst her mother was still in the kitchen so she reached for the pile of letters, found the next one, and started to read.

Grand Hotel,
Scarborough,
9pm, 16th August, 1899

Dear Ma,

What an exhausting day! And here was I thinking we'd come to Scarborough for a holiday. We'd barely got over all the excitement of the fair when Mr Hartright (he says we're to call him George, but I can't quite bring myself to be so familiar) invited us to accompany him on a trip to Whitby which is about twenty miles further up the coast.

Alice was terribly excited to see the place where Dracula came ashore. She and Mr Hartright talked all the way about Mr Stoker's novel and whether it was strictly necessary to chop off Lucy's head. I never heard such a load of gory nonsense in all my life. I never thought I'd say this, but maybe Henry Blackwood has a point when he says ladies shouldn't read fiction. I still don't like him, mind!

The first thing that hit me in Whitby was the noise! Honestly, I thought Scarborough had more than enough seagulls but you should have heard them in Whitby! My ears are still ringing from their blooming screeching.

Now, to be fair, there were some very nice little tea shops along Church Street and if we could have just popped into one of those I'd have thought the trip more than worthwhile, but of course we had to go and climb the steps to the Abbey. You're not going to believe how many steps there were. One hundred and ninety-nine! I know, because I counted them. And what did we see when we got to the top? Yet another ruin, in the same sad state of repair as Scarborough Castle.

Well, I was fair jiggered by the time we reached the Abbey so I sat down on a bench and let Alice and Mr Hartright wander off. He was telling her all about the geology of the place, a subject about which he seemed to know a ridiculous amount and I really wasn't interested in hearing about a load of old rocks. I know you're thinking I shouldn't have left them on their own, it's not proper and all that, but really Ma, I don't see the harm in it. It's almost the twentieth century after all.

As they say, what goes up must come down, so when they'd finished looking round the Abbey ruins, we had to walk back down all those steps, all one hundred and ninety-nine of them (I don't think my legs are going to recover in a month of Sundays) and I thought surely now it's time for a nice cup of tea and a cream scone, but Mr Hartright insisted on taking us to a jet workshop where they make jewellery from the jet stone that comes from this area. It all sounded a bit mournful to me because jet is what the Queen has been wearing ever since Prince Albert died, but anyway, we went to this workshop. Now, to give him his due, Mr Hartright is nothing if not generous and after we'd looked around and admired the skill of the craftsmen, he insisted on buying us both a small gift. Mine is a jet brooch in the shape of a rose and I thanked him kindly for it. For Alice he bought a jet necklace, and very fine it is too, with delicate black beads in a series of intricate loops.

Now I'm going to let you into a secret. I think Alice might break off her engagement with Henry Blackwood, and no bad thing that would be either. Keep that to yourself, mind, and don't go spreading rumours. I don't want to cause trouble.

Love to all,

Mary.

~~~

Dan stood under the hot shower, letting the water pelt him on the shoulders. He'd finished washing long ago, but was in no hurry to leave the comfort of the steamy cubicle. His mind was stuck on an infinite loop, going round in maddening circles, replaying the events of last night.

It had all been going so well until he'd had the crazy idea to go and follow those two crooks, for Dan had no
~~~

doubt that that was what they were. And what must Rose have thought? Probably that his family had connections with Scarborough's criminal underworld. He cringed with embarrassment. He'd wanted her to enjoy herself yesterday evening, had thought they were getting on great, that there was even some chemistry between them, and instead he'd dragged her into this dangerous situation where they could have been shot. Never mind his dad nearly running her over, he was doing a pretty good job of endangering her himself. That was why he'd suggested fish and chips when they got back into town, as a way of putting things right again but that gesture now seemed totally inadequate as a way of making amends. If she had any sense she'd steer well clear of him from now on.

Stop worrying, a small voice inside his head tried to argue back. S*he agreed to meet you again today. What's the problem?* But a louder voice argued that she only said that to be nice. If he was her, he'd be having second thoughts about meeting him again.

He turned off the shower and grabbed the towel from the heated towel rail. Pushing thoughts of Rose to one side for the moment, he turned his attention to the problem of his dad. Despite what he'd agreed with Rose, now in the cold light of day he was in two minds whether or not to say anything to his dad about the events of last night. Ryan would probably try to dismiss the whole thing and just tell him he shouldn't have followed the men in the first place. And besides, it was highly unlikely that his dad would willingly admit to any business dealings with a man like Max. But did his dad really know what sort of man Max was? That he employed armed thugs? If he kept quiet and something terrible happened to his father, he'd never forgive himself. He went downstairs resolved to speak up, but found only his mum in the kitchen.

"Is Dad around?"

"What?" Fiona glanced up from her mobile phone.

"There's something I wanted to speak to him about."

She clicked her phone off and dropped it into her handbag. She was wearing a bright pink Lycra sports top and cropped leggings.

"He left early," she said. "Said he had business to see to. Can it wait till later?"

For a moment Dan was tempted to blurt everything out to his mum. She might not be the overly maternal type, but she wasn't bad in a crisis. She could be surprisingly level-headed if the situation demanded it.

She fished her car keys out of her bag and said, "There's some leftover curry in the fridge. You can warm it up in the microwave whenever you want it." And the moment for speaking evaporated. She was on her way out and wouldn't want to be held up. She probably had a class to get to, yoga or Pilates.

"Cheers," said Dan. He really didn't feel like eating leftover curry in the house on his own. He'd get some chips in town later on.

"Right, must dash." She picked up her sports bag and headed for the front door. "Have a nice day." The door banged shut behind her.

Dan sighed. Some teenagers would think him lucky that his parents weren't breathing down his neck all the time and that he was free to come and go as he pleased, but sometimes he just wished they would act a bit more like they cared.

He ate some cornflakes and put the bowl and spoon into the dishwasher. What now? He wandered back out into the hallway. The house suddenly felt very large and very empty. It was absurdly big for just the three of them and most of the rooms were never used on a daily basis. All the doors that led off the hallway, to the lounge and dining room and morning room (whatever that was supposed to be) were closed, except for one: the door to his father's study. It stood ajar, casting a beam of sunlight onto the parquet floor from the room's south facing window. *Like an invitation,* thought Dan, as he walked towards it.

He had no plan of action as he stepped into his dad's study, certainly no intention of prying. But something was going on and if his dad was involved with an armed gang, then that could land them all in serious trouble. There had to be something that would give him a clue to what was wrong.

~~~

Grand Hotel,
Scarborough,
5pm, 17th August, 1899

Dear Ma,

When I woke up this morning my legs had seized up. I blame those steps in Whitby! At breakfast, Alice said that the best thing would be to take a gentle stroll along the prom. I noticed straight away she was wearing her new necklace, the one Mr Hartright had bought for her in Whitby. It looked very fine against her white dress.

So after breakfast we took the funicular railway down to the sea-front (for once I was glad of this little train) and started walking towards the spa buildings. We hadn't gone far when we encountered a photographer, a young fellow who was doing his best to attract the attention of the ladies and gentlemen walking past and, from the looks of it, not having much luck. He tried to persuade us to have our photograph taken. I wasn't at all sure I liked the sound of that, but Alice agreed at once and we had to stand there, side-by-side, squinting into the bright sunlight whilst this photographer fiddled around with his big black box and hid himself under a black curtain. I felt such a fool what with everyone staring at us! He said the photograph would be ready to collect tomorrow from his studio in Queen Street, so I suppose that means I'll have to walk over there and pick it up. I shall need a holiday after all this!

Take care,

Love,
~~~

Mary.

~~~

Dan couldn't remember the last time he'd been in his dad's study, possibly not for years. The room smelt of his dad's aftershave and extra-strong coffee. A vase of roses on the windowsill had dropped half its petals onto the floor. Next to the vase stood a framed photograph of himself aged eight riding a donkey on the beach. That must have been about the time his dad took over the amusement arcade, buying it with the money he'd inherited after the death of his own father. The arcade had been in a state of gradual decay for years and Ryan had put a lot of money into doing it up, buying new slot machines and replacing all the neon lighting on the front. It wasn't exactly Las Vegas but it was the nearest thing Scarborough had.

Dan turned his attention to the rest of the room. It was sparsely furnished with a mahogany desk, a high-backed leather swivel chair and a bookcase stacked with non-fiction hardbacks which Dan didn't think he'd ever seen his dad reading. Dan walked over to the desk and sat down in the chair. The centre of the desk was occupied by a state-of-the-art Apple Mac. Dan tried switching it on but it was password protected. He switched it off again. Pushed to one side of the desk was a pile of letters. He picked them up and flicked through them. They looked to be invoices from the companies his dad did business with. Dan recognised the names of some of the companies who made slot machines, the company that supplied the teddy bear prizes and the cleaning company. He put the letters back. The desk had a set of three drawers down one side. He hadn't intended to go rifling through drawers or anything like that, but now that he was here he found it hard to resist. *Just get on with it,* he told himself. *Yes, you're being nosy and no, it's not right. Get over it.* He tried the top
~~~

drawer. It was locked. Was he relieved or frustrated? He wasn't sure. He tried the next drawer and it slid open on smooth runners. Inside was a Smythson diary and a Montblanc fountain pen. Dan picked up the diary and opened it to today's date. *9 am meet Max at Highcliff House.*

The appointment was written in his dad's hand and underlined three times. Dan broke into a cold sweat. His dad was meeting Max *today*. What about the armed men? Would they be there too? What kind of crazy trouble was his dad mixed up in? Dan checked his watch. It was ten to nine. His dad must be on his way there now. But where was Highcliff House? He was sure he'd seen the name recently but couldn't think where. Then it came to him in a flash.

He dropped the diary back in the drawer and went to the kitchen, opening the cupboard where they kept the recycling box. Buried under pizza boxes and juice cartons he found what he was looking for: last week's edition of the *Scarborough News*. The headline on the front cover was all about the *Tour de Yorkshire,* the new cycle race that had sprung up in the wake of the *Tour de France.* Dan was sure he'd seen something about Highcliff House on one of the inside pages. He flicked through the newspaper until he found what he was looking for. On page five was a picture of a derelict Victorian mansion and the headline **Former Lunatic Asylum At Risk of Collapse.** Highcliff House was an abandoned Victorian asylum about a mile and a half north of Scarborough, off the main road to Whitby. The article explained how coastal erosion was threatening the foundations of the Victorian building so the council had authorised its demolition. Work was due to start in the autumn. It didn't sound like the sort of place you'd want to go to meet a man who employed armed thugs.

He dialled his dad's mobile number. He had to warn him to stay away from Max. His dad's phone went straight to voice mail.

There was nothing for it. He was going to have to cycle

to Highcliff House as fast as he could. He ran out the front door, pulled his bike from the garage and started pedalling furiously down the hill.

~~~

Grand Hotel,
Scarborough,
4pm, 18th August, 1899

Dear Ma,

We are in the gravest danger! I went to the photographer's studio this afternoon to collect the photograph of us on the promenade and when I saw it I nearly died of shock for it clearly shows Henry Blackwood's man, Jackson, leaning against the railing, watching us! So I was right. We are being followed, and by that scoundrel no less.

I hurried back to the hotel and showed the picture to Alice and Mr Hartright, who were taking afternoon tea with Mrs Goodly. Alice nearly fainted when she saw the photograph and Mrs Goodly had to revive her with a bottle of smelling salts. Mr Hartright wanted to whisk us away there and then but I said that wouldn't do because Jackson would be onto us. It was then that I came up with a plan to get Alice safely away from him. I can't say any more about it now, but I will write again in a few days when all is well and we are far away from Scarborough. Wish us luck, Ma. We are going to need all the help we can get.

Love,
Mary

Rose picked up the scrapbook and turned to the photograph of Alice and Mary, wanting to see if she could spot the man Mary called Jackson.

She looked once again at the two women. Alice's jet necklace, the love token from George Hartright, was, as Mary had said, clearly visible against her white dress.

There were other people in the photograph, passers-by
~~~

strolling along the prom, the women with parasols and the men absurdly over-dressed for the seaside in suits and bowler hats, but there was one figure who caught Rose's attention. A man in the ubiquitous dark suit and bowler hat was standing about twenty feet behind Alice and Mary, off to their right. He was accompanied by a pretty young woman in a dress decorated with frills and bows, but he was ignoring her. Instead he was leaning against the railing of the promenade, arms crossed, staring directly at Alice and Mary. The other passers-by in the photograph were out of focus because they would have been moving when the picture was taken, but this man and his companion were almost as sharp as Alice and Mary themselves, and that was why they stood out so. Was that Jackson? A shiver ran up Rose's spine. She wanted to shout at the women in the photograph, *He's behind you!* But they were separated from her by more than a hundred years and besides, it was only a picture.

CHAPTER NINE

At four o'clock Rose turned onto the sea-front. She could see Dan waiting for her outside the amusement arcade. He stood slightly hunched, biting his lower lip, kicking the paving stone with the toe of his shoe, but when he caught sight of her approaching through the crowds of holiday-makers he straightened up and his face broke into a huge smile that lit up his eyes. *Maybe he thought I wouldn't show up after what happened last night,* thought Rose. *But we survived didn't we?* She had already started to think of the incident with the armed men as nothing more than a bit of a scrape.

"Hi there," she said.

"Hi." He leaned forwards and gave her a peck on the cheek. It was friendly, nothing more.

"So what's happening?" asked Rose.

"How's the ankle?"

"Much better thanks. It wasn't a bad sprain."

"Good." He looked relieved. "In that case, can we go for a walk?"

"Sure." She'd spent most of the day lying on her bed deciphering Victorian letters so she could do with some exercise. Andrea had received a call from work and had shut herself away in her bedroom to deal with it and her grandmother had gone for a lie down in the afternoon saying she felt tired. That wasn't surprising: it must be exhausting having Andrea around all the time.

"Where are we going?" asked Rose. "Anywhere in particular?" When he suggested a walk, Rose hoped it would be a gentle stroll along the beach but Dan set off at a brisk pace towards the headland and Rose had to work hard to keep up with his longer stride.

"There's this place I want to check out," said Dan. "It's an abandoned Victorian lunatic asylum."

"A lunatic asylum? You sure know how to give a girl a good time."

He stopped. "Sorry. We don't have to go there if you don't want to."

She could see the disappointment in his face. "No, I don't mind, really. But why there of all places?" They started walking again.

Dan hesitated for a moment then said, "I cycled there this morning because Dad had gone there for a meeting with Max. But by the time I got up the hill, they'd already left. I saw Dad's Ferrari coming back down and Max's Jaguar was shooting off in the opposite direction."

"Max? As in *gangster-boss-have-a-gun* Max?"

"Yeah, him."

Rose stopped and took hold of Dan's arm. "And he hangs out in an abandoned asylum when he's not in his luxury camper van or on his yacht? What kind of madman are we dealing with here?"

"I don't know why he would want to use the asylum," admitted Dan. "The place is falling down actually. The council have condemned the building. They're going to demolish it."

"And what about his two cronies? The ones with the guns, remember?"

Dan shuffled his feet. "I promise you we'll turn around immediately if there's any sign of anyone at the asylum."

Rose looked into his face. Could she rely on him? She barely knew him, and yet she felt so comfortable with him. She didn't want to become like her mother, always worrying about things. "OK," she said. "Let's go."

They crossed over the headland and followed the road that ran along the North Bay, Scarborough's quieter, less commercial beach. The road descended towards Peasholm, an Edwardian park with a lake that Rose had vague memories of having visited as a child, and then climbed steeply as it headed north out of the town. They passed a sign for the Sea Life Sanctuary, then the houses thinned and petered out, giving way to open fields. The footpath narrowed to a single track beside the road on which cars shot past at increasingly hazardous speeds. Rose fell into step behind Dan, not wishing to risk life and limb a second time. *Or should that be a third time?*

"It's down here," said Dan suddenly, turning off the main road onto a lane that led towards the coast. The lane was little more than a dirt track, rough and stony. Stinging nettles growing along the edge had been recently flattened by car wheels. They turned a corner and Rose saw a large Victorian house, more of a mansion, built out of age-blackened stone. The land around the house was cordoned off with a chain-link fence. A sign attached to the fence read, *Danger! Demolition in progress. Do not enter.*

Lonely and unloved, the house still retained something of its former architectural splendour. With a gabled roof and circular turrets on each of the four corners, it could have been turned into a luxury hotel if it hadn't been left to decay. A flight of stone steps led up to an arched doorway above which hung a clock with the hands stopped at twenty to nine. A number of slates were missing from the steeply sloping roof. Most of the windows were broken and ivy was climbing up the walls as if trying to reclaim the house for nature.

"Welcome to Highcliff House," said Dan.

"I know it's a bit dilapidated," said Rose, "but couldn't

it be restored? Why does it have to be demolished?"

"The house itself is OK I guess. But the land on the side facing the sea has been eroding for years. Eventually the whole place will fall into the water. That's why they're going to knock it down."

Hard to imagine such a solid building tumbling into the sea, thought Rose. But then it was even harder to imagine the land under one's feet just falling away.

"Why would your dad come here to meet Max?" Rose avoided asking the bigger question which was, why is your dad mixed up with a guy like Max in the first place?

"I don't know. That's what I was hoping to find out."

"So why don't you just ask him? Your dad I mean."

Dan grunted. "Last time I mentioned the name of Max to him he went into a rage and nearly ran you over, remember?" He started to walk around the perimeter of the fence.

"Yeah, I remember." Every time she saw a red car now it reminded her of the Ferrari zooming towards her.

She followed Dan around the side of the fence. Now she could see just how close the building was to the edge of the cliff, only a couple of metres, less in some places. The drop down to the sea was a sheer one. No one would have built such a large house this close to the edge, so the cliff must be disappearing at quite a rate.

"Look." Dan pointed to a gap in the fence big enough for a vehicle to drive through. "Security's not up to much is it? We can go in this way."

"Is that a good idea?"

"Why not? What's the worst that could happen?"

"Well…" *Falling masonry, aggressive squatters, those guys with guns,* thought Rose, but Dan was already walking through the gap in the fence towards the house. Rose pushed her fears to the back of her mind and followed him.

~~~
~~~

Jackson had long dreamed of setting up his own business. He fancied a shop in London, selling luxury items such as imported tea or silks to wealthy customers. Two years working for Henry Blackwood had taught him that rich people were often fools when it came to money, spending it like it was going out of fashion. Jackson reckoned he could make a tidy profit by catering to the Henry Blackwoods of this world.

He'd been putting aside money for years and almost had enough to buy a small corner property in one of London's better streets. With the money Henry had promised him for fulfilling this assignment in Scarborough, Jackson would have enough to resign his position as Henry's valet and general dogsbody and go it alone. Well, not entirely alone. He hadn't known Kitty for long but he'd known her long enough to know that she was the woman for him. Smart, funny and a looker to boot, she'd make a perfect wife and mistress of a boutique. She'd confided in him that she was tired of performing on the Scarborough stage; said she was getting too old to be singing about boys in the gallery. Jackson had taken the hint. She'd told him that she'd never been to London. Well, he would change all that for her. It wasn't so much that he would make an honest woman of her, more that she would make an honest man of him. It was time to put his dark ways behind him before he ended up in prison or worse.

But there was still this business with Alice to see to. He needed the money from this job if his plans with Kitty were going to come to fruition. He leaned over the railing of the promenade and watched the bathing machines making their way down to the sea. He was alone this afternoon whilst Kitty rehearsed for tonight's show. That was just as well given what he was about to do. At breakfast he had received a letter from Henry. Henry was angry about how much time Alice was spending in the company of the painter. Jackson knew from experience that when Henry was really cross about something, he often took matters into his own hands. And if that happened, the consequences for Jackson would be much worse than not just being paid. Henry had the power to ruin any man he chose. His last valet had been reduced to begging in the streets. Jackson feared that he knew too much about Henry's debauched lifestyle for Henry to let him walk away on bad terms. The only way to escape from Henry's employment without dire consequences was for Jackson to apprehend Alice and deliver her back to her future husband without delay.

By now the bathing machines had reached the water's edge. Alice and Mary were in the third machine on the right. Jackson was keeping a close eye on that one, determined not to muddle it up with any of the others. He wished he could have nabbed Alice before they'd gone to bathe, but he'd missed them by seconds and now there was nothing to do but wait for them to return. He couldn't very well fish her out of the sea - it was too public. He'd let them have one last dip and then he'd grab hold of Alice when she returned to the promenade. Mary would follow wherever her mistress went so he had no concerns about her.

Half an hour later the bathing machine was on its way back up the beach. Jackson sauntered towards the hire place, doing his best to maintain a low profile. No point drawing attention to himself. He didn't want there to be any trouble, but at the same time he reached into his inside pocket and felt for the handle of his knife. It was reassuringly solid. He'd never used it on a woman and didn't intend to hurt Alice, but he had to make her see that he meant business. He needed her to fear him.

He hung back a short distance because there were too many people milling around for him to grab hold of Alice right here. He'd have to wait until she was away from the crowds. The boy leading the horse opened the door of the bathing machine and Alice and Mary stepped down.

They had changed out of their bathing costumes, back into their normal clothes, Alice in her white dress and Mary in black. They had their backs to him, but he knew it was them. From days of following them around, he recognised their clothes instantly. Alice wore a wide-brimmed hat and a white lace parasol hung from her right forearm. Mary wore a black bonnet over her hair that shielded the side of her face.

Jackson kept his distance as the two women made their way along the promenade. There were still too many people around and also that damn photographer was photographing people willing to pose long enough. Jackson didn't want his actions captured on film for all to see. Alice and Mary walked close together, their heads bowed in conversation. Then suddenly they stopped, clasped hands, exchanged a few words, and went their separate ways. Mary headed up the hill towards St Mary's church and Alice set off in the direction of the harbour.

All the better if Mary's out of the way, thought Jackson. *Alice will be easier to handle on her own. She's probably going to meet that painter.*

With his prey in sight, Jackson set off in pursuit of Alice.

~~~

Ryan waited until half past four, when he was sure that Dan would have left the amusement arcade, then he pulled up on the pavement, leapt out of the Ferrari and went inside. Dave, who did the evening shift, was in the booth, busy handing out prizes to a family who had got lucky on the machines. The little girl couldn't make up her mind between the beaded bracelets and a fluffy rabbit which meant that Dave was distracted and barely noticed Ryan. *That's good,* thought Ryan. *The less attention I get the better.*

Ryan let himself into the booth and retrieved the cardboard box from under the counter. The little girl
~~~

decided at that point to go for one of the fluffy rabbits and Dave turned to fetch the one she wanted from the shelf at the back. Ryan slipped out of the booth, making sure the door shut locked behind him, and carried the box outside to the waiting Ferrari.

As usual, an appreciative crowd of holiday-makers had gathered to admire the sleek lines of the bodywork, the enormous tyres and the plush interior. If there was one day he could have done without an audience it was today and for the first time in his life Ryan wished he didn't own such a conspicuous car.

It had always been a dream of his to own a real sports car and he'd bought this beauty a few years back, when times had been good, from a dealership in York. Years ago the arcade had been making a ton of money, but things had taken a turn for the worse in the global economic downturn and now look where he'd ended up: clandestine meetings with a self-styled mafia boss and boxes to smuggle around the country in return for what? A pittance of a loan with exorbitant interest rates just to prop up his failing business and pay for his wife's expensive taste in home design. He should really sell the car but in Ryan's eyes that would be admitting defeat. The car reminded him of better times and gave him hope that one day he'd hit life's jackpot again.

Ryan dumped the box on the passenger seat and climbed into the driver's side, vowing to himself this was the last time he would do a job for Max. When Max lent money he expected more than just interest payments in return. He demanded favours, like delivering these boxes to his "clients" as he called them and if you refused to do the jobs he asked of you, things could get very ugly very quickly. One arcade owner on the sea-front had had his premises burnt down in an arson attack the previous year. Ryan had no doubt that Max was behind it.

Well, Max could threaten him all he liked, but Ryan wanted out. Sooner or later they were going to get into serious trouble and Ryan needed to think about Dan and Fiona. He didn't like it when Dan asked questions about Max because he didn't want to drag Dan into this bloody mess. He glanced at the box, but the packaging gave nothing away. He started the engine and the car responded with a satisfying, deep-throated roar. Ryan smiled in spite of himself and pulled away from the curb. A little boy with ice cream plastered all over his face waved him off.

He drove carefully along the sea-front, heading north. He was anxious to get going, but today of all days he couldn't risk an accident or being pulled over for speeding. It had never happened before but there was always a first time. He cursed under his breath at tourists who stepped off the pavement without looking where they were going and tapped his fingers impatiently on the steering wheel at every red light. He was rounding the headland when the sound of a siren and the flash of blue lights in his rear-view mirror caused him to break out into a cold sweat. The police. Ryan gripped the steering wheel tighter, his mind in a whirl of panic. Behind him, cars were pulling over to let the police car through. It bore down on him and his heart rate went through the roof. This was it. He was done for. Might as well get out of the car with his hands in the air. He slowed and pulled over to the side, waiting for the police car to swerve in front of him. His luck had finally run out.

But then the white and blue car with the flashing light on its roof zoomed straight past and disappeared round the corner. For a moment Ryan expected to hear the screech of tyres and the smell of burning rubber as they executed a sharp U-turn, but, after a few seconds when the police car didn't return, it slowly sunk in that they hadn't been chasing him after all.

Shit, he thought as he let his head fall forwards onto the steering wheel. The police car had really freaked him out. He was obviously more anxious than he'd realised. The sooner he reached his destination and delivered this box the better. Only then would he be able to relax.

Ryan restarted the engine and drove off. As soon as he was out of the built-up area and on the country roads he hit the accelerator pedal and the car sprang forward like a caged tiger let loose.

~~~

The reek of fish was overpowering. Jackson breathed through his mouth so as not to inhale the rotting stench that emanated from the stacked lobster baskets and piles of old nets. A boat had just docked in the harbour and burly fishermen were hauling crates of silvery fish onto the jetty, some of the creatures still twitching. The smell of a fresh catch had attracted every seagull for miles around and the air was swarming with screeching, pooping birds. The fish fixed him with their half-dead eyes, silent witnesses to the action he was about to commit.

Jackson turned away in disgust and focused on Alice, who was only a short distance ahead of him now. He could see the white bow on the back of her dress and the lace that edged the bottom of her skirt; the brim of her hat fluttered in the breeze; her parasol hung from her right wrist, swinging by her side as she walked. She must be going to a rendez-vous with that painter and her brazenness surprised even him, who was no stranger to independently-minded women. It was strange too that her maid had left her and gone off elsewhere, but that would make what he was about to do only easier. For once it seemed that luck was on his side.

Alice walked by the crates of fish and started making her way towards the lighthouse at the far end of the jetty. It was time to make his move.

He sidled up to her and grabbed her firmly by the upper arm.

"Miss Hawthorne," he said. "Please don't make a scene..."
~~~

The woman spun around and he saw her face. It was the maid. Mary screamed at the top of her voice, a sound so piercing it frightened even the noisiest of the seagulls, and hit him over the head with the parasol.

~~~

The asylum may once have been surrounded by a beautiful garden. Rose could make out pathways and the occasional hardy clump of lavender or a rose bush gone wild. But now weeds were choking the paths, the grass had grown long, and brambles had invaded the flower beds. She stepped around a patch of scorched earth littered with broken beer bottles, cigarette stubs and a discarded syringe.

They walked around to the front of the building. The blackened stone façade loomed over them, sucking the heat out of the day. Vertical iron bars covered the ground floor windows, presumably to keep patients from escaping rather than to keep intruders out. The upper storey windows were too high for any sane person to consider using them as a means of escape.

A chill ran up Rose's spine. Imagine being put away here. She'd seen a TV programme once about Victorian asylums, how they were regarded as a huge step forward in the treatment of mental illness, but also how regimented and institutional they were. Many of them survived well into the twentieth century. And how many people were put here under false pretences? What dark secrets were buried inside the walls of this building? How many lives had been blighted by its harsh regime and the experimentation of doctors who treated patients like human guinea-pigs?

"Hey, this is like one of those YouTube videos about urban exploration." Dan's voice jolted Rose back to the present.

"Except we didn't bring a flashlight," said Rose.
~~~

"Those people always have backpacks with survival equipment in them and they carry professional-looking SLR cameras." She'd seen videos of people exploring abandoned warehouses, factories and asylums. The explorers always crept around as quietly as possible as if expecting to encounter the former inhabitants. And the buildings themselves always exuded an air of sadness, as if the walls still held the memories of the lives of those who had lived and worked there. Buildings were never just bricks and mortar. They were repositories of human lives, hopes and dreams. "Are you going to record this?" she asked.

"I have a pretty good video camera on my phone," said Dan, pulling his mobile from his pocket. "Come on, let's see if we can get inside."

The main door was locked with heavy rusting chains and a padlock. They explored the far side of the building, finding a smaller door that looked like a tradesman's entrance. Dan tried the handle. The door rattled in its frame but refused to open. *The house doesn't want us to enter,* thought Rose, secretly relieved.

They continued round the back of the building. They were barely a couple of metres from the edge of the cliff now. Below them the waves crashed against the cliff-face, eroding it particle by particle. *How soon before it collapses completely?* Rose wondered. She stayed close to the house, wanting to feel its solidity.

"This looks more like it," said Dan. He was standing in front of a window boarded up with a rain-damaged piece of old hardboard. There were no iron bars. Rose's heart sank. Dan thumped the edges of the board and it fell away from the window frame in a cloud of dust.

"That wasn't secured very well," he laughed. "You go first. I'll give you a leg up."

"Are you kidding?"

"Nope. We came here to check this place out and that's what we're going to do." He interlaced his fingers and held out his hands. Not quite believing she was doing this, Rose stepped onto his hands and hoisted herself up onto the window ledge.

"Watch out for broken glass," said Dan.

There was no glass in the window frame but broken shards on the floor inside glinted amongst bits of plaster and a scattering of dried leaves. Rose crouched on the sill, judging the distance to the floor below. No more than a metre. The board had fallen a little way to her right. If she landed on that she'd avoid the broken glass. She took a deep breath and jumped, managing to land on the corner of the board. Underneath she heard the crunch of breaking glass. She stood up and dusted herself off, wishing she'd worn trainers and not open-toed sandals. Next time she went on a date with Dan she'd wear something suitable for running and climbing, since that was what they always ended up doing.

"You coming then?" she called. For one brief moment she wondered whether Dan was actually going to join her, or if she'd fallen into a trap. Then his lean figure appeared in the window frame and he sprang lightly onto the floor beside her.

"Wow," he said. "Just look at this place."

~~~

Mary gave Jackson another sharp whack just for good measure. The parasol buckled but she didn't think Alice would mind, given the circumstances.

"Please stop," he cried, bringing his hands up to protect his head. He took a step back, lowered his arms and stared at her in disbelief.

"I thought you were Miss Hawthorne," he spluttered.

"Yes, well, you thought wrong!" said Mary. "How dare you try to accost a lady in public!"

"Are you all right there, Miss?" One of the fishermen from the boat that had just docked came running over and
~~~

stood beside her, glowering at Jackson.

"This brute just tried to kidnap me," said Mary, turning to the young man. He was still wearing his oilskin trousers and had his shirt sleeves rolled up, revealing strong, tanned arms. She looked up into his face and saw a resolute, square jaw and sun-bleached blond hair.

"How dare you assault a lady," said the fisherman, turning on Jackson. He raised his right arm and in one well-aimed strike, landed a punch on Jackson's nose. Jackson reeled backwards with a grunt of pain, a stream of blood spurting from his nostrils.

"She's no lady," croaked Jackson. He pulled a handkerchief from his pocket, balled it into a fist and rammed it against his nose. "She tricked me into thinking she was one."

"She looks like a lady to me," countered the fisherman. "And a very fine one too!" Mary blushed at the compliment. "Now get your ugly face out of here," continued the fisherman, "before I put you in a boat, sail out to sea and toss you overboard!"

Jackson didn't need telling twice. With one last scowl at Mary he turned on his heels and fled. Mary watched his retreating back, savouring her moment of triumph.

"Now, Miss." The handsome young fisherman turned to Mary and inclined his head. "If you'll permit me to take you back to my cottage, my sister will make you a nice cup of tea to calm your nerves."

"Well, thank you," said Mary. "That would be most agreeable." She took the proffered arm and let the young man guide her across the street. As they walked she looked into the smiling face of her rescuer and remembered the words of the fortune teller. *You are going to meet the man of your dreams when you are least expecting it.* Maybe the fortune teller had spoken the truth after all.

~~~
~~~

The room could have been a comfortable doctor's consulting room with its alcoves, high ceiling and large fireplace. But now a dead bird lay in the grate, the plaster was peeling off the walls and a damp patch under the window was stained green with mould.

"Careful where you walk," said Rose, pointing to the broken glass on the floor. There was no furniture in the room to give a clue to its former use, but a wooden cabinet, like a large bathroom cabinet, hung on one wall. Curious, Rose pulled open the doors and peered inside. Rows of bare shelves stared back at her and an enormous spider darted out from the corner of the top shelf. Rose shut the cabinet doors quickly and turned around. Dan had taken his mobile out of his pocket and switched on the video camera. He was already filming her. She gave a smile and a wave. He panned slowly around the room, then beckoned Rose to follow him through the door.

A corridor with a high, vaulted ceiling ran the length of the house. It made Rose think of a monastery. She almost expected to see the ghosts of black-clad monks, heads bowed, emerging from the walls. Like the room they had just left, the corridor was a mess of peeling paintwork and falling plaster, as if the building was gradually shedding its soul. Given enough time it would just crumble to dust. Their footsteps echoed on the tiled floor and Rose found herself walking on tiptoe to avoid making too much noise, even though there was no one to hear them.

Dan stopped in front of a pair of double doors, the camera still held aloft in his right hand.

"This way?" he whispered.

Rose nodded. She pushed at one of the doors. It swung open to reveal a large hall. At one end was a small stage framed by moth-eaten red velvet curtains. In the centre of the stage stood an old upright piano. The piano lid and half the keys were missing. Had they held entertainments here? It was hard to imagine.

They returned to the corridor, peering into each room

as they went. Most were empty but occasionally they came across a metal bed frame or an abandoned hospital trolley.

Dan kicked open a door that was ajar and stopped in his tracks.

"What is it?" asked Rose, trying to see over his shoulder.

"I don't know," said Dan, walking over to the room's single object. In the middle of the floor was a free-standing wooden cabinet about the size of a large chest-of-drawers. It had glass panels and inside was a metal wheel attached to a handle on the outside of the cabinet. Protruding from the front of the cabinet were two rods, about a foot apart, each with a brass sphere attached to the end.

Dan tried turning the handle and the wheel inside started to rotate. "It looks like a machine for generating static electricity. But what's it doing here?"

"They used machines like that on patients," said Rose, remembering the TV programme.

Dan stopped turning the handle immediately and took a step back. "Let's move on," he said, leaving the room. "I've still got no idea why Dad would come here for a meeting with Max. There doesn't seem to be anything here, except that torture chamber." He indicated the room they had just left with a nod of his head.

They were now at the foot of a staircase with an ornate metal balustrade. Rose peered up the stairwell, following the zigzag of the stairs up to the top floor. Dan was already starting to climb so with more and more misgivings in her heart, Rose followed him.

A room on the first floor that must have once been a dormitory contained dozens of metal beds minus their mattresses. Further along the corridor was a tiled bathroom with a line of chipped and stained sinks, a row of toilets separated from each other by low screens, and three claw-footed bath tubs. *So much for privacy,* thought Rose. But in the next room they got a surprise.

The room, which looked out onto the front of the

house, had been swept and in the corner was an old mattress and a pile of folded blankets. Empty baked bean cans were stacked on the floor in a little pile beside a small gas stove. There was a plastic bowl and a spoon, the sort of thing you might take on a picnic or camping trip. A dog's rubber bone lay on the floor, beside a box of dog biscuits. "Looks like someone's living here," said Rose. She stopped in the doorway, reluctant to intrude on the person's private space. Despite the humbleness of the objects, the blankets had been folded with care and for the first time she really felt that they were trespassing.

"And I think they're coming back," said Dan. "Listen." From somewhere in the bowels of the building a dog barked, the sharp sound reverberating around the empty house. "Come on," said Dan, pulling Rose down the corridor. "Time to be going."

~~~

Jackson fumed with rage as he stumbled back to the Grand Hotel. The women had played a dirty trick on him, a mean sleight of hand worthy of the lowest of fairground charlatans. It was like one of those ridiculous operettas where two gentlemen changed hats and everyone mistook them one for the other. The women must have been onto him and had played him for a fool. How humiliating!

In his defence, he had only glimpsed them from behind and they were remarkably similar in height and stature. No one could blame him for following the woman in white. Alice always wore white. Only a numbskull would have followed the woman in black. And yet, they had deceived him and he was now at risk of losing them and of incurring Henry's wrath. If that happened then his plans to buy a shop and marry Kitty would all come to nothing. In fact, Henry was likely to make sure Jackson never worked again.

As for Mary! Some lady indeed. The real Alice would
~~~

never have hit him over the head with her parasol. And where was she anyway? Probably making plans to run away with that dandy fop of a painter. His only hope was to run as fast as he could back to the Grand Hotel and pray that he hadn't missed her. Returning to London without her was unthinkable; Henry would have his guts for garters.

Jackson arrived at the hotel red-faced and out of breath. Blood from his nose had sprayed across his white shirt and there was a dent in his hat from where Mary had hit him with the parasol. He tried to cover the blood stains with the lapels of his coat, and did his best to punch his hat back into shape. Then he entered the hotel, went straight to the front desk and demanded to be shown to the room of Miss Alice Hawthorne.

"I'm sorry, sir," said the clerk, barely bothering to look up, "but she checked out this morning."

"She can't have!" shouted Jackson, leaning across the counter. The lapels on his coat fell open and the clerk recoiled at the sight of the blood on Jackson's shirt. Reaching for the hand bell that hotel guests used to attract attention when there was nobody on the desk, the clerk rang it with all his might. At once two uniformed porters appeared. Jackson reached for the knife inside his breast pocket, but the men were too quick for him. They grabbed hold of his upper arms, and forcefully marched him outside, making it quite clear that riff-raff like him were not welcome in the genteel environs of the hotel.

"You don't understand," called Jackson as the two men turned and walked back into the hotel. "I…Damn and blast!" He kicked at a passing pigeon with the toe of his boot, sending the bird into a flurry of flapping feathers. Jackson had had enough. He dusted himself off, straightened his hat and walked away with as much dignity as he could muster, which wasn't very much at all.

From the window of the hotel lounge Mrs Goodly watched Jackson's retreating figure, sipped her tea and smiled to herself. It was terribly thrilling to be part of a conspiracy. Alice's luggage was safely stored in Mrs Goodly's room and Mrs Goodly had promised to send it on in due course when Alice and Mr Hartright were safely out of Scarborough. It was all so romantic. Mrs Goodly had always fancied herself as a woman of letters and this, she thought, would make a terrific plot for a novel.

~~~

Rose's mind flashed back to the dog at the fair, the one that had almost savaged her; the one that had had its brains blown out by a bullet. The barking they could hear now was nothing like as aggressive, but Rose still had no desire to meet this new dog and its owner. Whoever was sleeping rough here, they might not take kindly to her and Dan snooping around.

They ran back to the main staircase and peered over the banister.

"There's no one coming up yet," said Dan. "We'll be all right if we hurry."

"Maybe there's another way down," said Rose. But Dan was already leaping down the stairs two at a time. Rose was determined not to be left behind a second time, especially not with another dog on the loose. Holding onto the banister she ran down the stairs, jumping the last half dozen steps in an effort to keep up with Dan.

The barking was coming from the side of the house that they had not yet explored. A door banged shut and the barking intensified. They hurried along the corridor, heedless of the sound of their footsteps, and back to the room where they had entered the building. Dan interlaced his fingers and held out his hands so Rose could hoist herself onto the window sill. Then she held out a hand and pulled him up beside her. They jumped down onto the ground and ran along the back of the house towards the gap in the fence.

This is insane, thought Rose. *Why does every date with Dan*
~~~

have to end with us running away from someone?

Once they reached the lane they slowed their pace.

"We're on a public right of way here," said Dan. "No one can challenge us now."

"So were we trespassing back there?" asked Rose. She hadn't seen any *Trespassers Will Be Prosecuted* signs.

Dan shrugged and Rose decided to let it go. What did it matter? They'd got out safely enough. At least they hadn't encountered any armed men so Rose supposed they could count the evening a success. But had they learnt anything useful? Not that she could tell.

~~~

When she was sure that she wasn't being followed, Alice slowed her pace. She didn't want to arrive at the church hot and out of breath. George had suggested they meet there since it was close to his lodgings and, as the site of their first meeting, it seemed like an appropriately romantic spot from which to embark on their new lives. He had warned her that she must not return to the hotel under any circumstances because as soon as Jackson realised he'd been tricked, he would go there first.

Alice paused for a moment in the graveyard and looked out across the sea. George had said he would take her abroad. They would go to Italy and visit Venice and Florence and Rome. He wanted to show her the masterpieces of Leonardo da Vinci and Michaelangelo. They would go to St Mark's in Venice and the Coliseum in Rome. They would be free spirits, going where the wind chose to take them. Her heart swelled with joy at the prospect of so much freedom. And to live a life like that with a man she loved. It was more than she could ever have hoped for.

She turned and walked towards the church. The oak door was heavy and creaked on its hinges, as if the building did not want to admit her to its sanctuary. She
~~~

pushed it open just far enough to allow her to slip inside. The door banged shut behind her.

The church smelled of old paper, tallow candles and dust. She waited a moment for her eyes to adjust to the gloominess of the interior after the bright light outside. Once her vision had settled, she took a few tentative steps down the aisle, resting her hand as she went on the backs of the oak pews, needing to feel their solidity. Stone pillars blocked her view of the side aisles, giving her an uneasy feeling in case someone should be hiding behind them. *Don't be silly,* she told herself. But the echo of her own feet on the stone floor caused her to spin around, scared that Jackson had followed her after all. A starling flew out of the rafters, startling her, then disappeared again into the roof space.

She sank down onto the nearest pew and took a few deep breaths to calm her nerves, telling herself that so far everything had gone according to plan. Swapping clothes had been Mary's idea. Alice had protested at first, knowing that Jackson would follow Mary, and not wanting to put her maid - *her friend* - in danger. But Mary had been insistent, even viewing it as a game. Dear Mary. Alice wondered where she was now and hoped she had escaped Jackson's clutches.

Sitting there in Mary's plain black dress, Alice couldn't help but think how much simpler life was for girls like Mary. Not that it was an easy life, being a maid, but Mary was free to fall in love with and marry whoever she liked, whereas Alice's proposed marriage to Henry had been a foregone conclusion ever since she was fifteen. The fact that he was twenty years her senior did not matter to her father who viewed the match as highly desirable and couldn't understand why his daughter wouldn't want to devote herself to a man who came from a family with a long, noble heritage. But she had come to Scarborough and fortune had smiled on her, had given her the courage to take her fate in her own hands for the first time in her life. It was a truly liberating experience.

The church door opened and banged shut. Alice heard the rap of footsteps on the stone floor, a man's step, sure and solid. Alice jumped to her feet and stepped out into the aisle. "George, is that you?" Her voice sounded small and childlike in the large stone building. A man appeared from behind a pillar, striding into the central aisle. Alice froze. It wasn't George.

With her path to the door blocked, Alice lifted the skirts of Mary's dress and ran towards the altar, looking frantically from left to right. There had to be another way out. But the man caught up with her easily and grabbed her by the arm.

"Hello Alice," said an all too familiar voice. "You didn't think you could escape from me did you?"

~~~

The dog could smell them. Two distinct smells: a flowery smell that reminded him of girls, and a stronger scent that he picked up around older boys. He stood at the bottom of the staircase and sniffed the air. Someone had been here.

The girl who looked after him was following, calling him to be quiet, but it was his job to protect her. If there were intruders then he would attack them. He bounded up the stairs and into the room where he slept curled up on the bottom of the girl's mattress. The two smells were strongest in here and mingled with something else. He sniffed. The smell of fear. He ran back out into the corridor but the smell was growing fainter now.

The girl reached the top of the stairs. "What's the matter Lucky?" she asked, bending down to stroke the top of the dog's head. He barked to tell her that someone had been here, but as usual she didn't understand a word he said. Humans could be so stupid sometimes.

"Come on," she said. "It's dinner time."
~~~

He followed her into the room they shared and waited whilst she opened a tin of dog food. Whoever had been here had gone now, but he would stay on his guard and sleep tonight with one ear cocked. It was a cruel world and you couldn't be too careful.

~~~

Mary gratefully accepted a second cup of tea from Ellie, the fisherman's younger sister. He was called Walter Fairbright, and on their way to the cottage he had explained to her that he lived with Ellie, their parents having died some years ago. It was the most delightful little cottage, with exposed beams and a log hearth and Mary could see Ellie kept it spick and span. There was a spinning wheel in one corner and a vase of hand-picked flowers on the parlour table. Mary settled back in the armchair, thinking how much she would like to live in such a place.

"So if you're just here on holiday," pondered Ellie, "why was that horrible man following you around?" Walter had given his sister a brief explanation of the morning's events and Ellie was bursting with questions.

Mary sipped her tea and related to an astonished Ellie and Walter how she and her mistress, Alice, had come to Scarborough on account of Alice's recent poor health, and how Alice's future husband, the thoroughly despicable Henry Blackwood, had sent his man, Jackson, to spy on them.

"But we managed to fool him by swapping our clothes in the bathing machine," said Mary, unable to suppress a smile of satisfaction.

Ellie clapped her hands in delight. "What a brilliant idea! Did you think of it?"

Mary nodded. It had indeed been her idea and she was rather proud of it. After spotting Jackson in the photograph and guessing his business, Mary, Alice, George
~~~

and Mrs Goodly had discussed how they could outwit Jackson and give Alice time to make an escape with George.

"We saw the metamorphosis show at the fair," said Mary. When her listeners looked blank she explained, "It's a magic trick where the magician's assistant is in a box and the magician swaps places with her. Well, that gave me the idea of swapping places with Alice. The bathing machine was the perfect opportunity. We went for a quick paddle in the sea and I looked out of the machine's peep holes to make sure that Jackson was watching us. Then, after bathing, we swapped dresses so that Jackson would follow me instead of Alice. Alice and Mr Hartright planned to meet in St Mary's Church, so I led Jackson down to the harbour to give Alice and Mr Hartright time to get away."

"But weren't you scared?" asked Ellie.

"Well, just for a moment," admitted Mary, remembering the feeling of panic when Jackson had grabbed hold of her arm. "But parasols make surprisingly good weapons. And then your brother came to my rescue and I wasn't afraid at all." Mary smiled at Walter who smiled back, blushed and looked away.

"But what about Alice?" asked Ellie, looking serious. "Will she have made it safely to the church?"

A flicker of doubt sparked in Mary's mind. But what could go wrong? The plan had been so carefully worked out. She'd successfully diverted Jackson away from Alice and George had promised to meet Alice at the church. The next step was to take a train to Whitby and spend the night there before travelling on the next morning to Gretna Green where Alice and Mr Hartright were to be married. Mary was due to meet them at Scarborough Railway Station. They had left nothing to chance.

"I'm sure she's fine," said Mary.

"In that case, would you like another cup of tea?" asked Ellie, picking up the pot. The clock on the mantelpiece chimed the hour. Mary still had another forty-five minutes before the train left Scarborough and Walter had promised to give her a lift in his pony and cart. But should she leave now and make sure Alice was all right?

But then Walter said, "Yes, please do have another cup," and Mary said, "Oh, go on then. Just one more."

~~~

With the wind in his hair, the sun on his face and one and a half tonnes of high-powered machinery at his fingertips, Ryan started to relax. Driving the Ferrari always did that to him. It was a dream car, responding to the most minuscule movement, the slightest pressure from his foot on the accelerator pedal, the gentlest turn of the steering wheel. The tyres gripped the road surface and the car handled corners beautifully. Ryan loved the feeling of being in control of this monster, particularly on empty country roads like the one he was on now.

He glanced down at the box on the passenger seat beside him. In the busy centre of town it had seemed to draw too much attention to itself, like a thief's bag stamped with the word SWAG in bold letters. But out here, away from prying eyes, he could see that it was just a harmless cardboard box with nothing to give away its contents. And to think that he had thought the police were after him! He laughed out loud at his foolishness. They were probably just responding to some minor traffic accident caused by an old person doddering about behind the wheel of an ancient hatchback. Nothing for him to worry about.

The late summer sun was just starting to dip in the perfect blue sky, a fiery ball of orange that cast a shimmering glow over the fields of ripe wheat. It was a beautiful evening to be out driving. There was a turning coming up on the left. The steering wheel glided under his fingers as he pulled it anti-clockwise. As the car turned there was a brief moment when the sun's rays caught in
~~~

the rear-view mirror and the glaring reflection hit the back of his retinas, blinding him. It only lasted for a second until the road straightened out but when he regained his vision his heart leapt into his mouth.

He was right in the path of a giant tractor that was heading his way. In an instant Ryan registered the enormous five-foot high tractor wheels, the look of horror on the farmer's face and the fact that the tractor was occupying about three quarters of the narrow country road. Then everything happened at once: the screech of tyres, the stench of burning rubber and the crunch of metal against metal.

The Ferrari's airbag exploded into Ryan's face and everything went black.

~~~

George was desperate to get away from his lodgings and meet Alice at the church, but his landlady, Mrs Barker, was so sorry to see him leaving early that she had insisted on making him a packed tea to take on his journey and he didn't have the heart to tell her not to bother. She'd been so good to him during his stay, cooking him hot meals and seeing to his laundry, that it would have been ungrateful to have denied her this one last act of charity. But as she carefully wrapped up pies and slices of cold meat into a clean muslin cloth and laid them in a picnic hamper, George hopped impatiently from one foot to the other and hoped that Alice wouldn't think he had abandoned her.

At last, the packed tea was ready. George picked up the hamper, silently cursing its weight. The food it contained could have fed a whole boatload of invading Vikings. At least he had left his painting things at the Grand Hotel in the care of Mrs Goodly. An easel would have been far too much to manage under the circumstances.

George thanked Mrs Barker for her kindness, picked
~~~

up a small bag containing his few personal belongings and walked as fast as he could up the hill towards St Mary's Church.

He arrived half an hour late, hot and flushed. He dropped his bag and the picnic hamper beside one of the gravestones and entered the church. Blinking in the dim light, he pulled a handkerchief from his pocket and mopped his brow. "Alice?" he called. "I'm here."

The sound of his voice echoed off the stone pillars and was lost in the rafters. Somewhere high above a small bird fluttered.

"Alice?" he called again, more hesitantly this time. There was no reply.

He walked down the aisle, conscious of the clicking noise his boots made on the stone floor. Something was lying on the steps in front of the altar. He rushed forwards, knelt down and picked it up. It was a woman's shawl. Being a painter, he had a good eye for detail and he recognised the design. It belonged to Mary, Alice's maid. But what was it doing lying here in a heap on the floor? As he held the shawl in his hands, he touched something wet and sticky. He held his fingers up to the light and saw that they were smeared with blood.

~~~

Mary accepted Walter's hand as he helped her down from the cart outside Scarborough Railway Station. He seemed to be as reluctant to say good-bye to her as she was to take her leave of him. There was still plenty of time before the train to Whitby and there was no sign yet of Alice and Mr Hartright, so Mary and Walter passed the time talking about his life as a fisherman and what it was like out on the open sea. Walter came from a long line of fishermen who seemed to prefer life on the waves to life on land.

"If you're ever back in these parts," he said, shyly, "I'll
~~~

take you out in my boat for a trip around the bay."

"That's very kind of you," she said. "But I prefer to keep my feet on dry land."

Mary would have liked to prolong their conversation indefinitely, but at that moment they were interrupted by the arrival, in a state of considerable distress, of Mr Hartright. He ran up to them, clutching his side. For a moment or two he was so out of breath that he couldn't speak. Mary became increasingly agitated.

"Where is Alice?" she demanded. "What have you done with her?"

"She … wasn't … in … the … church," gasped George when he had recovered sufficiently to get a few words out.

"What do you mean, she wasn't in the church? She must have been. That's my shawl you've got there!" She pointed at the garment that was scrunched up in Mr Hartright's trembling hands.

"Was Alice definitely wearing this?" he asked.

"Of course she was," snapped Mary. "It was part of our plan to trick Jackson."

George's face crumpled. "Then I fear something terrible has happened to Alice. Look, there is blood on the shawl!"

Mary clutched the side of Walter's cart for support, but he was already behind her, supporting her with his strong arms.

"We must go to the police," said Walter who was the only one of the three still in possession of his wits. "Get in the cart, both of you, I'll take you there now."

~~~

Rose and Dan walked back along the road towards the town. This time they were going downhill which made it easier and the traffic had died down a bit too.

"You didn't find what you were looking for at the
~~~

asylum, did you?" asked Rose.

Dan shook his head. "No. But it doesn't matter. I'm sorry I put us in danger a second time."

"That's OK," laughed Rose. "We made it out. But you're worried about him aren't you? Your dad I mean."

"I just don't like the look of Max and his two thugs and I don't know what Dad is doing getting involved with them."

"You don't suspect your dad of criminal activity do you? I mean, I know he breaks the speed limit now and again, but surely he's not doing anything really serious?"

Dan shrugged. "I honestly don't know," he said. Rose didn't like the sound of that and decided not to push her questioning any further. She was interested in Dan, not his father.

They came to the North Bay. The tide was out and the long stretch of sand beckoned. Maybe now, thought Rose, they could take that walk along the beach that she had imagined earlier. "Walk along the sands?" she asked.

"Sure," said Dan, cheering up at the suggestion.

They followed the path that led down to the beach and Rose took off her sandals, carrying them by the straps.

"Race you!" cried Rose, heading off at a sprint towards the sea.

"Hang on, I have to take my trainers off."

Despite her head start, Dan soon caught up and overtook her. He'd removed his socks and trainers and rolled up the legs of his jeans. He ran straight into the sea.

"Come on, slow coach," he called to her.

Rose's feet hit the edge of an incoming breaker and the water splashed over her legs and skirt. She had been expecting it to be freezing cold, but the shallow water was actually quite warm.

Dan caught hold of her, swinging her into the air and threatening to throw her in. Rose screamed and laughed. "Put me down!"

Dan placed her gently down in the shallow water.

Waves lapped at their ankles but Rose barely noticed the water as Dan put his hands on her shoulders, pulled her towards him and kissed her on the lips. She kissed him back as their feet sunk into the wet sand.

A bigger wave came in then, almost causing them to lose their balance and topple over.

"Whoa!" cried Rose as Dan held onto her. They pulled their feet out of the squelching sand and started to walk along the edge of the water with their arms around each other.

As they walked, the wind carried the sound of an ambulance siren over their heads and out to sea.

CHAPTER TEN

"I thought we'd take Gran to Peasholm Park this afternoon," said Andrea when Rose came down for breakfast the following morning. "The fresh air will do her good. It's the Naval Warfare show today. She'll enjoy that."

"Sure," said Rose. She was still floating in a cloud of happiness after yesterday evening on the beach with Dan and right then she'd have agreed to anything her mother suggested. "But what's the Naval Warfare show?"

"It's a battleship show on the lake with man-powered model boats," said Andrea.

"Um, right," said Rose, not really getting it.

"It's quite a Scarborough tradition," said her grandmother, walking in from the kitchen and joining the conversation. "It's been going for over eighty years now. We took you once when you were little, but the bangs scared you."

"I don't remember."

"You've caught the sun a bit," said her grandmother, caressing Rose's face. "You've got more colour in your cheeks than when you arrived."

Rose glanced in the mirror over the fireplace and

touched her fingers to her cheek. It was true, she *was* looking a bit brighter. *It's not just the sun, sea and sand though,* she thought, thinking about Dan. They had arranged to meet again later that day. Six o'clock outside the amusement arcade. Hopefully this date wouldn't involve any armed men or abandoned buildings.

As they were finishing breakfast Andrea's mobile phone rang and she ran outside to take the call. When she returned five minutes later she looked harassed. "Something's come up at work," she said. "I'll have to go and sort it out. But we're still going to Peasholm Park this afternoon."

"I wonder what that was about?" said her grandmother to Rose as Andrea disappeared upstairs.

"Oh, it's probably nothing," said Rose. "She's always getting calls from work. They can't manage five minutes without her. Here, let me clear the breakfast things away."

Rose spent the rest of the morning ferrying boxes of books to the secondhand bookshop in town, whilst dreaming about Dan and wondering what they'd do this evening. The weather was looking good, like it might actually stay warm and dry for a few days.

"Thank you, Rose," said her grandmother when she had removed the last of the boxes. "You've been a huge help."

"No problem, Gran. Is Mum still working?"

Upstairs a door slammed shut and they heard Andrea's heavy tread on the stairs. "Sounds like she's finished," said her grandmother. "Come and have lunch. I've made sandwiches."

Andrea was unusually quiet over lunch but as soon as they'd finished eating and had cleared everything away she snapped back into her organisational mode. "Is everyone ready?" she asked, gathering together her handbag, keys and mobile phone. "We don't want to miss the start of the show."

"Yes boss," said her grandmother, getting to her feet.

"Has anyone seen my walking stick?"

"Here it is Gran," said Rose, picking it up from where it had fallen onto the floor.

Rose helped her grandmother into the front passenger seat and then climbed into the back of the car. They set off towards the park.

It didn't take them long to reach the entrance of Peasholm Park, near the North Bay. Andrea signalled and pulled over. "You two hop out here. I'll go and park up the hill."

Rose jumped out of the car and helped her grandmother out of the front seat. Outside, her grandmother seemed much smaller and frailer than she did in her own home and Rose suddenly felt the responsibility of looking after her.

"I'll meet you by the lake," called Andrea. "Save me a seat." A queue of traffic was already building up behind the car. Rose closed the passenger door and her mother drove off.

"Are you all right, Gran?" asked Rose, taking her grandmother's arm.

"Right as rain," said her grandmother. "Just as long as we don't have to run to the lake." She gave a faint laugh. "I'm not as quick on my feet as I used to be."

"We'll go at your speed, Gran," said Rose. The bruise on her grandmother's face from the fall she had suffered had faded to a dull browny-yellow over the last couple of days, but Rose was acutely aware of how unsteady her grandmother was on her feet, particularly now they were out in public and the pavements seemed to be full of small children careering around on scooters. They started to make their way through the park.

The path followed the edge of the boating lake where paddle boats in the shape of dragons and swans glided past at a leisurely pace. They passed an oriental-style footbridge that led to a steep man-made island with a red and gold Chinese pagoda on the top. Rose was just thinking what a pleasant place Peasholm Park was when a small dog on a long lead scampered past so quickly that her grandmother almost stumbled.

"Am I going too fast?" asked Rose.

"No, no, you're all right," said her grandmother. But Rose thought her grandmother's breathing sounded a little ragged and she slowed her pace anyway. There was no hurry. The naval display didn't start for another half an hour. Andrea was always in such a flap about getting to places early.

But even so, by the time they reached the part of the lake where the show took place, all the seats in the front rows were already taken.

"What about up there," said Rose, pointing to a space halfway up. "Can you manage the steps?"

Her grandmother nodded but didn't speak. Rose helped her up the steps and they sat down in the first available row.

"Ooh, that's better," said her grandmother, flopping down on the bench.

"I'll just send Mum a text to tell her where we are," said Rose, fishing her mobile from her back pocket.

"All right, dear." Her grandmother pulled a handkerchief from her handbag and dabbed her forehead with it.

"We've got a good view from up here," said Rose when she had sent the text. In the middle of the lake was a square bandstand with a roof that turned up at the corners, like a Chinese pagoda. In the centre of the bandstand, a man was playing a medley of film music on an electronic organ. Rose recognised *Star Wars*, a couple of Bond tunes and *Frozen*, but most of the music was from films before she was born. Her grandmother identified the theme tune to *Doctor Zhivago* and the *Dam Busters March.*

Ten minutes later Andrea arrived, hot and puffing from having *run all the way* and complaining that the car park up the hill had been *chock-a-block*. She'd had to *drive around for ages until someone eventually left.*

Rose listened with half an ear to her mother ranting on about drivers who hogged two spaces and how the council really ought to provide more parking. She wished her mother would just drop it. They were here now weren't they? They were supposed to be enjoying themselves. She turned to her grandmother to ask if she recognised any more of the melodies when her grandmother suddenly swayed in her seat as if she was about to topple over. Rose grabbed her grandmother's arm. "Gran, are you all right?"

"And it's not as if parking is cheap. The council is making a killing…"

"Mum, shut up! I think there's something wrong with Gran."

"What?" asked Andrea, jumping to her feet. "My God, Mum, are you all right?"

Rose put her arm around her grandmother. "What's the matter Gran? Do you feel ill?"

Her grandmother mumbled something incomprehensible, clutched her chest and crumpled over onto Rose's lap.

"For Christ's sake, where's my mobile?" shouted Andrea. "Someone call an ambulance! Help!"

~~~

Henry Blackwood felt very pleased with himself as the horse and carriage jolted up the hill.

"Not much further now," he said to the woman sitting opposite him. Alice turned her head away and refused to look him in the eye.

Never mind, thought Henry. *She's mine now and that's all that matters.* He shuddered at how close he had come to losing her and her money. He should never have entrusted this assignment to that oaf Jackson. If he ever got his hands on him he'd make sure he spent the rest of his life crawling in the gutter. Thanks to the incompetence of that
~~~

idiot, Alice had almost got away from him. Of course, he should never have let her come to Scarborough in the first place. But Henry was not a man who dwelt on past mistakes, particularly his own. He had decided to come to Scarborough himself and see with his own eyes what was going on. He had been there that morning, on the promenade, when Alice and her maid had gone bathing. He had watched the bathing machine making its way down to the water's edge, had watched its return and had seen his fiancée and her maid emerge from the bathing machine wearing each other's clothes. God, how he hated the cunning of women.

Jackson, of course, had been fooled by the deception, but not Henry. He had followed Alice to St Mary's church suspecting that she was preparing to meet her lover. And she had proved his suspicions right as soon as she had uttered those words, "George, is that you?"

George! Henry would see to him soon enough. But first he had to teach Alice a lesson. Show her that he was not to be meddled with.

She sat opposite him in the carriage, clutching her right arm where the blade had cut her. Hurting her had been a necessary evil: it was the only way he could bring her under control. She had been hysterical when she'd seen it was him in the church. But as soon as the blade had sliced through the fabric of her dress and drawn blood, she had fallen to her knees begging him to spare her life. How pathetic she was! Of course he was going to spare her life. She was no use to him dead.

The carriage turned off the main road, bumped over a rough path and came to a halt outside a large house. Henry looked at the building with its heavy oak door and iron bars on the ground floor windows and knew he had found the perfect place in which to keep her secured whilst he made arrangements for their departure. Highcliff Asylum. A private establishment.

The oak door opened and Dr Collins, the man with

whom Henry had communicated earlier, appeared and walked briskly towards them. He was followed by a pair of male orderlies in matching blue overalls.

Henry opened the door to the carriage.

"Where are we?" asked Alice. It was the first time she had spoken to him since begging him to save her life in the church, and there was an edge of fear in her voice that Henry savoured.

"Oh, just somewhere that will teach you the error of your ways," said Henry. He took hold of her arm and pushed her towards the carriage door.

"I don't understand," said Alice, the panic audible in her voice.

"As you can see," said Henry, addressing Dr Collins, "she's somewhat confused."

The male orderlies pulled her down from the carriage and led her towards the house, Alice writhing in their grasp like a captured animal.

"Please do not concern yourself," said Dr Collins to Henry. "They're all a little confused when they first come to us. If you'd like to step inside and sign the paperwork, I'd be most obliged."

"It will be my pleasure," said Henry, following the doctor into the building.

~~~

Rose wrinkled her nose at the hospital disinfectant smell, a pervasive, clinging odour that hit you as soon as you walked in and became stronger the further you penetrated into the labyrinthine maze of corridors. The rubber-soled shoes of busy nurses squeaked on the linoleum floor as they hurried from room to room, attending to the sick and dying. Somewhere in the distance an alarm started to beep. The nurse who had been walking down the corridor at that moment turned on her heel and ran towards the source of the sound.
~~~

Rose and her mother were sitting in the waiting area outside the Intensive Care department, too stunned to say anything to each other. Rose couldn't believe how suddenly everything had changed. One minute they had been enjoying the sunshine in the park, listening to the theme tune from *Star Trek*, and the next minute her grandmother was being lifted into an ambulance on a stretcher. Life was precarious. It was as if someone had flipped a coin and suddenly her grandmother's life was hanging in the balance. Rose found herself sending up a silent prayer to a God she wasn't sure she believed in. *Please let her be all right.*

The events between her grandmother collapsing and Rose and her mother arriving at the hospital were already crystallising into distinct memories: her mother shouting for help, people nearby jumping to their feet, park attendants running onto the scene. One of them carried a large green first-aid kit with a white cross printed on the side. All this time Rose had cradled her grandmother in her arms, aware of the bones poking through the thin flesh and trying to see if the old lady was still breathing. The first-aider did his best to make her grandmother comfortable and minutes later the ambulance arrived and the paramedics, two men and a woman, were lifting her onto a stretcher. They gave her an oxygen mask to help her breathe and whisked her away in the emergency vehicle, lights flashing. Rose and her mother had run up the hill to the car park and then driven as fast as possible to the hospital where the receptionist informed them that Mrs Shawcross had been admitted to the Accident and Emergency unit and was now undergoing tests. They spent an anxious hour in the A&E department surrounded by an assortment of the walking wounded. Eventually the nurse in charge of triage had informed them that they were transferring Mrs Shawcross to Intensive Care. Rose and her mother then spent fifteen minutes following the overhead signs and navigating the maze of corridors until they reached the heavy double doors that admitted them to the Intensive Care department. The nurse on the desk asked them to wait, indicating a row of plastic chairs, and promised that a doctor would be with them shortly. That had been almost an hour ago. Time seemed to be standing still.

A door down the corridor swung open and a white-coated doctor emerged and started walking towards them. "At last," muttered Andrea under her breath.

"Mrs Jenkins?" His accent was a pleasant blend of clipped Yorkshire vowels and an Indian lilt.

"Yes?" said Andrea, jumping to her feet.

"I'm Dr Patel." He held out a hand. "I'm in charge of your mother's care."

"How is she?"

"I'm afraid your mother has suffered quite a severe heart attack. We've stabilised her and moved her to the Intensive Care ward."

"Can we see her?"

Dr Patel smiled, obviously practised in offering reassurance to worried relatives. "I'm afraid she's heavily sedated right now. The best thing would be for you to go home and get some rest. We'll call you if there's any change."

"But is she going to be all right?" asked Rose. She had to stop herself from clutching hold of the doctor's arm and begging him to make her grandmother better.

The smile on Dr Patel's lips slipped a little. "We'll do our best for her." He held her gaze for a moment before looking away. *There's something he's not telling us,* thought Rose.

At that moment a little electronic tag on his belt beeped. "Sorry, I have to go. Like I said, we'll contact you if there's any change." With that he disappeared down the corridor, his white coat flapping behind him.

"I suppose we should go home," said Andrea, although she didn't sound like she wanted to. They drove back to

Tollergate in silence, both too stunned to speak.

Rose went straight up to her room and sank onto the bed. She wanted someone to talk to. She took her mobile phone out of her pocket and dialled Dan's number. It went to voice mail. She tried a couple more times but got the same response. In the end she just texted him. *Can't meet you today. Something bad has happened. Please call me. Rose.*

~~~

Jackson picked up the copy of the *Scarborough Evening News* that another customer had left lying on a table in *The Three Mariners* and scanned the article on the front page. **Lady Goes Missing, Feared Dead**, read the headline. Inspector Booth of Scotland Yard had been assigned to the case. They were searching for a man called Jackson who was the prime suspect. Fortunately there was no picture of him. Still, he folded the paper carefully and tucked it inside his coat. No point leaving it lying around for every Tom, Dick and Harry to see. He finished his pint, pulled his hat down low over his brow, picked up his bag and headed for the door. He had already left sufficient money at his lodgings to pay his landlady, not wishing to compound his difficulties by being accused of unpaid debts.

Something had happened to Alice and it was no surprise he was a wanted man. The irony was, he was completely innocent and it baffled him how his fortunes could have changed so suddenly. If everything had gone according to plan he would have delivered Alice safely back into the hands of his master, Henry Blackwood, and he would have received his reward. As it turned out, he found himself a hunted man; a fugitive on the run.

He walked down to the harbour, keeping a lookout for that brute of a fisherman who had caused him so much pain. His nose was still swollen, although the disfigurement made him less recognisable so there was that to be
~~~

thankful for. To his relief, the coast was clear.

Last night in *The Three Mariners*, Jackson had got talking to the captain of a cargo boat that was due to set sail for the Continent. The captain, an old sea-dog, had agreed to take Jackson on board in return for a gold ring that had belonged to Jackson's mother and the promise of help below decks because the captain was one man down, having lost a crew member to dysentery on the last voyage.

The boat, a clipper, was docked in the harbour, its sails at half mast. Standing on the jetty with a fine view across the water, Jackson took one last look at the seaside town that had been the backdrop to his downfall. There was the Grand Hotel, proud and majestic, the scene of so much personal humiliation. Up on the headland was St Mary's Church and the ruined castle where he had first spied Alice with the painter. Confound the pair of them! He turned his gaze southward towards the Spa and sighed. He had spent many a happy hour there, in the theatre, listening to Kitty sing. Kitty, with her cherry lips, rosy cheeks and infectious laugh was his one regret.

He turned and walked up the gangplank.

~~~

The next morning Rose and her mother were both up early. Rose hadn't slept well and, judging from the dark rings under Andrea's eyes, neither had her mother.

"There's been no news from the hospital," said Andrea over breakfast. There was no bacon today, just a bowl of cornflakes and a cup of coffee. "As they say, no news is good news."

Rose could tell her mother was trying hard to put a brave face on things, but there was no doubt this was a serious situation. Rose kept hearing Dr Patel's words in her head - *a severe heart attack* - and had to choke back the desire to cry.

They'd cleared away the breakfast things and got ready
~~~

to go back to the hospital. On the way to the car Rose suddenly remembered the text she'd sent Dan yesterday. She checked her mobile but there was no reply. *Story of my life,* thought Rose as she climbed into the car. *Why can't guys reply to text messages? What's wrong with them?* She pushed the thought from her mind. She had more important things to think about now. All she wanted was for her grandmother to recover and come home. The cottage wasn't the same without her.

The receptionist on the hospital's main desk checked her computer screen and informed them that Mrs Shawcross had been moved from Intensive Care to the High Dependency Unit. Rose had no idea if that meant her grandmother was getting worse or better. Neither Intensive Care nor High Dependency sounded like great places to be. They followed the signs through the corridors to the HDU where they encountered yet another reception desk. The nurse on duty, a cheerful red-faced girl with *Roxanne* printed on her name badge, checked her notes and said that yes, they could go through and visit. "Although Mrs Shawcross might be a bit sleepy," she chirped. "She's quite heavily sedated."

Rose wondered how Roxanne could be so cheerful working in a place like this with sick and dying people all around. But then, she supposed, you couldn't let it get to you otherwise you'd never be able to do your job. Hospitals needed more people like Roxanne, she decided.

They found her grandmother, as predicted, asleep. She was in a small ward with three other beds, each occupied by elderly, dozing patients hooked up to drips and monitors.

Rose stood by her grandmother's bedside and looked down at the small, frail figure tucked into the large hospital bed. She was wearing a hospital gown that looked to be two sizes too big for her and her wispy hair had been brushed back off her face, emphasising the high forehead and hollow cheekbones. Surrounding the bed was a bewildering array of machines and monitors connected to her grandmother's thin arms by a tangle of wires and tubes. A screen behind the bed showed a series of fluorescent lines and numbers. Rose guessed from the little peaks and troughs in the lines and the rhythmic beeping of the machine that it was monitoring her grandmother's heart rate. *Her life reduced to a series of beeps and dashes.* She found herself listening to each beep, dreading the continuous alarm that would sound if her grandmother's heart stopped for good.

Andrea had brought along a pile of magazines for her mother to read but with all the machinery there was nowhere to put them and Gran was obviously in no fit state to read anything at the moment.

"It's very warm in here," said Andrea, flopping down onto one of the plastic chairs beside the bed and fanning herself with a copy of *Hello!* "We should have brought some water."

"I'll go and buy a bottle," said Rose. There was a vending machine in the main reception area.

"Oh, would you love?" Andrea rummaged in her purse and found some loose change. "That should be enough."

Rose retraced her steps through the maze of corridors. The High Dependency ward had given her the goosebumps, seeing her grandmother and the other old people wired up to all those machines. What would happen if there was a power cut? Would everyone just die? Or did hospitals have generators that were supposed to kick in? Rose didn't want to think about it. What upset her most was seeing her grandmother lying there so helpless and vulnerable. *Gran would hate it,* thought Rose, *if she was aware of what was happening.*

Rose fed the money into the vending machine and punched in the number for water. An ice-cold plastic bottle thudded into the dispensing tray at the bottom of the machine. Rose bent down to pick it up and heard a familiar voice calling her name.

She spun around.

"Dan? What are you doing here?" He was standing behind her, hands thrust into his jeans pockets. She hadn't told him she'd be at the hospital so how did he know where to find her?

"I was just thinking the same thing about you," he said. It was then that she saw how awful he looked. His hair was unbrushed and there were dark circles under his eyes.

"What's the matter?" she asked, going up to him and tentatively placing a hand on his arm.

"Let's go and sit down," he said. Rose followed him to a nearby seating area where more of the ubiquitous plastic chairs were arranged around a low table covered in leaflets on how to quit smoking and the dangers of obesity. Dan sat with his shoulders hunched, biting his lower lip. She wanted to tell him about her grandmother but she could see he had something on his mind. She waited for him to speak first.

"It's Dad," he said, at last. "He crashed the car."

"Oh my God, is he OK?"

"Well he's alive," said Dan, trying to smile, "but he's in a coma. The car's a write-off."

"I'm so sorry." Although Rose had firsthand experience of his dad's terrible driving, still she wouldn't wish something like this on her worst enemy. No wonder Dan looked so dreadful. "Do they…do they think he's going to be all right?"

Dan shrugged. "The doctor says we have to wait for him to come round. It hasn't been long yet, apparently. I found out about it when I got home the other night after…after…" The words stuck in his throat. *After we visited the asylum,* thought Rose. *After we kissed.* She had a vague memory then of hearing an ambulance siren, carried on the wind.

"So what about you?" he asked. "What are you doing here?"

It was such a relief to have someone to talk to that her

words came tumbling out as she related what had happened at the park yesterday. "So it was a heart attack," she finished by saying, "and I'm just so scared. I don't know what's going to happen."

"I know," he said, taking her hand in his. "I'm scared too."

They sat hand in hand for a few moments, not saying anything. Rose wanted to reassure him, but she didn't want to come out with a stream of platitudes like Dr Patel had yesterday. She knew nothing about coma victims and their chances of pulling through, let alone elderly heart attack patients. If they were lucky then both Dan's dad and her grandmother would be fine. But was that asking too much, for both of them to make a full recovery? It seemed like tempting fate.

After a couple of minutes Dan said, "I was just on my way to see Dad now."

"Of course," said Rose, standing up. "And I'd better be getting back or Mum'll send out a search party."

They walked back down the corridor together. The hospital was already starting to feel eerily familiar and Rose hardly noticed the disinfectant smell any more. They came to a T-junction with Intensive Care one way and High Dependency the other.

"Call me if there's any news," said Rose, squeezing Dan's hand.

"Sure. You too."

They kissed, briefly and awkwardly, a light peck on the cheek, nothing more. Then he was gone, pushing open the doors to the Intensive Care Unit. Rose sighed and turned in the direction of the HDU, feeling as if all the world was crashing down around her.

~~~

Dan pushed open the door to the private room where his dad lay in bed and stepped inside. Ryan was wired up
~~~

to machines that beeped and hummed in the background, monitoring every sign of life, no matter how fragile.

It had seemed like a stroke of luck, bumping into Rose like that in the hospital foyer, and for a moment he had thought she must be there because she'd heard about his dad's accident. But it had quickly become apparent that she had reasons of her own for being in the hospital, and not good ones either. *Christ, what a shitty mess.* Life had served them both a couple of backhanders, and just when everything had been going so well.

Dan's mum was already in the room, sitting next to the bed, holding her husband's hand which lay limp on the blanket. The doctor in charge of Ryan's care, Dr Wilson, had told them they should talk to Ryan as much as possible because it might help him to wake up. Fiona was babbling away about everything from the sauna at the health spa to the flowers in the garden to whether or not they ought to repaint the hallway a brighter shade of green. Her words just tumbled out in a never-ending stream of consciousness. Dan had never heard her talk so much, particularly not to his dad, and he wondered if she was just in a state of shock and this was her way of dealing with it. She paused for a moment at the sound of Dan's footsteps and smiled wanly at him. She looked deadbeat.

"Hello love," she said. "Would you mind if I just popped out for a minute to get myself a cup of tea? All this talking is making me thirsty."

"No, of course not."

She stood up and offered the chair to Dan. "You should talk to him," she said. "He might be more interested in what you have to tell him."

"Oh, I don't know, I…"

Fiona was already at the door. "I won't be long." Then she was gone.

Dan sat down awkwardly on the plastic chair and cleared his throat. The idea of talking out loud to someone who was in a coma felt like a really weird thing to do.

What was he supposed to talk about for goodness' sake? It wasn't like he and his dad were in the habit of having great man-to-man conversations when Ryan was awake, never mind when he was unconscious.

Dan glanced around the room. There were so many machines in here, it was like something out of a sci-fi movie. A clear plastic bag hung on a hook above the bed and was connected to his dad's arm by a thin plastic tube. A monitor with what Dan guessed to be his dad's heartbeat showed a red line with a little peak of activity every other second or so. That was good. He knew from hospital dramas on the TV that when the peaks stopped and the line went straight that the patient was dead. Watching that red line with the little peaks was mesmerising, as if it was measuring out his dad's life. Dan worried that if he looked away the peaks would cease. *Don't be stupid,* he told himself. *Nothing you do or don't do will make any difference.* Except talking, apparently.

He turned his attention back to his dad who was lying there so still. It wasn't like Ryan to be still. He was always on the go, always rushing around from one appointment to the next. Always driving too fast.

He really ought to start talking. But what was there to talk about? Well, apart from his dad's accident, there was only one thing on his mind at the moment so he might as well talk about that. He cleared his throat and began.

"Hey, Dad, remember that girl you nearly ran over the other day? Well you're not going to believe this, but…"

~~~

Rose and her mother shared the bottle of water between them whilst the nurses bustled around the room, monitoring the machines, checking the drips and making notes on the clipboards which hung at the end of each bed. Roxanne carried out the check on her grandmother and Rose was astonished at how quickly she worked, and
~~~

always with a smile on her face.

"She's a tough old bird," said Roxanne, adjusting the sheet and tucking it in where it had come loose.

"Will she get better?" asked Rose, trusting Roxanne to give her an honest answer.

Roxanne tilted her head sympathetically to one side and said, "The next twenty-four to forty-eight hours will be critical." Then one of the other nurses called her over to another bed, leaving Rose wondering what exactly Roxanne had meant by that. Roxanne hadn't said *yes* or *no*. She'd said they'd have to wait and see. Rose didn't know if she could wait that long to find out. Already time seemed to be crawling slower than a snail on crutches.

Rose looked at her gran's face. The skin had an unhealthy greyish tinge to it and looked paper thin over the hollowed out cheekbones. Her lips were dry and cracked, her wispy white hair like a halo around her head. If it wasn't for the machines indicating that life was still present, Rose wouldn't have believed it. And what about Dan's dad? You heard about people staying in comas for years, as good as dead and yet clinging to life by the slenderest of threads. But what did that do to the relatives waiting by the bedside?

Andrea laid a hand on Rose's shoulder, rousing her from her morbid reverie. "I'm just popping to the ladies. Will you be all right here?"

"Yes, I'm fine, Mum."

Rose watched her mother walk from the ward. Her shoulders drooped and there was a heaviness to her step that Rose had not seen before. *This must be really hard on her.*

Rose leaned forward, resting her forearms on the crisp white sheets and bringing her head close to her grandmother's face. She had no idea if her grandmother was aware of anything at the moment, but she so much wanted to talk to her. Keeping her voice low so as not to disturb the other patients and visitors, Rose said, "Hey, Gran, remember that boy I went to the fair with? Well you're not going to believe this but I bumped into him just now, in the hospital foyer, by the vending machine."

Was that a flicker of movement in her grandmother's face? Had she heard Rose speak? It was impossible to know for sure, but for the first time since her grandmother's collapse in the park, Rose felt a glimmer of hope. Encouraged, she quickly told her grandmother about his dad's car accident and how worried she was for him.

"I really like him, Gran," she said. "Part of me wishes I didn't have to go back to London. I'm going to miss him."

Rose was so sure that her grandmother was going to speak some words of comfort and support that she felt the ensuing silence as a desperate blow. Her grandmother's eyes remained closed and there was no sign that she'd heard what Rose had said.

~~~

"I've never felt this way about anyone before. She's not just pretty. Rose is really smart and fun to be with."

Once Dan started talking he found that it wasn't so hard after all. In fact, once he got going, the words just wouldn't stop. And talking about Rose had made him realise how much he cared about her. He told his dad all about their meeting in the café and how he'd asked her to go to the fair with him. He talked about the Kamikaze ride and how dizzy she'd been afterwards. He didn't mention Max and the guys with the guns, obviously. It didn't seem appropriate under the circumstances.

"The only problem," said Dan, "is that she's just here on holiday and she'll be going back to London in a couple of weeks and then I probably won't see her again. I bet she has loads of friends back in London, maybe even a boyfriend, I don't know, but I'm really going to miss her when she's gone."

Dan stopped. There was nothing more to say. It was just his luck to fall for someone who wasn't going to be
~~~

sticking around. He wondered if she felt the same way. He'd probably never know.

The beeping of the heart monitor filled the silence. Then something unexpected happened. His dad's eyelids started to flicker.

"Dad?" called Dan, leaning closer to his father. "Dad, can you hear me?"

Was it just an involuntary twitch of the muscles, or was his dad actually waking up? Dan took hold of his father's hand and gave it a gentle squeeze. "Dad? It's me, Dan."

His dad's eyelids flickered once more, and this time the lashes parted and Ryan slowly opened his eyes.

Dan leapt to his feet. "Dad, it's me. Can you see me Dad?"

Ryan blinked as if the light in the room was unbearably bright for him, then he turned his head a fraction and looked straight at Dan.

"Dan," he croaked.

"You're awake," cried Dan, grasping his father's hand.

The door opened and Fiona walked back in carrying a styrofoam cup. "Have I missed anything?"

"He's awake," said Dan. "He's awake." It was only then that he realised his cheeks were wet. Tears of relief were streaming down his face.

~~~

Rose and her mother took it in turns to go down to the cafeteria for a tasteless hospital sandwich and an insipid cup of tea. Walking through the corridors, Rose kept a lookout for Dan but didn't see him again. Maybe he'd gone home, or was working at the amusement arcade. She thought about his dad and hoped for Dan's sake that he would pull through.

Back at her grandmother's side, Rose tried to remember happier times she'd spent in Scarborough as a child. Donkey rides on the beach, sandcastles, ice cream.
~~~

Those memories seemed so far away now, like they'd happened to someone else. *Oh Gran,* she thought, *please come back to us.* Beside her Andrea was flicking through one of the magazines she'd brought along. Rose didn't know how she could read anything at a time like this, but then maybe she was just staring at the pictures?

Did her grandmother's eyelids flicker just then? Rose looked more closely, hardly daring to hope. Yes, there it was again. A twitching around the eye muscles. "Gran?" she called in a soft voice. Her grandmother blinked once, then opened her eyes.

"Mum," said Rose urgently, "Gran's awake."

Andrea dropped the magazine onto the floor and hurried to the other side of the bed.

Her grandmother tried, unsuccessfully, to sit up, and flopped back down onto the pile of pillows. "Where am I?" Her voice was barely audible, a thin rasping sound.

Rose was overjoyed to see her open her eyes. There was hope after all. "Gran, you're in hospital. But it's OK. We're here." She grasped her grandmother's hand and the old lady turned her head to look at her.

"What happened?"

"You had a heart attack in Peasholm Park," said Andrea in a voice that was too loud. "You gave us all quite a turn, I can tell you." She sounded as if she was scolding her mother for falling ill.

Andrea then launched into a monologue about the paramedics and the ambulance and the A&E department, how she'd been in Intensive Care and was now in the High Dependency Unit. She described Dr Patel in glowing terms (*Does she fancy him?* Rose wondered) and how the nurses were all kind but busy. Couldn't her mother shut up for a moment? Rose could see her grandmother's eyes starting to glaze over.

It was a relief when Roxanne arrived and Andrea was forced to be quiet. "Now then, Mrs Shawcross," she said in her sing-song voice, "how are you feeling?"

"Tired," croaked her grandmother.

"Well, that's not surprising after all you've been through. Now, it's time for your medication." She looked pointedly at Andrea. "You've both been here all day. You must be dead beat. Why don't you go home and get some rest yourselves?"

"We'll come back tomorrow, Gran," said Rose, leaning over to kiss her grandmother on the cheek.

Her grandmother smiled at her but there was a look in her eyes as if she was trying to tell Rose something that couldn't be spoken out loud. Rose could barely bring herself to leave.

They stopped to pick up fish and chips on the way home. But the chips were stodgy and greasy and the batter on the fish was overcooked. "I can't eat this," said Rose, rising from the table and throwing the unwanted food in the bin.

"No, me neither," said her mother. They washed up in silence, then Rose climbed the stairs to her room.

Even though she'd done nothing all day except sit by her grandmother's bedside, she felt exhausted and could feel the beginnings of a headache. She supposed it was the mental strain of not knowing if her grandmother was going to be all right. She flopped down on the bed and pulled her mobile from her pocket, wondering if Dan had got in touch, but there were no messages or missed calls. *No news is good news,* she tried to tell herself, but it sounded like a lie.

She needed something to take her mind off images of hospital corridors and life support machines. The only thing she had were Mary's letters. She picked up the pile from her bedside table and flicked through until she found the next one, written on the 22nd of August 1899, a gap of four days since the previous letter. It wasn't like Mary not to write daily and Rose wondered what had happened to cause such a delay.

Fisherman's Cottage,
Scarborough,
10am, 22nd August, 1899

Dear Ma,

Oh, Ma, I don't know where to begin. Something terrible has happened! Now, make sure you're sitting down before you read any more of this.

There's no easy way to say this, so I'll just come straight out with it. Alice has gone missing! We had this plan to get her away from Jackson, Henry Blackwood's man, and it worked up to a point, but when Mr Hartright went to meet her at the church, she wasn't there. He found her shawl (well it was my shawl, but Alice was wearing it) splattered with blood. But of Alice, there was absolutely no sign. We can't think what has happened to her.

We have reported her disappearance to the police and an Inspector from Scotland Yard has been assigned to the case, but so far they have found no clues. The blood on the shawl indicates that something bad happened in the church, but the police cannot say she has been murdered unless they find a body. It really is too dreadful to think about.

I am going to stay in Scarborough and do everything I can to find her. I have moved out of the Grand Hotel and am being taken care of by a very kind fisherman, called Walter, and his sister, Ellie. They have been very good to me and I have offered to help Ellie keep house in return for their kindness and generosity. I'll never forgive myself if Alice isn't found alive, safe and well. Please don't worry about me, I'll be fine.

Love to all,
Mary.

What a terrible letter to have to write. Rose tried to imagine doing the same in similar circumstances - the confusion, the worry. The guilt. The next few letters were more of the same: the police were doing what they could, making enquiries, but there was no sign of Alice; no body had been found (*a good sign,* according to Mary); Walter kept an eye out every time he went fishing in case a body should wash up on the shore, but so far there had been nothing. Alice had vanished without trace.

There was a tap on Rose's door and her mother came in, pale and trembling.

Rose dropped the letter she was holding and jumped to her feet. "What is it Mum?"

"That…that was the hospital on the phone," said her mother, her voice cracking.

Rose's stomach turned over. "Is it Gran?"

Her mother nodded. "She passed away peacefully ten minutes ago."

Rose felt her knees go weak. She fell into her mother's arms and they stood there hugging each other tight, letting the tears fall.

~~~

The boy I love is up in the gallery,
The boy I love is looking now at me,
There he is, can't you see, waving his handkerchief,
As merry as a robin that sings on a tree.

Except he wasn't in the gallery anymore. And neither was he at his lodging house. Kitty knew because she had called round there earlier in the afternoon and the landlady had told her, whilst looking down her nose at the frills on Kitty's dress, that Mr Jackson had left. Then she had shut the door in Kitty's face.

The audience burst into rapturous applause as they did every night and Kitty bowed and blew kisses out into the auditorium, all the while smiling graciously. But her heart wasn't in it. She was a good actress so she hoped it wouldn't show, but underneath the rouge and the lipstick, her heart was breaking.

She picked up the roses tossed onto the stage,
~~~

pretending to sniff them, then she bowed once more and made her exit, running back to her dressing room. She closed the door and sank down on the chair in front of the mirror. She didn't know how much longer she could keep up this life of singing and acting. It was taking its toll on her and that was why she'd gone to St Mary's Church a few days ago. To think things through somewhere quiet. She had hoped God might tell her clearly and plainly whether or not Jackson was *Mr Right* and whether she should leave the stage and marry him. Not that he'd asked her yet, but she was confident she could wangle a proposal out of him. He just needed a little encouragement, but the question was, was he worth it?

She had chosen a quiet spot in the church, on the far right hand side, behind a pillar, because she didn't want to be disturbed. She wasn't a regular churchgoer and she felt a little guilty entering the building, as if she didn't have as much right to be there as other people. The last thing she wanted was to be accosted by some matronly do-gooder who would look at the bows and flounces on her dress and judge her badly for it.

So she'd sat there on her own, thinking over her life from blacksmith's daughter to star of the Scarborough stage, when she'd heard the door opening and footsteps coming down the aisle. Dainty footsteps. Peering out from behind the pillar, she had been surprised to see the lady Jackson had been *keeping an eye on*. Miss Alice Hawthorne. Kitty had thought it rather a funny business to be monitoring the activities of a lady on holiday, but Jackson had assured her that he meant Alice no harm and he was only doing this job at the behest of his employer, Sir Henry Blackwood. Kitty had seen for herself that Jackson kept his distance from Alice and so she had trusted him. On her strolls around Scarborough with Jackson, Kitty had become familiar with Alice and her maid, Mary. They did everything together and were more like companions than mistress and maid. But now here was Alice all alone. And it looked to Kitty as if Alice was wearing Mary's plain black dress instead of her own fancier, white one. Why was she on her own? Was Jackson about to appear too? Or had Alice given him the slip?

All these questions were spinning around Kitty's head when the door had opened a second time and she heard a man's footstep on the stone floor. Heavy and resolute. Naturally, she had thought it must be Jackson, but Alice had thought it was someone called George and had called out his name. Not wishing to disturb a love tryst, Kitty had remained hidden from view.

But then it had turned out not to be George, the painter, or Jackson for that matter, but another man entirely. Someone that Alice was clearly afraid of. He had followed Alice to the front of the altar and grabbed her by the arm. In a fit of female solidarity Kitty had jumped to her feet, but then she had glimpsed the blade of the knife in the man's hand. He lashed out at Alice, wounding her on the arm. Alice had pleaded with him not to kill her and he had dragged her outside, muttering something about Highcliff House.

It had all happened so quickly that Kitty had been too shocked to react. When she had finally pulled herself together and run outside, Alice and the man were nowhere to be seen.

Now she was in a dilemma.

She had tried to find Jackson to tell him what had happened but he too had vanished. She should have gone to the police straight away, but was now worried that she had left it too late and they would charge her with dereliction of duty if such a crime existed. Her only hope was to find Mary and tell her what she had seen.

~~~

The next day at the hospital, Dr Wilson talked to Dan and his mother about the cognitive tests he would be
~~~

carrying out on Ryan.

"There may be some short term memory loss," he explained, "and with severe cases of concussion like this I would expect spells of dizziness and tiredness, but he should make a full recovery in the long run."

Dan wondered how much, if anything, Ryan would remember about what Dan had been telling him just before he woke up. Remembering how he'd opened his heart up about Rose made him cringe with embarrassment. A bit of short term memory loss would be no bad thing as far as Dan was concerned.

Dan and his mother sat outside in the corridor whilst Dr Wilson carried out the first round of tests.

"What were you talking to him about when he woke up?" asked Fiona.

"Oh, just stuff," said Dan. Talking to an unconscious person was one thing but he wasn't about to reveal his deepest thoughts to his mother of all people.

"Well it did the trick," she said, taking hold of his hand and giving it a squeeze.

Dan checked his phone to see if Rose had got in touch, but there was nothing. He'd give her a call later, see how she was doing.

There was a sound of men's voices down the corridor. Dan looked up to see two men, an older one with thinning grey hair, broad shoulders and a square jaw; and a younger one with a ginger beard. They were talking to a nurse who nodded and pointed towards Dan and his mother. The men both wore dark suits and had an official-looking air about them. Dan was reminded of detective shows on the television: the Detective Inspector and his Sergeant. The older man nodded his thanks to the nurse and then both men strode towards Dan and his mother. Something was going on, but what? Dan shifted in his seat, feeling uncomfortable. Fiona was oblivious, too busy checking her mobile to pay any attention to the arrival of the two men.

They stopped in front of Dan and his mother. "Mrs

Grigson?" said the older of the two.

"Yes?" said Fiona, stuffing her mobile phone back into her handbag.

"Detective Inspector Crawford." He flashed an ID card in front of their faces. "And this is Sergeant Peterson." He indicated his colleague. "We'd like a few words with your husband if that's possible."

Fiona jumped to her feet. "What about? My husband is very ill. He's only just woken up from a coma."

"We understand the situation, Ma'am," said the Inspector. "But this relates to the car accident that put him in here in the first place."

"What about it? Look, if the tractor driver wants to press charges then I think we're all agreed that Ryan was probably driving too fast. I never did like him driving that bloody Ferrari. Good riddance to it is what I say."

"Ma'am," said Inspector Crawford in a tone that made Fiona shut up immediately. Dan felt a tightening in his chest. He thought he could guess what the Inspector was going to say next. "This is not directly about the accident. It relates to another matter that has come to light since we impounded the car."

At that moment the door to Ryan's room opened and Dr Wilson stepped out into the corridor. The Inspector introduced himself and asked if he was the doctor in charge of Ryan Grigson's medical care.

"I am," said Dr Wilson. "How can I help you?"

"We need to speak to your patient," said the Inspector. "Is he in a fit state for us to see him?"

"Well, he's quite tired, but yes, he's awake at the moment," said Dr Wilson, looking warily from the Inspector to Fiona and back to the Inspector.

"What's going on?" asked Fiona in a shaky voice.

"If I may…" said Inspector Crawford, moving towards the door which was blocked by the doctor.

Dr Wilson stepped to one side. The Inspector and his Sergeant went into the room, followed closely by Dan and his mother.

"Mr Grigson?" said Inspector Crawford, looking down at the prone figure of Dan's father and flashing his ID card at him.

"Yes?" croaked Ryan.

"Mr Grigson, I am arresting you on charges of drug trafficking. You do not have to say anything, but it may harm your defence if you do not mention when questioned something which you later rely on in court. Anything you do say may be given in evidence."

Fiona let out a strangled scream and fell against Dan who only just managed to catch her in his arms.

CHAPTER ELEVEN

For the next few days Rose and her mother were busy preparing for the funeral. Andrea, in particular, threw herself into activities, such as contacting everyone in her mother's address book, with her usual vigour, but once or twice Rose caught her mother just staring vaguely into empty space, a tear trickling down her cheek. Rose did her best to stay cheerful for her mother's sake and made them both endless cups of tea, but most of those were left to go cold. Inside, Rose felt numb with shock. She woke every morning expecting to see her grandmother downstairs and then remembered that she was gone forever and the sadness would hit her afresh.

Rose accompanied her mother to the undertaker's funeral parlour where a sympathetic lady called Cynthia took them into her office, served them tea and biscuits, offered her condolences, and asked whether they were looking for a cremation or a burial, what sort of music they would like and whether or not there should be flowers? Rose had no idea there would be so much to arrange. All this talk of music and flowers made it sound more like a wedding than a funeral.

"Mum wanted to be cremated," said Andrea. Rose

wondered how her mother knew such a thing. Had they discussed it whilst Rose was out at the fair? Cynthia nodded encouragingly as if this was the correct answer, although Rose suspected she responded like that whatever bizarre requests grieving relatives put to her. In the end they settled on a simple service at the crematorium chapel with, at Cynthia's suggestion, some *quiet but uplifting* organ music whilst the coffin was carried in, and just one hymn during the service, *The Lord's My Shepherd*, which Andrea thought was her mother's favourite.

On the way back from the undertaker's they called in at *The Fisherman's Arms*, a modern flat-roofed pub not far from the crematorium, which had a private function room, a large car park and no atmosphere whatsoever. Andrea spoke to the manager about booking the private room for the wake. Rose thought it a dreary place but Andrea said no one would come if there wasn't anywhere to park.

"Just a simple buffet," said Andrea to the manager. "Nothing too fancy."

The manager nodded and noted down her request. *Gran would have liked a bit of a bash*, thought Rose, but didn't say anything. She wondered about inviting Dan, but then decided not to. She'd texted him to let him know what had happened and he'd texted back to say how sorry he was but he hadn't been in touch since. *He's probably got better things to do*, thought Rose, *and I guess we'll be going home once the funeral is sorted out*. A knot tightened in her stomach at the thought of leaving Dan and going back home to…what? Joe? That relationship was well and truly over and Rose knew in her heart of hearts that it had been for a long time, even before coming to Scarborough.

Neither Rose nor her mother had brought clothes suitable for a funeral, thinking they were coming to Scarborough for a holiday, so the day after their visit to the funeral parlour they walked into town and went shopping together. Shopping for clothes was not an activity they normally shared and Rose was doubtful it would be an experience she'd want to repeat.

"How does this look?" asked Andrea, emerging from a changing room at *Marks and Spencer* wearing the only black dress available in the shop. The summer sales were in full swing and the racks were bulging with T-shirts and strappy tops. Trying to find a black dress was almost impossible.

"It's fine, Mum."

"It's not too low-cut?"

"Of course not."

"I suppose I could always wear it with a scarf."

"It would look better without."

"I don't want people to think I haven't dressed appropriately."

"Mu-um! No one's going to think that."

"Well, if you're sure…" Andrea disappeared back into the changing room. When she re-emerged Rose marched her to the check-out before she had time to change her mind about the dress.

Rose found a cute little black dress in one of the more fashionable chains.

"Don't you think it's a bit short for a funeral?" asked Andrea.

"It's only *just* above my knee." Rose looked at herself in the full-length mirror. The dress had short sleeves, a square neckline, fitted bodice, a swinging skirt and showed off her figure without being too revealing. *Gran would have liked this dress,* she thought, and a lump came to her throat. *But Gran's not here to stick up for me anymore. It's just Mum and me now.*

The day of the funeral dawned grey and foggy. Rose put on her new dress and a pair of black ballet pumps that she'd bought in the same shop. She checked her appearance in the mirror, wanting to look her best for her grandmother's sake. Her mother was already downstairs, tugging at the neckline on her new dress and fussing with her hair in the living room mirror.

"You look lovely, Mum," said Rose. "That dress really

suits you." At forty-eight, her mother still had a figure to be proud of.

"Are you sure it's all right? Wouldn't it be better with a scarf?"

"No. It's perfect just as it is." Then they were in each other's arms, hugging each other tightly. "I miss Gran," said Rose.

"I know, sweetheart. I miss her too."

There was the throb of an engine in the street, a car door opened, and then a measured knock on the front door.

Rose glanced out of the window and her stomach contracted. A black, shiny hearse was outside, bearing a coffin. Behind the hearse was another black car, a limousine. The funeral cortège would start from here. Gran was leaving Tollergate for the last time.

"Ready, Mum?"

Andrea nodded. They linked arms and stepped outside.

The little chapel at the Crematorium was packed. Rose was astonished to see so many people, but it seemed her Gran had a good many friends from having lived her whole life in Scarborough.

The minister, a young woman with a smiley face, spoke warmly about her grandmother's life, how she had worked as a chamber maid then as a receptionist at the Grand Hotel and in her retirement had worked as a volunteer at the charity shop attached to the Royal National Lifeboat Institution.

"And now," said the minister, giving Rose an encouraging smile, "Janice's granddaughter will read a poem by Christina Rossetti."

Rose stood up and walked to the front of the chapel, clutching the book of poems she had found in her grandmother's bedroom. Dozens of pairs of eyes were on her. She took a deep breath and looked down at the book in her hands. Then she started to read.

Remember me when I am gone away,
Gone far away into the silent land;
When you can no more hold me by the hand,
Nor I half turn to go yet turning stay.
Remember me when no more day by day
You tell me of our future that you plann'd:
Only remember me; you understand
It will be late to counsel then or pray.
Yet if you should forget me for a while
And afterwards remember, do not grieve:
For if the darkness and corruption leave
A vestige of the thoughts that once I had,
Better by far you should forget and smile
Than that you should remember and be sad.

~~~

Fiona had wasted no time in hiring the best lawyer she could find. Charles Baker-Howard was a senior partner at the law firm *Baker-Howard & Carmichael* despite being only in his early forties. She had extolled his credentials to Dan at great length the previous evening over take-away pizza which was the only food they ate at home these days. Dan didn't think there was much any lawyer could do for his dad whatever his or her credentials. If the police had found a stash of cocaine on the passenger seat of the Ferrari then Ryan was up shit creek without a paddle and that was that.

"That'll be him," cried Fiona as the doorbell chimed. "Can you let him in? I just need to check the morning room." *So that's what a morning room is for,* thought Dan. *Impressing lawyers so that they'll get your husband off in court.*

Dan opened the door. A tall, dark-haired gentleman who looked like he might be auditioning to be the next James Bond was standing on the doorstep. He carried a slim, leather briefcase in one hand. Dan speculated for a moment whether or not it would explode if you opened it
~~~

the wrong way.

"Good evening. I hope I'm not late." Baker-Howard glanced at his watch. *A Rolex,* noted Dan. *This is obviously the business to be in.*

"Please come in," said Dan. "We're just in here." He led the lawyer through to the morning room where Fiona had set a tray with filtered coffee and wafer-thin chocolate biscuits on the coffee table. She was sitting on the sofa, fiddling with the rings on her fingers. She jumped up to greet their guest.

"Please take a seat, Mr Baker-Howard. Would you like some coffee? Do help yourself to a biscuit."

She's nervous, thought Dan. *And not without reason.* The news that Ryan was being arrested on charges of drug trafficking had come as a terrible shock to both of them, even to Dan who already had misgivings that his dad was mixed up in some bad business with Max. One minute his dad was fighting for his life and, having successfully conquered that battle, he was now under arrest for dealing in cocaine. How unlucky could you be!

No, not unlucky, thought Dan bitterly. *Just incredibly stupid.* Luck had nothing to do with it. The accident was the result of recklessness, not bad luck. It was bad luck there'd been a tractor in the middle of the road, for sure, but it was recklessness that had caused his dad to take the turning too quickly. The tractor driver, who was unhurt due to the fact that he'd been driving a much bigger vehicle at a very slow speed, had told the police that the Ferrari came *tearing round the corner like a bat out of hell.* Ryan hadn't stood a chance. But why was he driving like an idiot? It had to be because of the box on the passenger seat. Dan found it hard to believe that his dad didn't know what the box contained, and maybe that knowledge had made him jittery at the wheel. Fiona in particular had taken the news very badly. Quite a few pieces of crockery had hit the kitchen floor before she'd calmed down and phoned the lawyers.

What really worried Dan was that he had been behind

the counter at the amusement arcade when those guys had brought the box in. Dan had taken possession of it and stored it under the counter. Did that make him an accessory to drug trafficking? Was there such an offence?

Doctor Wilson was insistent that his patient was still too fragile to be moved so Ryan remained in his hospital bed and a uniformed constable was on duty in the corridor to make sure he didn't escape. *Not very likely with a broken leg,* thought Dan. The police had gone through his dad's office looking for whatever evidence they could find. They'd confiscated Ryan's computer and mobile phone.

Dan didn't know if he was expected to leave the room or stay, but as neither his mother nor the lawyer said anything Dan decided to just sit quietly in the corner and listen. This situation affected all of them, after all.

Baker-Howard sat back in the best armchair and casually crossed one leg over the other. "I've just come from the hospital."

"Does he have a good chance of getting off?" asked Fiona.

"I'm afraid the situation doesn't look good," said the lawyer. "He can't deny the cocaine was in the car. It looks as if his best bet would be to plead guilty, maybe say that he was coerced into this or something, apologise profusely and hope that the judge will give him a reduced sentence for honesty. They like a repentant sinner. It makes their job easier."

And yours, thought Dan. *It'll save you having to plead his case if Dad confesses everything to the judge.* There was something about Baker-Howard that Dan instinctively didn't like. He hoped his mother had made a wise choice in picking him.

"Oh," said Fiona. "That doesn't sound too promising."

"There is one thing that could help his case." The lawyer reached for a biscuit and snapped it in half with his long fingers.

"What's that?" asked Fiona, perking up.

"If he can lead them to the real criminals behind this

operation then the judge would be more inclined to reduce his sentence, maybe even give him a suspended sentence for a first offence. I've explained this to him and he's thinking it over at the moment."

It's Max, thought Dan. *He's behind all this. He's the reason that Dad almost got himself killed and is now facing a jail sentence. Why does Dad have to think it over? Why doesn't he just shop Max to the police?*

Dan decided there and then that if his dad wasn't going to snitch on Max, then he would.

~~~

"I've always enjoyed the poems of Christina Rossetti," said a voice at her shoulder. Rose turned from the buffet at *The Fisherman's Arms* to see a tall, elderly man standing behind her. He was dressed in a well-cut, dark suit and when he held his hand out to shake hers she noticed a dolphin-shaped silver cuff-link in his shirt sleeve. "David Drinkwater," he said, taking Rose's hand in his. "I'm your grandmother's younger brother. You read that poem beautifully, by the way."

"Thank you," said Rose. "I was quite nervous."

"It didn't show." Rose had the feeling he wasn't just saying that to be nice, but really meant it. She smiled at him. She didn't remember meeting this man before but there was something about his manner, charming but relaxed, that put her at ease. If he was her grandmother's brother then she supposed that made him her great uncle. "Do you live in Scarborough?" she asked him, wondering why she hadn't encountered him before now.

"Sadly no," he said, shaking his head. "I live in the centre of York."

"I like York," said Rose. She hadn't been there often but she had a memory of old, medieval streets, a Roman wall and a huge Minster.

"Then you must come and visit sometime," said David.
~~~

"You and your mother would be most welcome."

"We will," said Rose.

David bowed slightly and then said, "You'll have to excuse me, but I must go and catch my train. It's been a pleasure meeting you."

Rose watched him go over to Andrea on the other side of the room and take his leave. She would have liked to talk to him for longer and wondered if they would ever visit him in York. She supposed it was unlikely. After David had gone, Rose picked at the food on her plate, not really hungry. She didn't know most of the people there, except for one or two neighbours from Tollergate, and Rose found herself shaking hands with people whose names she immediately forgot.

After an hour of eating and drinking and reminiscences of Janice as a young, vibrant woman in Scarborough, people started to make their excuses and leave. Soon Rose and her mother were the only ones left, surrounded by a litter of half-empty wine glasses and sandwiches that were starting to curl at the edges. The pub staff began to clear away the dirty plates and glasses. Andrea was sitting on her own at one of the tables, wine glass in hand, looking sad. Rose went to join her.

"I tried to get her to come and live with us in London," said Andrea suddenly, staring into the middle distance.

"I know."

"She would never have come, though. Scarborough was her home." Andrea set the wine glass down on the table. "You know, as a teenager growing up here I couldn't wait to get away from the place. I thought it was boring and provincial and I wanted the excitement of living in London. But it's not so bad here really."

"Scarborough's a great place," said Rose, surprising herself. She hadn't really considered it before, but she'd grown very fond of the bustling seaside town in the last few weeks. Or maybe she'd just grown fond of one person who lived here? Either way, she found herself missing

London less and less.

"Come on," said Andrea, reaching for her handbag and standing up. "We should go home."

They ordered a taxi and, when it arrived, sat in the back in silence, each lost in their own thoughts. Rose had the feeling that her mother had something else on her mind beside the immediate concerns of the funeral and sorting out her grandmother's will, but she knew her mother would tell her when she was ready. They let themselves into the house that now felt so silent and empty, but still contained so many reminders of her grandmother, from the ornaments on the mantelpiece to the lingering smell of lavender and Pears soap.

"I'm tired," said Andrea, kicking off her high heels and leaving them in front of the fireplace. "I'm going to lie down."

Rose listened to the creak of the stairs and heard her mother's door click shut. She felt restless and was unable to just sit still. She roamed the downstairs rooms, still expecting to see her grandmother sitting in her favourite armchair, reading a book, or at the dining table, coffee cup in hand, scouring the local newspaper. She tiptoed upstairs and gently pushed open the door to her grandmother's bedroom. The smell of lavender was strongest in here and for a moment Rose stood, breathing in the scent and remembering. She sat down at her grandmother's dressing table and picked up the ivory-handled mirror and hairbrush, inlaid with mother-of-pearl. How long had these been in the family? A century? Rose knew very little about her ancestors, other than what she'd gleaned from Mary's letters. She should have asked her grandmother more questions about her own life, but it was too late now. Maybe David would tell her stuff, if they ever did visit him in York. She went back downstairs.

The early morning fog had lifted and the day was now bright and sunny. Suddenly Rose felt hemmed in by all the memories. She wanted to be outside, to feel the sun on her face, to feel alive. Her grandmother would have understood. She scribbled a note for her mother to say she was going for a walk, then without bothering to change out of her black dress and pumps, she slipped outside and started walking up the hill towards the North Bay.

It had been a week since she'd been here with Dan, running into the sea, kissing him, walking hand in hand along the sand. So much had happened since then, and none of it for the better.

Dan. She hugged her arms around herself as she walked, thinking about him. Meeting Dan had been the best thing that had happened to her in a long while, but what was going to happen to them now? She didn't know how he really felt about her. Was it just a holiday romance or did they have something more? But even then, how would they manage to continue their relationship when she was back in London? And now with his dad in hospital, he had other things to worry about.

She'd walked further than she'd realised and found herself at the turning that led to the asylum. If she carried along this road she'd be out in open countryside, but she didn't feel like going back towards the town just yet. She hesitated a moment, then turned down the path to the asylum, careful to avoid the nettles touching her bare legs. She arrived at the chain-link fence and stood looking at the old house. Its air of abandonment and isolation matched her mood perfectly. It looked even more dilapidated than last time. There was a hole in the roof that she hadn't noticed before and one of the chimneys was broken off. She couldn't believe she and Dan had been so foolhardy as to actually go inside. The place looked to her now like a death trap, as if it might fall down any minute. No wonder they were going to demolish it.

There was a rustling in the undergrowth behind her. She jumped and spun around just as a dog leapt out from behind one of the bushes. The animal stood in the middle of the path, a scruffy medium-sized dog, some sort of cross-breed that Rose couldn't identify. It had rough black fur, a long snout and pointed ears that folded over at the top. The dog took one look at Rose and bounded over, barking loudly.

Oh no! Rose pinned herself back against the wire fence, her mind flashing back to the dog at the fairground. That incident had left its mark on her and although this dog didn't look anything like as frightening, still you couldn't be too careful. She knew you weren't supposed to show fear in front of strange dogs, but that was easier said than done. The dog was standing in the middle of the path, blocking her exit. If it leapt at her it could easily bite her.

"Hey, Lucky, come here boy!" A girl shouted from somewhere out of sight. At the sound of the voice the dog stopped barking and looked around. Then it turned back to Rose, obviously torn between obeying its mistress and sniffing out the intruder.

"Good dog," ventured Rose in a voice that sounded high-pitched and thin. The dog took a couple of steps towards her.

"Lucky, I said come here!" A girl rounded the corner of the path and the dog trotted back to its mistress with its tail between its legs. Rose breathed out a sigh of relief. Thank goodness the owner had turned up and it wasn't a wild stray. Her palms were clammy with sweat and she wiped them on the skirt of her dress.

The girl, who looked to be about Rose's age, walked forward, keeping one hand on the dog's collar. In her other hand she held a plastic carrier bag that looked to contain a few items of tinned food. She was wearing ethnic-print cotton trousers and a tie-dyed top and her sandy-coloured hair hung in dreadlocks down her back. She wore a silver ring through one nostril.

"Who are you?" asked the girl, scowling at Rose. "What are you doing hanging around here?"

Rose wished it had just been the dog after all.

~~~

I have become familiar with the daily routines at the asylum.

We rise at six. Dorothy, the lady who talks to herself, is always the first to get out of bed. Sometimes the nurse in charge tries to put her back, but then she starts shouting and creating a fuss so it is usually best to leave her. She starts pacing the room and muttering to herself so it is impossible for the rest of us to get any rest after that time.

We take it in turns to wash in a bowl of water. We line up in order of who has been here the longest. As the newest arrival in the dormitory I am last in the queue so that when it is my turn to wash, the water has gone cold and a grey soap scum is floating on the top. Then we put on our blue woollen dresses. Everyone wears the same. We are given fresh underwear weekly.

When everyone is ready the nurse in charge escorts us down to the dining room for breakfast. We are not allowed to go on our own in case we try to escape and, anyway, the doors around the asylum are locked and can only be opened by keys which the nurses keep about their persons on long chains.

We dine in a large room on the ground floor. The women enter through a door at one end of the room and the men enter through a door on the opposite side. The male and female sections of the asylum are in separate wings of the building.

Breakfast is the same every day. A ration of coarse, brown bread, a small piece of butter and lukewarm tea served in a tin mug. Some of the women tear at the bread with their fingers and try to hide pieces in the pockets of their dress. Others spill their tea because their hands are shaking so much. For the first couple of days I couldn't eat anything, I was in such a state of shock at finding myself in this place. But then I nearly fainted through lack of food and I realised that I must keep my strength up if I am ever
~~~

to convince the doctors of my sanity and be released.

If the weather is fine the nurses take us outside for half an hour to walk around the garden. It is a pleasant enough space with perennial flowers, rose bushes and lavender, but it is enclosed by a high brick wall to prevent anyone from escaping. From the garden the house looks grand and imposing. It would be a fine building but the effect is spoilt by the bars on the windows. It is a prison.

The first day, Dorothy attached herself to me and gleefully pointed out some of the other patients. That one she said, indicating a woman with frizzy hair, was suffering from mania and was prone to fits of shrieking. Another one, grey-haired and pale-skinned, was, apparently, a victim of melancholy. Dorothy warned me in a conspiratorial whisper to keep away from a red-faced woman called Louise who was, she said, hysterical and apt to be violent. To me, they simply looked sad.

Dorothy then asked me what my complaint was and I responded that I didn't have a *complaint* as she put it. She shook her head at me and said not to worry, Dr Collins would soon diagnose my case and then I would have a *condition* just like everyone else. Then she laughed in a high-pitched shriek until one of the nurses came and slapped her on the face. After that she fell quiet.

Dinner is served at half past twelve in the dining room. The fare is invariably boiled mutton, boiled potatoes and boiled cabbage. The smell of cabbage never clears from the air. The food is served on tin plates so they do not break when some of the more violent patients throw them onto the floor. This happens a few times every week.

In the afternoon, if we do not have medical treatment, we may pass an hour or two in the day room where there are board games such as chess and packs of playing cards. There is an out-of-tune piano which some of the patients attempt to play but the result is always dreadful. There are a handful of books, however these are not to my taste. They are all *improving moral tales* and terribly dreary, but that is what the doctors here think we need.

Tea, at five o'clock, is the same as breakfast. More bread and butter and another mug of tea.

There is a rota for the weekly bath. The ladies in our dormitory have their bath every Tuesday. It is the same routine as the day I arrived - get wet, lather yourself in carbolic soap and then endure the scrubbing brush at the hands of either Nurse Barrett or Nurse Cooper. The only difference is that we are all in the bathroom at the same time. Modesty is a long-forgotten memory in this place.

On Friday evenings there is entertainment, or what passes for entertainment in these dreary walls. Sometimes the staff put on a play, usually a farce. It is hard to follow the dialogue because there is so much shouting from the audience. Other times visiting musicians or magicians come to the asylum. Last week a man brought a magic lantern to the asylum and showed us the German fairy tale, *The Heart of Stone*. It was a simple moral tale about the evils of pursuing material wealth. But the moving images were too much for some of the more sensitive patients and many of them, including Dorothy, screamed in fright when the projected images started to move. For my part, I was painfully reminded of an evening in happier times when I had witnessed a ghost show and other such marvellous illusions. I thought of Mary and George and wondered what they are doing now. Have they forgotten me? With every day that passes I fear that they will forget me and I will fade away to nothing. Some days I already feel as insubstantial as one of Dr Pepper's Ghosts.

~~~

Fiona saw the lawyer out of the house and then came back into the morning room.

"It doesn't look too good, does it?" said Dan. He didn't want to believe that his dad would go to prison. What would happen to the amusement arcade if that happened?
~~~

Fiona bent down to pick up the coffee pot. "Your father should have thought of that before agreeing to get involved in this business. I mean, what the blazes was he thinking of?"

"I guess he had his reasons," said Dan doubtfully. To be honest, he couldn't think of any good reasons for getting involved in drug smuggling.

Fiona looked Dan in the eye. "Your father's been an idiot, but we have to stick together and fight this. Even if it means selling the house to pay the legal fees. Mr Baker-Howard is good but he doesn't come cheap."

Dan was shocked that his mother could talk so calmly about selling the house. This house was her pride and joy, the ultimate status symbol of their success as a family. She always spoke with bitterness about how she'd grown up in a two-up-two-down in a poor mining village just outside Durham and how she and her sister had practically starved during the miners' strike in the 1980s.

"Mr Baker-Howard said the judge would be more lenient if Dad told the police who was behind the drug smuggling."

Fiona looked at him with a steely glare. "What are you saying?"

"I know who gave Dad the drugs," said Dan. "They came into the arcade. I could point them out in an identity parade if I had to. There are a couple of Geordies and a guy…"

"Stop right there," said Fiona, holding up a hand.

"But…"

"No. You listen to me. Whatever you do, don't get involved in this. Do you hear me? People like that are dangerous."

"But shouldn't we go to the police?"

"That's for your father to decide. But you stay out of this. Do you hear me?"

Dan didn't reply.

"Do you *hear* me?"

"Yes. I hear you." Dan turned on his heel and ran up the stairs to his bedroom, slamming the door behind him. He shouldn't have said anything to his mother. He wanted to speak to Rose. He dialled her number but it went straight to voice mail. He hung up.

~~~

"I'm Rose."

The girl was looking at her with a mixture of suspicion and hostility. Rose worried that if she said the wrong thing the girl might set the dog on her. The animal was straining at the collar, wanting to come over and sniff her out.

"What are you doing here?" The girl repeated her question, still on her guard.

"Nothing. I just came for a walk, that's all."

"That's a fancy dress for a walk." The girl took in the black dress and ballet pumps.

"I've been to a funeral. My grandmother just died."

The girl narrowed her eyes as if she was assessing the likelihood of what Rose had just told her.

"It's true," said Rose. "And I don't see why I have to justify myself to you." She was getting pretty fed up of this girl's attitude. *What was her problem?*

The girl dropped the carrier bag onto the ground and her whole expression changed from one of aggression to one of sympathy. "I'm sorry about your grandmother." She smiled and knelt down, wrapping her arm around the dog. "I thought maybe someone had sent you to find me, that's all."

"No, of course not." Rose had no idea what the girl was talking about but guessed she must be hiding out, was maybe on the run or something. She remembered the signs of squatters that she and Dan had seen in the asylum the other day. "So are you living here?" Rose indicated the derelict building behind them.

The girl jumped to her feet. "So what if I am? There's
~~~

no law against that is there? It's just an abandoned building. Better that someone should be making use of it."

"OK, calm down, can't you?" Rose held up her hands. God, this girl was a prickly character, whoever she was. Part of Rose wanted to leave, but part of her was intrigued by this weird, jumpy girl and the idea that she was living in this abandoned building. Didn't she get scared at night? Out here all on her own? Rose couldn't imagine staying in this building after dark. "Look, I don't mean to be nosey, but isn't this house going to be pulled down?"

The girl shrugged. "I guess we'll have to find somewhere else then." She patted the top of the dog's head. The animal looked at her with such trusting eyes, Rose got the impression he'd follow her anywhere.

The girl seemed calmer now so Rose carried on talking. "Have you been here long?"

"A couple of months. Ever since my step-dad beat up Mum and she had to go and live in a hostel."

"Oh." Rose didn't know what to say to that, never having met anyone in such a dire situation. "But how do you manage to live?"

The girl shrugged her shoulders. "There's always casual work on the sea-front in the summer. Selling ice creams. Hiring out deckchairs, that sort of thing." Then she seemed to come to a decision. She held out her hand to Rose. "I'm Zoe, by the way. Welcome to my home - the madhouse."

~~~

On Wednesday afternoons I have my treatment sessions with Dr Collins. Nurse Cooper escorts me to his office, always making a big show of unlocking the doors and locking them again behind her, as though she were escorting a convicted prisoner to the gallows.

Dr Collins sees me in his office which is on the ground floor and is furnished with a large mahogany desk, the
~~~

walls lined with book shelves. The doctor believes himself to be a man of science and learning and he treats his patients as laboratory specimens to be experimented on.

I believe it is the only ground floor room in the building without iron bars on the windows. I suppose there is no need for them because the room is always occupied by Dr Collins during the day and then locked at night. Besides, bars would spoil the doctor's view of the sea.

His first task was to diagnose my case. For a while he seemed uncertain as to whether I was suffering from melancholia, monomania or moral insanity and kept referring to a large leather-bound volume that he kept on his desk. I explained to him, in great detail, the events that had brought me here: how Henry was obsessive and jealous; how he wanted to marry me for my money; how he had sent a man to spy on me. At this last revelation, Dr Collins' face lit up and he nodded, I thought at the time, most sympathetically. I pressed home my case, describing Jackson, even telling him that I had a photograph which clearly showed Jackson watching me and Mary on the promenade. I was so desperate for Dr Collins to believe me that I started to sound a little obsessed, but I knew I was telling the truth and I had to trust in his judgement as a learned man, a man of reason. When I had finished speaking, Dr Collins got to his feet, took up a position of authority in front of the fireplace and gave me his verdict.

"Miss Hawthorne, it is quite clear to me from everything you have said, particularly the part about the man following you around Scarborough, that you are indeed under a fixed delusion, an *idée fixe* as we medical men like to call it. This is the clearest case of monomania I have ever encountered in my time as a doctor."

"No, Dr Collins," I protested. "Please, you have to understand me. I am not delusional. I am telling you the truth."

"Ah, yes," said Dr Collins. "In your own mind of

course you are telling me the truth. The truth as *you* see it. However, you cannot possibly expect me to believe that Sir Henry sent a man to spy on you. The idea is preposterous."

"I agree it is preposterous, but that doesn't stop it from being true." I was starting to tremble and grow hot. If Dr Collins would not believe me then my case was hopeless. Maybe it would have been better for me if I had stopped trying to persuade him, but I was fighting for my right to freedom, for my life, and I couldn't stop.

But having convinced himself of this diagnosis, it was impossible for me to persuade him otherwise. To him, my very denials of insanity were proof enough of the delusion that had supposedly taken possession of my mind. To my claim that Henry had brought me here as a punishment, Dr Collins was adamant that Henry had brought me to the asylum solely for my own good and anything that I might say to the contrary only served to incriminate me further. It seemed to me that if anyone here was suffering from a fixed delusion it was the doctor and not I.

"You cannot make me stay here," I said. "It is against the laws of human decency."

Dr Collins gave me a pitying smile as if I were a small child. "But your husband-to-be has signed the papers. Do you not think he knows what is best for you?"

"He is no longer my husband-to-be. I refuse to marry him."

Dr Collins shook his head. "Come, come, my dear. Mr Blackwood explained to me that you and he have a longstanding agreement that you will marry him when you reach the age of twenty-one and come into your inheritance. I have no reason to doubt the word of a man of his standing, a member of the Carlton Club no less. I consider it admirable in him that he chooses to stand by you given your current unfortunate circumstances."

"But Doctor," I protested, "can you not see that Henry only wants to marry me for my money? He will keep me here until my twenty-first birthday to ensure I do not marry someone else in the meantime."

"Miss Hawthorne, you must understand that when it comes to financial matters men, possessing a greater intellectual capacity than women, have a far better understanding of such things and that a large fortune, in the hands of a woman, is liable to be frittered away on mere fancies: ribbons and knick-knacks and such like."

"And are you telling me that men do not waste money, with their gambling and their drinking and…and… their *whores?*"

Dr Collins looked shocked that I had dared to mention the oldest profession in the world. But I am no fool and I know what Henry gets up to when he frequents the theatres around the Haymarket and Covent Garden.

"Miss Hawthorne," said Dr Collins, "you are becoming hysterical and if you do not curb these immoral thoughts then I will be forced to conclude that you are suffering from moral insanity as well as monomania."

It is hopeless to reason with Dr Collins. He has an answer for everything I might say to him. The fact of the matter is that he believes Henry because Henry is a man and no doubt Henry has paid him handsomely to keep me here.

I asked Dr Collins if I might be given paper and pen with which to record my thoughts as I have always been used to keeping a journal and I thought, although I did not tell him this, that it would help me to retain my sanity, of which I was still in full possession. Dr Collins refused my request on the grounds that patients are not permitted sharp objects like pens in case they harm themselves or others.

After each session Nurse Cooper escorts me back to the ward. I might as well be a convict being returned to her cell.

If only Mary knew where I was. But she probably has no idea and may even have returned to London without me. If that is true then I fear I really will go mad in this place.

~~~

Two days after the cremation, Rose, her mother, her grandmother's brother David, and a small group of her grandmother's closest friends gathered in the cemetery for the burial of the ashes. Rose had thought that they might scatter her grandmother's ashes out at sea, or something equally liberating, but Andrea was of the opinion that a dignified burial in the family plot was far more appropriate. So for the second time, they donned their new black dresses, Andrea teaming hers with a black and gold scarf this time, and stood in solemn silence as the undertakers performed the short ceremony.

Rose couldn't look at the small casket and imagine her grandmother's ashes inside. A coffin would have been a different matter, but this tiny box seemed totally inadequate to contain the remains of a human life, all its hopes and dreams and achievements.

The casket was laid to rest beside the remains of her husband, Rose's grandfather, Donald Shawcross. Rose had no recollection of him because he had died in 1999, a year before she was born. Rose placed a pot of bright pink geraniums on the spot in the ground that now held all that was left of her grandmother. Andrea had arranged for a local stone carver to re-do the headstone so that under the name *Donald Shawcross 1936-1999* was added *Janice Shawcross née Drinkwater 1938-2016 May They Be Together Forever.*

Whilst Andrea was saying good-bye to her grandmother's friends and thanking them for coming, Rose found herself once more with her great-uncle, David. Today he was wearing a cream linen suit teamed with a dark blue shirt and his relaxed manner put Rose at her ease.

"There are lots of our family buried here," he said in a
~~~

voice that was half wistful, half amused.

"Like who?" asked Rose. She had never really considered who had existed before her grandmother, but now that she was reading Mary's letters she found her curiosity aroused.

"Just about everyone," said David. "Let's see who we can find." They started to wander around the headstones, peering to read the inscriptions, some of which had become almost illegible with age. "Yes, look," said David, pausing in front of a headstone carved with a ship's anchor. "Here are my grandparents and your great-great-grandparents, Walter and Mary Fairbright."

"He died in 1914," said Rose, looking at the inscription on the moss-strewn stone. "At the age of thirty-nine. I guess he was killed in the First World War?"

"German warships bombarded Scarborough in December 1914," said David. "He was killed then."

"How terrible," said Rose, thinking of poor Mary. According to the inscription, Mary Fairbright née Brewer had survived Walter by forty-six years, dying in 1960 at the age of eighty-one. It was hard to imagine her living well into the Twentieth Century, Rose was so used to thinking of her as a Victorian. She was born before aeroplanes had been invented and had survived two world wars. Astonishing really, when you thought about it.

David had already moved off in search of other family members. Rose caught up with him, thinking it was like a slightly morbid version of hide-and-seek.

"Here's my mother and your great-grandmother," said David, standing in front of a more modern-looking marble headstone. "Her name was Lilian and she was Mary and Walter's daughter." Lilian Drinkwater née Fairbright was born in 1904 and had died in 1986, *a devoted wife and mother*. Her husband William, lying beside her, had died in 1945, at the age of forty. The men in this family didn't have much luck it seemed, dying at such young ages.

"Did Mary and Walter have any other children?" asked

Rose.

"Lilian had an older brother," said David. "His name was Frank. But he was killed in the First World War."

Another young casualty then.

"He's buried somewhere in France."

"You're the only man in this family to survive into old age," said Rose, and then immediately worried that she'd been tactless, but David chuckled.

"I do my best to keep going," he said as they walked back towards Andrea.

An unbroken chain, thought Rose, *from Mary to Lilian to Janice and then to my mother and me.* Rose already had a good idea what Mary had been like from reading her letters, and she was grateful that she had known her own grandmother well, but what about Lilian who came in between? What was she like? Rose wondered if there was any way she could find out.

"It's time we were heading back," said Andrea. She turned to David. "Would you like to join us for tea?"

"Thank you, most kindly," he said. "But I have to be getting back to York."

Rose was sorry to see him go again, this strange man who was so relaxed in some ways and yet formal in others. They walked to the exit where David took his leave of them.

"I've been thinking," said Andrea as they walked back to the car. "I'm going to have to stay on a while and put Mum's affairs in order, sort out her will, that kind of thing. I also need to put the house on the market. I'm afraid it's not going to be very interesting for you, so if you want to go back to London I'd understand. You must be missing your friends up here. It can't have been much of a fun holiday for you. I could get you a train ticket if you'd like."

Rose couldn't believe her mother was suggesting she go back to London on her own, that she would actually let her live there unsupervised. At the start of the summer Rose would have jumped at the chance, but now things were different. It was over between her and Joe, but there was still unfinished business with her and Dan. She'd barely got to know him and although they'd have to say good-bye eventually, she wasn't ready for it just yet. At the very least she wanted to make sure he was all right. And ever since meeting Zoe she'd been thinking about her living in that abandoned asylum and wondering if there was anything she could do to help.

"Thanks for the offer," said Rose. "But I'd rather stay here at the moment."

"Well, if you're sure."

"Positive," said Rose. "I'll give you a hand clearing out Gran's house."

"Oh, would you?" said Andrea, tears welling up in her eyes. "That would be fantastic." She patted Rose's hand. "Shall we pick up some fish and chips on the way back?"

~~~

On the way to see Dr Collins today, Nurse Cooper informed me that he wished to try a new treatment on me. When I asked what she meant she replied curtly, "Nowt for you to worry 'bout," which only made me worry even more.

Instead of taking me to his office, Nurse Cooper took me to another room on the ground floor of the building. The room was tiled, like a bathroom, but there were no sinks or baths. Dr Collins was standing with his back to us in front of a large rectangular wooden cabinet with glass sides. The cabinet was on legs and stood about shoulder-height. It resembled a museum display-case of the sort used to showcase porcelain or a collection of fossils. But it contained neither of those things. Inside the cabinet was a large metal wheel in an upright position, like something from a factory machine. On the side of the cabinet was an iron handle for turning, like one I had seen on a barrel organ at the fair. Protruding from the front of the cabinet
~~~

were two rods with metal balls on them. I had never before seen such a bizarre piece of furniture and had no idea what its use could possibly be. Standing beside the cabinet, by the turning handle, was a man I recognised from the dining room. He was a strong-armed man and his job at mealtimes was to restrain some of the more violent male patients. His presence concerned me. Was he there to restrain me? Why would that be necessary?

Nurse Cooper leaned close and whispered in a voice too low for the doctor to hear, "This'll make yer 'air stand on end!" I looked at her in alarm but she only pushed me forwards and said in her normal voice, "The patient's 'ere for you now, Sir."

Dr Collins turned around and beamed at me. "Miss Hawthorne, please do come in. Today I am going to try something that will revolutionise the care of patients in this hospital." I looked at the machine with trepidation. "Oh, do not be alarmed," said Dr Collins. "You will come to no harm. Trust me." He nodded at the male member of staff and the man brought forward a chair on wheels to which were attached thick leather straps. I had seen other patients wheeled around in such a contraption but they were the ones who could not be trusted to walk anywhere without lashing out or trying to make a bid for freedom.

I think I would have fled there and then but Nurse Cooper was standing in the doorway, her arms crossed over her bosom, her mouth pulled into a tight, thin line.

"Please be seated," said Dr Collins, indicating the chair.

When I hesitated to sit down, Nurse Cooper came forward, muttering under her breath. "Can't you do nowt for yerself?" She pushed me into the chair and before I could do anything, she and the strong man fastened the leather straps around my wrists, binding me to the chair. They pulled the straps tight so that when I tried to free my arms the edge of the leather cut into my skin. Then they did the same to my ankles, strapping them tightly to the base of the chair.

"What are you doing?" I cried at them. "I don't deserve this! I have never been violent."

"It is purely a precautionary measure for your own safety," said Dr Collins. "It is not a punishment." I narrowed my eyes at him.

The man returned to his position at the side of the cabinet, by the handle, and Nurse Cooper stepped back, looking as if she were about to enjoy an entertainment at the fairground. Dr Collins went to a small table beside the cabinet and picked up two long, thin metal rods with rounded ends which were attached to the cabinet by a system of wires. My palms became sweaty and my throat felt dry.

"Please begin," said Dr Collins to the man. The man began to crank the handle on the side of the cabinet, slowly at first but quickly gaining in momentum. As he turned the handle, the wheel inside the cabinet started to rotate and then, to my horror, what I can only describe as bolts of lightning flew between the metal spheres that protruded from the front of the cabinet. There was something mesmerising but also utterly terrifying at the streaks of blue light that sparked and crackled before my eyes. Dr Collins approached me then, holding the two long rods, one in each hand. I struggled in vain against the leather straps that were binding me to the chair. I tried to turn my head away from him but the rigid back of the chair gave me no space to manoeuvre.

Dr Collins stood right in front of me now. I could smell his hair oil and the scent of snuff on his fingers. I tried to look him in the eye, to plead for mercy, but his eyes were focused on the top of my head and he seemed to me like a man possessed. He brought the rods either side of my head. I heard a crackling sound close to my ears and felt my hair rising off my head.

And then, I don't know what happened. It was as if lightning was pulsating through my body. A force shook me so violently that I thought I would die. My body went rigid as if struck by rigor mortis. It was no longer under my own control but felt as if it were the plaything of some cruel god who wished to torture me. I screamed but I do not know if any sound came out, so loud was the buzzing in my head, as if a thousand angry wasps had entered my brain.

Then the buzzing stopped and the silence was deafening. I slumped in the chair and my head flopped forward onto my chest. I was breathing heavily, gasping for air. I heard Dr Collins say, "Ten seconds today. We'll try a longer session tomorrow." I was too stunned to reply.

Nurse Cooper undid the straps and heaved me to my feet. As she led me back to the dormitory she said, "Ooh, you should've seen yer face. Looked like you was gonna explode!"

~~~

By the time Rose climbed into bed that evening she felt physically exhausted. She'd spent the afternoon helping her mother clean and tidy the house ready for the first estate agent who was due to call round in the morning. Andrea had been checking house prices on the Internet and knew what would be a reasonable asking price for a property in the heart of Scarborough's old town, even if it was in need of a bit of modernisation. It would be weird having people looking around her grandmother's house, especially since Rose had started to think of it as home. Despite the physical tiredness, she wasn't quite ready to go to sleep just yet so she reached for the pile of Mary's letters on her bedside table and found the next one.

Fisherman's Cottage,
Scarborough,
2pm, 31st August, 1899

Dear Ma,
~~~

News at last! I was down by the harbour waiting for Walter's boat to come in when a woman approached me. I suspected from her fancy clothes that she was an actress or something from the theatre and at first I was suspicious of her. But she said she'd been looking for me and was I Miss Alice Hawthorne's maid?

When I said I was, she introduced herself as Kitty Simpson, star of the Scarborough music hall, and asked if she could speak to me, in private. Well, as there was no sign of Walter's boat coming in, I agreed to walk with her along the prom and she told me the most incredible story. She'd been sitting in St Mary's church on the very day that Alice and I had swapped places, and she'd actually seen Alice but Alice hadn't seen her. Then she said a man had arrived and I expected her to describe Jackson, but from her detailed description of a ruddy complexion, gingery hair and sideburns, I knew at once it was Henry Blackwood. She saw him drag Alice from the church by force! Those were her very words.

That horrible man! If I ever get my hands on him, I'll kill him myself. Anyway, I asked Kitty if she knew where he'd taken Alice and she said she overheard him mutter something about "Highcliff" but she didn't know any more than that.

I hurried back to the cottage and asked Ellie if she knew where Highcliff was and she turned pale and said, yes, it was the lunatic asylum just outside of town. Can you believe it? That scoundrel has locked dear Alice up in the madhouse! Tomorrow I will go there and see if I can find her. Wish me luck!

Love to all,
Mary.

~~~

Fisherman's Cottage,
Scarborough,
5pm, 1st September, 1899

Dear Ma,
~~~

Oh, what a dreadful place. I went to the asylum and I asked to speak to the doctor in charge. It's a huge building, all fancy turrets and whatnot but with bars on the windows! Inside it felt more like a prison than a hospital. Nurse Cooper, who had a mighty high opinion of herself, said the doctor was too busy to see me and would I care to come back tomorrow. I said I would not care to come back tomorrow since I was here now and said I would wait for him. I swear she was wondering whether to lock me up or throw me out, but I stood my ground and in the end she stomped off to find Dr Collins. When he eventually turned up I told him I was a friend of Miss Alice Hawthorne (well, I thought that would sound better than just saying I was her maid) and asked if I could see her. At first he was reluctant to let me near her but then I took a risk and told him that Mr Blackwood had sent me to check on her and that put the wind up him. The good doctor (if that is what he is) is scared of Henry Blackwood, that much was clear.

He asked Nurse Cooper to take me to Alice. She was quite huffy about it, complaining all the way there that it wasn't her job to show visitors around, but I ignored her. I know her sort, all they want is attention and it's best not to give them any. She took me to a large room that smelled of cabbage. Men and women were seated around the edge of the room, all of them sunk in the gloom of boredom. One woman was hammering the keys on a piano and another kept shouting at her to shut up.

Alice was sitting in a corner of the room, on her own, reading a book. Dear me, I hardly recognised her. Her hair was unbrushed and she had on the most dreadful blue gown, the same as all the women were wearing. She's a shadow of her former self, like one of Dr Pepper's Ghosts I thought when I looked at her all thin and pale like she's not properly there. Nurse Cooper shouted at her that she had a visitor and to put the book down. At first she was so surprised that I don't think she knew me. But then recognition dawned in her beautiful face and her eyes lit up and I knew that the old Alice was still in there. Thankfully Nurse Cooper went over to the piano to sort out a row that had broken out between the incompetent pianist and the shouting patient. I took the opportunity to lean close to Alice and whisper to her that now I knew where she was, I would find a way to get her out of there. I know she understood me. Then Nurse Cooper returned and told me it was time to leave.

I will talk the problem over with my new friends, Ellie and Walter, and, of course, Mr Hartright, and we will find a way to rescue her.

Love to all,

Mary.

CHAPTER TWELVE

"Have you considered renting this out as a holiday cottage?"

"Are you saying it won't sell?" Andrea bristled at the suggestion, causing the agent to falter. Rose watched the exchange not without some amusement. The agent, the first of three that Andrea had booked to value the house in Tollergate, was a gangly young man who looked flustered in his shirt, tie and shiny suit. He was obviously the most junior member of *Hardings & Shipman*, a fact which spoke volumes about how keen they were to get a poky Victorian mid-terrace house on their books.

"Well, no, I wouldn't say that," blustered the agent who had introduced himself as Paul and offered them both a sweaty palm to shake. "But it's a slightly tricky market right now."

"If you could just evaluate the property and give us a price," said Andrea, "that would be helpful."

"Sorry, yes, of course."

Rose stepped out of the way as Paul crossed to the other side of the tiny sitting room. With an electronic gadget he measured the distance from one side of the room to the other and tapped the results into his iPad. He measured the whole of the ground floor and then moved over to the stairs, banging his head on the low ceiling as he started to climb. Ten minutes later Andrea was showing Paul out the door, a look of relief on her face that he'd gone.

"It's a shame we have to sell this house," said Rose. "It reminds me of Gran."

"I know what you mean," said her mother. "But we can't look after it when we're down in London."

"What about his idea of renting it out as a holiday cottage?" Now Rose thought about it, it didn't seem like such a bad idea. For one thing, it meant they'd be able to come back whenever they felt like it. She could continue to see Dan.

Andrea sighed. "I don't know. It's all too much to think about right now." She made her way to the stairs. "I've been clearing out Gran's linen cupboards. Could you take some stuff to the charity shop for me?"

"Sure," said Rose. "Where is it?"

"Hang on. I'll get it for you."

Andrea came back downstairs with a pile of neatly ironed sheets and a soft blue blanket. Her grandmother had never taken to duvets, preferring to make beds up the old-fashioned way. She told Rose once that working as a chamber maid in the Grand Hotel she'd learnt to make beds quickly and easily. It wasn't hard once you got the hang of it.

"Can you manage all that?" asked Andrea. "I'll get a bag for you."

Rose walked up the hill to the charity shop, holding the bag in her arms and inhaling the scent of lavender. Her grandmother always put bars of lavender soap into drawers and cupboards to keep clothes and bedding smelling fresh. The charity shop was sandwiched between a Chinese takeaway and an ironmongers. She handed over the pile of sheets to a nice old lady who thanked her for her kind donation, but she kept the blanket in the bag. On the way to the shop she had decided to take the blanket to Zoe at the asylum. She didn't see the point in giving everything to the charity shop when there was someone who could benefit directly from a gift. It was the sort of thing her grandmother would have done.

When she reached the asylum, Rose peered through the fence. Lucky was digging in a patch of ground a little way off from the house. His front paws were working furiously, throwing lumps of black earth into the air whilst his tail wagged from side-to-side. *Someone is having fun,* thought Rose. This time she was actually pleased to see the dog because it meant Zoe must be around. She let herself into the grounds of the asylum through the gap in the fence.

"Hi Zoe!" she called. "It's only me, Rose." She hoped Zoe would hear her and come out. She didn't want to have to go back inside the building. It gave her the creeps.

At the sound of her voice Lucky came bounding over, wagging his tail.

"Hi Lucky," she patted him on the head. "Where's Zoe?" The dog cocked his head as if he understood, which of course he couldn't possibly, and started trotting towards the house. When Rose didn't follow him he turned round, barked once and continued towards the building. Did the dog want her to follow him?

Lucky trotted round to the back of the house, past the window she and Dan had climbed through and on to a small door. *If we'd known about this door we needn't have climbed in through the window.* The door stood ajar, just enough for the dog to slide its agile body through. Rose opened the door wider and followed.

Lucky was already halfway down a long, dark corridor and Rose hurried to catch up as her eyes adjusted to the gloom. She didn't want to lose sight of him. It was comforting to have company in a place like this, even if it was the four-legged kind.

They were in a part of the building that she and Dan

hadn't explored. They passed a room that looked like an industrial kitchen and another that must have been used for laundry because it had racks hanging from the ceiling.

They turned a corner and came to the back of the main staircase. Now Rose recognised where she was: the long corridor with the vaulted ceiling where it was all too easy to imagine the ghosts of patients and nurses roaming at night. She didn't know how Zoe could stand to live here, all by herself. Rose followed the dog up the stairs, two at a time, calling Zoe's name as she went. Noise helped to dispel the eerie quiet of the place.

Zoe met her at the top of the stairs. "Hello," she said, bemused. "I wasn't expecting you to come back."

"I brought you this." Rose held the blanket out to her. "I thought you might like it."

Zoe hesitated and Rose realised that Zoe might think she'd bought it, the blanket was in such good condition. "It was my grandmother's," she explained. "Mum asked me to take it to the charity shop but I thought you could use it instead. I can still take it to the charity shop if you don't want it, I don't mind either way."

"Thank you." Zoe smiled and took the blanket, holding it up to her face. "It smells nice. Do you want to come in?"

Rose followed Zoe to the room she and Dan had seen on their first visit, the one with the mattress and gas stove. Lucky curled up at the foot of Zoe's makeshift bed, chewing a mangy old rubber toy. *I should have brought some dog biscuits,* thought Rose.

"Look what Rose has brought us." Zoe bent down and showed Lucky the blanket. "Now we'll be nice and warm."

Rose walked over to one of the box-sash windows which was pushed up to let some air in. The room was at the front of the house and had a good view of the grounds and the lane. She could also see the hole, near an overgrown rose bush, where Lucky had been digging.

"What are you going to do when the winter comes?"

asked Rose.

Zoe shrugged. "Dunno. Hopefully Mum'll be sorted by then and we can find a place together."

Rose almost blurted out that her grandmother's house was going up for sale and would make a really nice home for two people, but then bit her tongue. Tollergate might be cheap compared to London prices, but it was unlikely that Zoe and her mother would be able to afford the asking price, whatever that turned out to be. When Zoe talked about *finding a place* she probably meant a council flat.

Lucky jumped to his feet, ears pricked, head cocked to one side. A low growl emanated from the back of his throat.

"He's heard something," said Zoe. She tossed the blanket onto the mattress and pressed herself against the wall so she could look out of the window without being seen. "Get back from the glass."

As Rose darted away from the window she glimpsed a black Jaguar car bumping down the lane, throwing up a cloud of dust behind it.

"Damn!" said Zoe. "We've got visitors."

"Do you know who it is?"

Zoe shook her head.

Rose took up a position similar to Zoe's at the adjacent window so she could watch what was happening. The car disappeared around the side of the house and then reappeared at the front. It must have driven through the gap in the fence. It came to a halt in front of the house, parking at an angle, and Rose saw the number plate: MAX1. The hairs on her arms stood on end. Then the driver's door and the passenger door opened and two men climbed out. *Shit!* It was the men she and Dan had followed at the fair, the thin one with the spider tattoo on his neck and the short, stocky one built like a bulldog. *The men with the guns. The men who had shot the mad dog.* She'd hoped never to see them again. What the hell were they doing here?

The men walked round to the back of the car, opened the boot and pulled out two large boxes.

"Where does this stuff go?" asked the short one. His Geordie accent carried loud and clear in the still air.

"In the basement," said the guy with the tattoo.

The men disappeared from view as they walked round to the side of the house. *They must be going in the door I just used,* thought Rose.

Zoe knelt down and put her arms around the dog who was looking anxiously towards the door as if awaiting his instructions to chase after the men. "We have to be very, very quiet," she whispered. The dog lay down, putting his head on his front paws, his ears twitching incessantly.

A few minutes later the men reappeared, this time without the boxes. For an agonising five minutes they leaned against the side of the car, smoking cigarettes and gazing up at the house. From her position at the side of the window Rose felt sure they were looking straight at her. She didn't dare move. But then they tossed their cigarette stubs onto the ground, stamped on them, climbed into the vehicle and drove away with a screech of tyres.

"They've gone." Rose let out a long breath. She'd been holding herself so tense that her stomach muscles hurt. "Have they been here before?"

Zoe shook her head. "Not as far as I know, but I'm not here all the time. If they make a regular habit of turning up I'm going to have to find somewhere else to live."

"What do you think is in the boxes?" asked Rose.

Zoe stood up with a grin on her face. "There's only one way to find out."

~~~

George Hartright sat at his desk, sketchbook in front of him, a pencil hanging uselessly between his thumb and forefinger. Ever since Alice's disappearance, he had been
~~~

unable to draw even the simplest of sketches. He turned the pages of the book, looking at the likenesses he'd drawn of her, as Titania, as Ophelia. As Portia.

He was back at the boarding house, having returned there after they had reported Alice missing to the police. His landlady had gladly taken him back in and had done her best to soothe his rattled nerves with large helpings of hot stew and steaming cups of tea. None of it did any good.

There was a knock at the door. He recognised his landlady's delicate *rat-a-tat-tat.*

"Yes?"

She opened the door and stood on the threshold, a letter in her hand. "Sorry to disturb you Mr Hartright, but a boy just delivered this. He didn't say who it was from."

George took the letter from her. The paper was thick and of high quality. His pulse quickened at the thought that it might have something to do with Alice. "Thank you," he said, retreating into the privacy of his room.

"Would you like me to fetch you anything?" she asked hopefully.

"No, thank you." She liked looking after him, enjoyed bringing him things to eat from the pantry, and he was sorry to disappoint her but he wanted her to leave so he could read the letter in peace.

The landlady gave him a worried look, then backed out of the room, closing the door behind her. He listened to her footsteps on the creaky stairs and waited until he heard the parlour door close shut.

Although he had been so eager to read the letter whilst she was standing there, now that he was alone he hesitated. What if the letter contained bad news? Was it better not to know? He stood by the window, gazing out over the rooftops at the masts of the boats docked in the harbour. All these years he had been coming to Scarborough to paint the coastline and never before had he met anyone like Alice. She had brought light and life into his world.

She understood what he was trying to achieve with his painting and she had a thirst for knowledge that he had never witnessed in a woman before. On their walk around the ruins of Whitby Abbey she had confided in him about her engagement to Sir Henry Blackwood, saying it had all been planned for her when she was too young to know any better, but as she had grown up she had seen what sort of a man Henry was and she dreaded being tied to him for the rest of her life. It was that confession that had prompted George to buy her the jet necklace.

George looked down at the unopened letter. It bore a coat of arms: a griffin, the mythical creature famous for guarding treasure. He tore open the envelope and pulled out the folded piece of paper inside. His hands trembled as he read.

The letter was from Sir Henry Blackwood. It did not take George long to digest its contents, and he knew in his heart of hearts he had anticipated something like this. Dreaded it. The letter was a formal challenge to a duel, tomorrow evening. Henry proposed a spot in the forest west of Scarborough, half a mile from Low Road and, as the offended party, Henry had decided they would fight with pistols. Henry was staying at the Grand Hotel and would wait to hear that George accepted the challenge, assuming, of course, that he was a man of honour.

The swine!

George flung the letter aside and started to pace the room. Now he had no doubt that Henry was responsible for Alice's disappearance. He should report him to the authorities immediately. He should tell Inspector Booth that Henry was staying at the Grand Hotel. He should…he stopped pacing. What good would it do to accuse a man like Henry Blackwood? Alice had told him that Henry had friends in high places. Men like that always managed to wriggle their way out of difficult situations. And besides, Henry was Alice's official fiancé. By the codes of decency and honour, George was in the wrong for having stolen another man's bride. He picked the letter up off the floor and dusted it down. If he wanted to win Alice fair and square then he would have to face Henry Blackwood. The fisherman, Walter, was a resourceful fellow. Maybe he could be persuaded to act as his second. George was not entirely familiar with the rules of duelling, never having found himself in this situation before, but he knew that both participants were required to bring along a supporter to ensure the fight was a fair one.

George tore a piece of paper from his sketch pad, picked up a pen and hastily wrote a response which he folded and sealed in an envelope. Then he pulled on his jacket and went out, determined to deliver his response to the Grand Hotel himself.

~~~

"I didn't mean…" Rose gave up. Saying she didn't want to go into the basement would just make her sound like a wimp and besides, Zoe was already halfway down the corridor, Lucky trotting at her heels. Rose followed, reluctant. When she'd said, "What do you think is in the boxes?" she'd just been thinking out loud. She hadn't actually intended that they go and look. She wasn't sure she wanted to know. Whatever those guys were storing in this deserted building, it had to mean trouble.

Zoe clearly already knew the way to the basement, navigating her way through the building as if she'd lived here all her life. Rose followed her back to the passageway by the former kitchens and laundry room. Zoe opened a door onto a descending stairway. Lucky poked his nose around the door, whined and sat down on his haunches. *He's scared,* thought Rose. *That's not a good sign.*

Zoe started to walk down the steps.

"Is it safe down there?" asked Rose.

"It's fine. There's enough light to see. There are some windows just above ground level."
~~~

Despite his earlier reluctance, Lucky started to follow his mistress down the steps. Not wanting to be left behind on her own, Rose went too, treading carefully on the worn stone steps.

It was cold and damp in the basement. The sun failed to penetrate the dirt-covered windows but, as Zoe had said, there was enough light to see by. Broken tables and chairs, old beds and mildewed mattresses were piled up around the edge of the room. Was this where Zoe had found the mattress she was sleeping on? On top of the mattresses was a tangle of leather straps and buckles. *Restraints for dealing with patients?* Rose turned away. This whole place gave her the creeps.

Pipes, thick with dust, ran around the walls at head height and up through holes in the ceiling. This must have been a state-of-the-art heating and hot water system when it was installed but now it looked ancient and defunct. In one corner was a huge, cylindrical metal tank covered in handles, levers and dials. It gave off a lingering smell of oil and Rose guessed it was the boiler. It was so old it looked like it had been salvaged from the Titanic.

Lucky ran around, sniffing in every corner and growling. "There are rats down here," said Zoe as if it was no big deal.

Super, thought Rose.

The boxes that the men had brought inside were standing on a dusty old table, along with about a dozen others. No attempt had been made to hide them. *They probably didn't expect anyone to come down here,* thought Rose. *Well, no sane person would.*

"Have you seen these before?" asked Rose.

"Nope," said Zoe. "But as I said, I'm not here every minute of the day."

Zoe tore at the tape sealing one of the boxes and lifted the flap. She reached inside and pulled out a clear plastic bag filled with white powder.

"Is that what I think it is?" asked Rose.

"Depends what you're thinking," said Zoe, tossing the bag back inside the box. "My guess is cocaine."

"No way!" Rose reached into her pocket for her mobile phone. "We have to call the police."

"What do you think you're doing?" Zoe suddenly turned on her, her eyes blazing. "Put that away." She pointed at Rose's phone.

"Why?" It was the old, prickly Zoe back again and Rose didn't like it.

Zoe looked at Rose as if she was stupid. "Because if you call the cops they'll start crawling all over this place and they'll find me and put me back into care. I'm not going back into a children's home. Ever!"

"But this is serious." Rose pointed at the boxes. "People die taking this stuff. It shouldn't be on the streets."

"It's not on the streets is it? It's here in this basement. Look, I'm sorry but this stuff isn't my problem." She kicked the nearest box. "Don't you think I've got enough problems of my own?"

Rose felt her resolve starting to wane. She didn't want to make life harder for Zoe than it already was. "But you can't stay here forever," she said in the end. "It's not safe."

Zoe shrugged. "It's safer here than it was at home."

"But you won't be safe now if those men keep coming back. Look, I didn't have time to tell you earlier, but I've seen those two before. They're criminals and they're armed. You don't want to get in their way."

Zoe stamped her foot and turned away from Rose. Having failed to catch any rats, Lucky trotted over and pressed his nose into Zoe's hand.

"I'm sorry," said Rose. "I didn't mean to upset you."

"Forget about it. But please don't call the police. Not just yet anyway. I need a bit of time to work out what I'm going to do."

"Sure," said Rose. "I understand. I should probably get going, before Mum sends out a search party. Look, why don't you come…" She didn't finish what she was going to say. They'd both heard it: the rumble of an engine and the crunch of tyres on the stony ground outside. Lucky let out a deep-throated growl. Zoe jumped onto one of the broken bedsteads and peered out of a grimy window. "They're back."

"We need to get out of here," said Rose.

"There isn't time."

"Is there another way out?"

"No, there's only one door to the basement."

The car doors slammed shut.

"They're coming this way," said Zoe. "And this time there are three of them. We have to hide." She grabbed hold of Rose's arm and Lucky's collar.

"Where?" Rose looked around frantically for a hiding place.

"Behind the boiler."

There was no chance to call the police now even if Rose had wanted to. As she squeezed into the filthy space between the boiler and the wall she just had time to tap out a hasty text to Dan. *@ asylum. Help.*

~~~

Henry was a crack shot with a pistol. He'd learnt to shoot as a child on his father's estate in the Cumbrian countryside, practising on pheasants who were too slow or stupid to move out of the way, baby rabbits who were too bewildered by the bright lights he shone in their eyes and young deer when they wandered too far away from the herd. Living in London he regretted the lack of opportunities to practise what he regarded as this gentlemanly skill. But the fact that Alice preferred another man to himself had wounded Henry's pride and there was only one way that Henry knew to restore his high sense of self-regard.

It hadn't been difficult for a man of Henry's stature to
~~~

discover the whereabouts of a lowly painter. Hotel porters, inn keepers and common people always kowtowed to his superior bearing and told him what he wanted to know. Henry had found a boy willing to deliver the letter for a ha'penny.

He was sitting now in the lounge of the Grand Hotel, sipping a whisky, when the Hotel porter brought him a letter on a silver platter. He allowed himself to finish his whisky before opening the envelope. It was as he had hoped. The painter had been fool enough to accept his challenge of a duel. Well, George Hartright was as good as dead. Henry ordered himself another whisky and settled back in his armchair, lighting his pipe.

~~~

Dan carried the bags to the car whilst his dad hobbled alongside on a pair of crutches. Fiona was waiting for them by her Volkswagen Golf which she had parked illegally in a disabled bay in front of the hospital. Mind you, thought Dan, if anyone needed the advantage of disabled parking right now it was his dad. Ryan was wearing a neck brace because of his whiplash injury and his right leg was in plaster from the ankle to the knee, having sustained a serious fracture to the tibia. He had spent the last couple of days learning how to manoeuvre himself around with the crutches, practising in the hospital corridor under the close supervision of the policeman on duty, as if he might suddenly throw the crutches away and make a run for it. Dan didn't think his dad would be running anywhere for a long time, if ever.

Dr Wilson had said that Ryan was well enough to go home, although he'd have to take it steady and not expect to be able to do too much. He was still suffering from severe concussion and would need lots of rest. As Ryan lowered himself awkwardly into the car his trouser leg rose up and Dan caught sight of the electronic tag around his
~~~

left ankle. Ryan might be free to leave the hospital but he was not a free man. Until his trial came to court Ryan would be under house arrest, not a prospect that Dan viewed with delight.

Dan put the crutches and the bags into the boot of the car and climbed into the back. As his mother reversed out of the parking space his phone beeped. A text. He had no idea who it might be from. He'd been incommunicado for so long he thought Rose would have given up on him by now. She'd probably gone back to London, to her real friends. Her boyfriend. He pulled his phone out of his pocket and tapped the messages icon.

Rose. So she was still in Scarborough and hadn't forgotten about him. His heart leapt with joy. He tapped the message.

@asylum. Help.

At first he didn't understand, had to re-read the message. And then he got it. *Shit!* She was at the asylum and she was in danger. But why had she gone to the asylum on her own? What on earth had happened to her? He couldn't think of any reason she might have for going back there. She hadn't exactly enjoyed their first visit and he didn't blame her. But she was there now and she was calling for his help. What if she'd gone there and encountered Max and his cronies?

Fiona pulled onto the main road heading back into town. It was five o'clock, the middle of rush hour and the traffic was crawling down the hill. The traffic was jammed up at the roundabout outside Peasholm Park. Dan bit his lip and thought about what to do. If he got out of the car now it would take him fifteen minutes to walk to the asylum, less if he ran. He was about to ask his mum to stop the car and let him out when Ryan spoke.

"You know, I really appreciate you both standing by me through all this."

"That's what families do," said Fiona. "We stick together. Isn't that right Dan?" She caught his eye in the rear view mirror and Dan grunted in agreement.

Dan sank back into his seat. He'd have to help his mum get his dad into the house. Also, if he disappeared now, his parents would want to know where he was going and he didn't want to say anything about the abandoned asylum. He'd have to sit tight for now and try and get away as soon as he could.

He texted back, *Be there soon,* but how soon was another matter.

~~~

It was filthy behind the boiler, the narrow space between the cylinder and the wall thick with years of accumulated cobwebs. The cloying smell of oil made it hard to breathe. Not that Rose dared to breathe too deeply in case the men heard her. She took short gulps of air through her mouth and tried not to think about the mess on the floor which was almost certainly rat droppings. Next to her, Zoe was like a statue. Lucky sat on their feet, his tail tickling Rose's bare legs. If the men were going to come into the basement, she just hoped they would leave quickly. She didn't know how long she could stand there without sneezing from the dust or getting cramp in her foot from Lucky's weight.

Rose had a very restricted view of the basement. She could see part of the staircase but nothing of the room itself. Zoe could probably see a little of the room but not the stairs. She squashed herself closer to Zoe, worried that she might be visible to anyone walking down the steps.

There were footsteps overhead; the rising intonation of a Geordie accent. Lucky pricked his ears and a growl started to rise from deep within his throat.

"Shhh, quiet boy." Zoe stroked the dog's head. Lucky fell silent.

The door was kicked open and Rose's breath caught in her throat, her heart thumping against her ribcage. The
~~~

blood sounded so loud in her ears she thought it must be audible across the whole basement. Zoe kept her hand on Lucky's head and fortunately the dog was quiet as a lamb.

Out of the corner of her eye Rose glimpsed three figures descending the steps. The first two were the guys who had dropped the boxes off earlier, the Geordies. The third was slower and heavier and the heels of his boots made a sharp clicking sound on the stone steps. Rose risked turning her head a fraction and recognised the man she and Dan had seen in the camper van at the fairground; the one with the name MAX tattooed on his knuckles.

The men walked over to the boxes. The boiler blocked Rose's view of them, but their voices sounded alarmingly close.

"Is this the last of the batch?" asked a deep voice. It wasn't a Geordie accent, so it had to be Max talking.

"Aye, boss, that's the lot," said one of the Geordies. Rose thought it was the tall one with the tattoo.

"Ryan's gone and screwed it all up for us, man." That had to be the other Geordie, the short fat one. "We'll need to get this shit out of here before he tells the police everything."

"I've got Ryan covered," drawled Max. "He knows he'll lose the amusement arcade if he says anything stupid."

Ryan? The amusement arcade? Are they talking about Dan's dad? Rose tried to think clearly, but fear was scrambling her brain. All she could think was that she'd sent Dan a text alerting him to the fact that she was here and asking for his help. If he turned up now things could go horribly wrong. If only those guys would hurry up and get out of here. She didn't know how much longer she could stand there. Her right foot had gone to sleep and the dust and oily smell was aggravating her throat, making her want to cough.

Something tickled the toes of her left foot and Rose had to suppress a scream which welled up from deep inside her. A rat was nibbling the leather at the edge of her sandals. *Get off me!* What if it bit her toe? What sort of diseases did rats carry? Not the plague these days, but what about rabies? Rose had no idea, but she had to get rid of the damn thing before she had a full-blown panic attack.

Lucky had stayed quiet until now, but the rat was obviously too much for him to tolerate. He sprang to his feet and spun around in the tight space, knocking Rose and Zoe off balance, and letting out a piercing sound somewhere between a bark and a yelp. The rat scuttled away into a corner.

"Who's there?" shouted Max.

Zoe put out a hand to try and restrain him but Lucky was too quick for her. The dog darted out from behind the boiler and started barking furiously at the three men. "Shit!" muttered Zoe under her breath. The guy with the tattoo lunged at the dog, grabbing hold of Lucky's collar. Lucky went wild, straining to pull himself free, his barks ringing out like machine gun fire.

The short man pulled out his gun and pointed it at the dog.

"NO!" Zoe ran forward, throwing herself between the man with the gun and Lucky. "Don't you dare shoot my dog!"

The man's face registered a moment of surprise and then broke into a grin. "All right, pet. How about I shoot you instead?"

"Stop it!" Rose stepped out from behind the boiler and went to stand next to Zoe.

"Bloody hell," said the man. "It's like the fookin' TARDIS. How many more are hiding behind there?" He cocked his head towards the boiler without taking his eyes off Rose, all the time pointing the gun at her and Zoe.

"There's no one else, I swear," said Rose. Her legs were shaking so much she thought she might collapse onto the ground. Lucky was still barking.

"Be quiet Lucky," said Zoe, and the barks dropped to an occasional yelp. The man holding Lucky let him go and he ran to Zoe's side.

"What we gonna do with them, boss?" asked the man with the gun.

Max came to stand in front of Rose and Zoe, regarding them with a smirk on his face. Rose didn't like the way he was looking them up and down, his eyes resting too long on her breasts. Then he turned and walked over to the pile of mildewed mattresses. He picked up one of the leather belts, wrapped the ends around his hands and pulled it tight as if to test its strength. Then he let one end go and whipped the strap through the air. It made a whistling sound and the metal buckle rang out on the stone floor. For one terrifying moment Rose thought he was going to flog them. Then he tossed the strap to the man with the tattoo and said, "Tie them up. Over there." He pointed at the pile of old bedsteads. "I'll decide what to do about them later."

The guy with the tattoo caught the strap with one hand and grabbed hold of Rose with the other.

"Let me go," she screamed. She tried to pull away from him but his grip on her arm was too tight. He pulled her sharply towards the nearest bedstead. Rose jerked her head around and saw the man with the gun grab hold of Zoe. Max was handing out leather straps like candy.

As soon as the fat guy had Zoe in his clutches, Lucky went berserk, barking and snarling like Cerberus on steroids. He leapt at the man holding his mistress, jaw open wide revealing all of his teeth. He tried to bite the man's throat, but the man hit him over the head with the barrel of the gun. For a moment the dog was stunned and slunk away. Then he crouched low on his haunches and sprang at Max, biting him on the thigh. Max swung one of the leather straps at Lucky's side, whipping him hard. The dog yelped in pain, an ear-splitting cry that bounced off the stone walls. The man holding Zoe pointed his gun at the dog, his finger on the trigger.

"Go, Lucky!" shouted Zoe.

No, please don't go, thought Rose. As far as she could see the dog was the only weapon they had. Lucky cocked his head to one side and looked at his mistress for a moment, clearly reluctant to do as he was told. *But they shot the dog at the fair,* said a more reasonable voice in her head. *They can't shoot Lucky!*

"Go!" repeated Zoe in a louder voice. "Out!" This time the dog obeyed her, turned tail and bounded up the steps, the sound of his paws clattering down the corridor.

Lucky was safe! But it seemed to Rose that their last hope had disappeared with that dog. She cried out in pain as the man holding her wrenched her arms behind her back. Her mobile phone fell from her hand and the man kicked it across the floor to Max who casually picked it up and put it in his pocket.

"Give me that back," shouted Rose.

"Oh, I don't think you'll be needing it for the moment," said Max. "It's difficult to use a phone when your arms are tied behind you." He laughed a cold, cruel laugh and Rose felt such hatred for this man that she wanted to blow his brains out.

The man holding her pushed her onto the ground and used the leather strap to fasten her wrists to the leg of one of the beds. The other man tied Zoe up next to her.

Then the three of them left without another word.

~~~

George climbed into the carriage beside Walter and they set off at a steady trot. It had been a sultry day and now clouds had gathered, blotting out the last of the evening sun. George had spent the day trying to remember everything he'd ever learnt about firing a pistol, which wasn't much. He should have practised, he knew, but he didn't know anyone in this town who owned a pistol and Walter had urged him to keep the duel a secret from Mary. At the time, George had acknowledged this to be good
~~~

advice. From what he'd seen of Mary he knew her to be quite a forceful character who would try to dissuade him from the undertaking. But with every moment that took him closer to his destination, he wondered if telling Mary would have been the right thing to do, after all. She might have come up with a better plan.

"Just remember," said Walter once they were out on the open road, "keep a steady hand. Imagine you're painting a tiny detail on a picture."

"He'll kill me," said George. "The man's bound to be a good shot, otherwise he wouldn't have suggested this."

"Then you need to kill him first," said Walter, matter-of-factly.

George nodded glumly. Walter was doing his best to be supportive, but George felt that nothing short of a miracle could save him now. But he couldn't back out. To do so would brand him a coward and he couldn't live with that. He tried to focus on thoughts of Alice, tried to picture her fair face, her smile, her dark eyes. According to Mary she was alive and well, albeit locked up in the asylum. But they were going to get her out, Mary had convinced him of that. But freeing her from the asylum wouldn't be enough, George could see that. He had to deal with Henry man to man. It was essential that he didn't miss.

They turned off the main road and followed a track towards the forest.

"Is this it?" asked George, surprised that they had reached the wood so quickly.

"This is the place," said Walter in a tight, grim voice. The cart trundled over the rough ground and followed the path in amongst the trees. After a short distance they emerged into a clearing. Walter pulled on the reins and the cart came to an abrupt halt. On the far side of the clearing was a black carriage bearing the same coat of arms, the griffin, that George had seen on Henry's letter. Standing beside the carriage, smoking a pipe, was a man with gingery whiskers and a paunch. He turned at the sound of the approaching cart and smirked at them. George would have liked to wipe the smile off his face with a punch, but standing beside Henry was a brutish-looking fellow in black who looked like he was used to a few rounds in the boxing ring. George didn't rate his chances.

"Are you sure you want to go ahead with this?" asked Walter.

Could he back out now? Could he live with himself if he did? It was tempting to tell Walter to just turn the cart around and make a hasty retreat. He was a painter, for goodness' sake, not a soldier. But then Henry laughed and the sound carried across the clearing, harsh and mocking. If he ran away now, he'd hear that laugh for the rest of his life. "Yes, I'm sure," he told Walter.

They climbed down from the cart and stood, waiting. Then Henry's second started to walk towards them and Walter walked out to meet him. George watched as they greeted each other coldly. They conferred for a moment, then walked further into the clearing and marked, with sticks, the two spots from which Henry and George would fire their weapons.

George felt as though he were in a dream, or a nightmare to be more precise. He wished he could just wake up and find himself tucked up in bed. Surely this couldn't be happening to him?

Walter returned and led him towards the centre of the clearing where Henry and his man were waiting for him. Walter checked Henry's pockets to make sure he was not concealing another weapon and Henry's man did the same to George. The formalities dispensed with, both men took their positions by the sticks. Walter handed him a pistol. It felt heavy in his hand. He was never going to be able to fire it. The rule was that each pistol was to be loaded with one bullet. If they missed each other, that was too bad.

"You gents ready?" Henry's second looked approvingly at his master and then disdainfully at George. It was clear that in his eyes George was already as good as dead.

"Yes," said Henry, loud and clear, full of confidence.

"Ye-es," said George. He felt his head nod, although he was not conscious of choosing to make the movement. It was as if everything were happening to someone else.

"Take aim."

Henry lifted his right arm. George did the same.

"Fire!"

George had never killed a man in his life. But he wasn't himself anymore. He had become a stranger, an automaton. He was playing a game of chance and his fate was in the lap of the gods. He took a deep breath, curled his finger around the trigger and pulled. He was jerked backwards by the force of the shot. A cloud of smoke obscured his vision. And then a searing pain shot through his left arm. The pistol fell from his hand and he dropped to his knees, aware of nothing but a sensation of agony. He clutched his left arm with his right hand and his palm came away bright red.

~~~

It took forever to reach Oliver's Mount. Even when they were through the town centre and free of the traffic, Fiona drove at not a fraction over the speed limit as if she was on some sort of mission to prove to her husband that it was better to drive slowly and get from A to B in one piece than to drive like a madman and end up in hospital. Dan was silently willing her to put her foot down and groaned inwardly as she braked for yet another set of traffic lights that was only just changing from green to amber. But then he reminded himself that they wouldn't be in this predicament if it wasn't for his dad's reckless driving. He'd just have to sit tight. He checked his watch for the umpteenth time. It was half an hour since Rose had sent the text and he couldn't for the life of him think what sort of trouble she might be in. Why had she texted *Help!?* He wished he hadn't told her he'd be there soon. She'd
~~~

think he hadn't meant it; that he'd let her down.

Eventually, Fiona turned into the driveway and pulled up in front of the house. Dan jumped out of the car, retrieved his dad's crutches from the boot and yanked open his dad's door. Fiona was still sitting in the car, rummaging in her handbag for something. She pulled out her mobile phone and started checking it for messages.

For God's sake, hurry up, thought Dan. *Can't you do that later?*

Ryan slowly manoeuvred his legs out of the car, holding onto the open car door to pull himself into an upright position. It was painful to watch and Dan stared at the ground, not able to bear the look of helplessness on his father's face.

"All right there Dad?" Dan held out the crutches and helped his father slot his arms into position.

"Cheers, son," said Ryan. "Bit of a wreck aren't I?" He grinned and just for a moment Dan caught a glimpse of his dad's old self, the devil-may-care Ryan who liked to work hard and play hard, who would always drive too fast and take risks, but who was still his father, and Dan felt a surge of love for his dad that was so strong he had to turn away because his eyes were welling up.

At last Fiona came round to join them and they helped Ryan inside. Fiona had converted the lounge sofa into a bed so that Ryan wouldn't have to climb the stairs. Dan sat his dad down in the nearest armchair, made sure the TV remote control was within easy reach and gave him a footstool for his broken leg, all the time aware of just how on edge he felt. He had to get going. Rose hadn't texted back which wasn't a good sign. He poked his head in the kitchen where his mum was putting the kettle on. "Just off out. Got some stuff to do."

"But aren't you going to stay and…"

"Sorry. Something's come up."

Before his mum could ask him where he was going he was out the front door. He jumped on his bike and pedalled as fast as he could back down the hill.

~~~

Rose struggled against the bonds, twisting her wrists from side-to-side, but the strap was buckled too tightly and the edge of the leather cut into her skin. There was also a sharp pain in her shoulder from when the man had jerked her arms behind her back.

"This is hopeless." She sank her head onto her knees. "The straps are too tight."

"Same here," said Zoe.

Their only hope now was Dan. But where was he? It was at least half an hour since Rose had sent the text and he'd said he'd be there soon. It depended where he was coming from of course. He might be working at the amusement arcade or visiting his dad in the hospital. She should have texted her mum, but then her mum had no idea what or where the asylum was so that wouldn't have helped much.

They sat there in silence for a while, then Zoe said, "What do you fear most in the world?"

Rose gave a strangled laugh. "Well, if you'd asked me that yesterday I would have said something trivial like spiders, but right now the thing I fear most is being left here to die and no one knowing where we are. What about you?"

"Never seeing Lucky again."

"My great-great-grandmother knew a woman who was sent here," said Rose.

"Your *great-great-grandmother?* Like, how long ago was that?"

"At the end of the nineteenth century. 1899 to be precise."

"Was she mad?"

"Who? My-great-great-grandmother?"

"No, the woman who was sent to the asylum."
~~~

"Well Mary didn't think so. Mary was my great-great-grandmother. The woman's name was Alice."

"So why did she end up here?"

"As a punishment. She didn't want to marry the man she was engaged to. She wanted to marry someone else and tried to run away with him, but her fiancé was a powerful man and didn't like to be made a fool of, so he put her in here to teach her a lesson."

"I'd have kicked him in the balls and told him where to get off."

Rose laughed. "I guess ladies just didn't do that kind of thing in those days."

"So did she get out?"

"Well Mary planned to rescue her but I'm not sure how it went. I've been reading Mary's letters and I haven't got that far yet."

"Let's hope someone comes up with a plan to get us out of here," said Zoe.

Quite, thought Rose. *A plan would be good.*

~~~

By the time he had cycled back down Oliver's Mount, through the centre of town and out the other side, Dan was dripping with sweat, his T-shirt sticking to him. The weather had turned hot and muggy, the sort of day when sensible people went into the sea instead of cycling at breakneck speed uphill as if they were trying to win the *Tour de France*. Each rotation of the pedals was a huge effort, like he was cycling in the wrong gear, but he forced himself to keep going up the hill towards the asylum. His pulse pounded in his temples. He hadn't thought to bring a bottle of water and now regretted this oversight. He reached the brow of the hill and turned into the lane that led to the abandoned building, the narrow tyres of his road-bike bumping over the rough ground. He hit a sharp stone and wobbled so hard he almost fell off. After that he
~~~

got off the bike and pushed it the rest of the way.

A black Jaguar car was parked in front of the house and one look at the number plate told him whose car it was. MAX1. If it wasn't for the text from Rose, Dan would have turned around straight away and got the hell out of there. But he had to find her; she was in trouble and needed his help. He walked through the gap in the fence and suddenly a large black dog ran from round the back of the house, barking furiously. Dan stopped where he was. The dog was about twenty feet away and it looked angry. He could see the whites of its eyes. That was all he needed, a crazy dog. The thing with dogs, Dan knew, was not to show any fear. You had to let them know who was boss. That way they respected you.

"SIT!" shouted Dan. The barking stopped and the dog just stood there staring at him, its head cocked to one side. "Sit," said Dan again, quieter this time but with as much authority as he could muster. Unbelievably, the dog sat down on its haunches. That was better. Maybe the animal wasn't crazy after all, not if it responded to clear instructions. Dan approached slowly. The dog stood up. Was it going to let him past or not? The dog barked a couple of times, but not so ferociously as it had done before. Dan held out a hand and decided to try the friendly approach.

"Good doggy, come here." The dog trotted over to him and sniffed his hand. Dan risked patting the animal on the head and the dog nuzzled up against him. Dan breathed out a sigh of relief. The dog wasn't going to eat him for dinner. But where was Rose? Quite possibly the dog would know, but that wasn't much use. Dan thought he might just ask the animal anyway, when there was the sound of men's voices, a clear Geordie accent, and footsteps from round the side of the house. *Shit!* He glanced around but there was nowhere to hide.

~~~
~~~

"Of all the crazy things to go and do," said Mary for the umpteenth time. "He could have killed you!"

George smiled weakly at her and didn't try to argue. There was no denying she was right and only good luck had enabled him to escape with nothing more than a flesh wound.

"Keep still," said Ellie as George winced in pain. She was tending to his injury with water and vinegar. The bullet had sliced through the skin of his upper arm, tearing at the flesh, but had missed the bone and, thankfully, was not lodged in the muscle. She bound his arm tightly with a long strip of muslin cloth and put it in a sling.

According to Walter, he'd missed Henry by miles. In a way George was relieved. He'd shown courage in agreeing to participate in the duel but at least he wouldn't have a man's death on his conscience for the rest of his life. But Henry's shot hadn't been as assured as it might have been which was why the bullet had merely wounded him and not killed him outright. It seemed that for once, fortune had been on his side. As far as George was concerned, the matter of the duel was over and they could let Alice decide who she preferred to marry. All that mattered now was rescuing her from the asylum, and Mary had been formulating a plan to that purpose.

"The front door is kept locked and there are bars on the downstairs windows," said Mary.

"It sounds more like a prison," said George.

"Exactly," said Mary. "But the patients take a walk around the garden every morning between ten and eleven."

"Aren't they closely supervised?" asked Walter.

Mary smiled at him. She had forgiven him for his part in taking George to the duel. "Yes, but here's my plan." Everyone looked at her in anticipation. "Ellie will dress like one of the nurses and join the patients in their daily walk. Alice can pretend to stumble and Ellie can lead her away. We'll be waiting nearby with the horse and cart. We only need a moment to separate her from the group."

"It sounds highly risky to me," said Walter.

"Not as risky as taking part in a duel," replied Mary.

There was no argument to that, so everyone agreed they would go to the asylum tomorrow morning and take their chance.

~~~

At the sight of Max and his two cronies, the dog went into a frenzy of barking, at the same time cowering beside Dan's leg. Dan wasn't sure which of them was more afraid of the men, him or the dog.

Max took one look at Dan and sauntered over. "It's busier than Scarborough Fair here today," he said, blowing smoke from the side of his mouth. The men laughed at their boss's joke, although it wasn't a very good one, thought Dan. They must be real pricks to work for this jerk.

"This is a demolition site," said Max. "Didn't you see the signs? I'd run along now if I were you."

Dan ignored him. Like he had with the dog, Dan was determined not to show any fear. "Where's Rose?" he asked. "What have you done with her?"

"Rose?" Max tapped his chin with his forefinger. "Now, would she be the dark-haired one or the blond one?"

Dan looked from Max to the two men but their faces were giving nothing away. Dan didn't know what Max was talking about. What did he mean, *the dark-haired one or the blond one?* Who else was here?

"How's Ryan?" Max tossed his cigarette aside and ground it into the dust with his steel-capped boot. "Recovered from his little bump has he?" His eyes never left Dan's face and his lips curled at the corners as if he knew this question would unsettle Dan. "Guess he won't
~~~

be running a marathon any time soon. Very unfortunate, that accident of his."

Dan saw red. He dropped his bike onto the ground and approached the big man. "Well he's alive," said Dan, "but no thanks to you. He could have got himself killed carrying out your dirty business."

The two Geordies moved towards Dan, one on either side of him, but Max held up a hand to hold them off. "And what dirty business would that be?" he asked innocently.

"You know perfectly well what I mean," said Dan through gritted teeth.

"Do I?"

"The drugs business." The words tasted foul in his mouth. "Why else did Dad have a box of cocaine in his car?"

Max was completely unruffled by Dan's allegations. "You won't find a single drug on me," he said. "I'm completely clean."

"That's because you get other people to do your dirty work for you!"

Max shrugged and reached into his jacket pocket for his packet of cigarettes. "You can't prove anything."

Dan knew he wasn't going to get anywhere standing here accusing these thugs of drug smuggling. They'd kill him in an instant if they thought he knew anything. Right now the important thing was to find Rose.

"Where's Rose?" he asked again. "Tell me where she is."

Max turned his back on him and started walking towards the car. Before Dan knew what was happening the two Geordies had grabbed hold of his arms and were marching him towards the Jaguar.

"Get your hands off me!" Dan struggled to free himself but the men were too strong for him. One of them punched him in the back causing him to double over in pain. The dog was barking its head off but was helpless to do anything and seemed reluctant to approach the men. Max opened the boot of the car and the men pushed Dan inside. He tried to kick out at them, but they slammed the boot down and Dan was plunged into blackness.

A moment later the engine started and Dan felt the car bumping over the rough ground. He had no idea where they were taking him. But worse than that, he had failed Rose. She was still there, he was sure of it. And now there was nothing he could do to help her.

~~~

Rose wanted to cry. She had caught most of the exchange between Dan and Max, when Lucky wasn't barking, and from the sounds of a struggle at the end she could guess that the men had bundled Dan into the boot of the car and driven off with him. All this time she'd been wishing Dan would hurry up and get there, but now she wished he could have arrived just five minutes later, after the men had gone. He was in danger now and it was all her fault for texting him in the first place. And she and Zoe were no nearer getting free.

How much longer would it be before her mother wondered where she was and called the police? Maybe she already had, but Andrea would have no idea where she was and wouldn't be able to tell the police anything useful. The police could enquire at the charity shop and no doubt the nice old lady who worked there would confirm that she had dropped off some sheets, but after that there would be no trace of her. Rose could see the headlines already. *Girl Goes Missing.* Like Alice. But Alice hadn't been tied up without access to food and water.

"Was that your friend who was going to rescue us?" asked Zoe.

"Yes," said Rose. "And now they've got him."

"So what now?"

~~~

"Let's just run through this one more time," said Mary. Her previous plan to get Alice away from Scarborough had failed miserably and she didn't want the same thing to happen again.

"Walter," she said, "you're going to stay with the horse and cart so we can make a quick escape."

Walter nodded, patting the pony on her flank. "Don't worry, we'll be there waiting for you."

Mary turned to Ellie who was dressed as a nurse. On her previous visit Mary had observed the dark grey dresses, white aprons and white caps worn by Nurse Cooper and her colleagues and had managed to improvise an outfit for Ellie that, at first glance, was close enough to that worn by the nurses of the asylum. "Your job will be to get Alice away from the other nurses. The patients will come outside for their walk in a few minutes. Are you confident you know what Alice looks like?"

"Absolutely," said Ellie. "I studied her photograph all last night. I'd recognise her anywhere."

"Good," said Mary. "And remember to show her the brooch so that she knows I sent you."

"I've got it here," said Ellie, taking Mary's Whitby jet brooch out of her pocket.

"Splendid." Mary turned to George. "For now you're Alice's brother. If we can't extract Alice from the garden then we'll have to go inside and you'll have to distract Doctor Collins whilst Ellie and I track her down. Dr Collins won't be able to refuse entry to a close family member like a brother, but if he finds out you're the man Alice was planning to run away with, then he'll have you evicted from the premises."

George nodded. His arm was still bound and in a sling.

"All right," said Mary. "Let's do this."

They climbed into the cart, Mary sitting up front with Walter, George and Ellie in the back.

Walter squeezed Mary's hand. "Everything will work

out fine in the end," he said. Mary wished she shared his optimism, but her heart was all aflutter and she'd barely slept a wink last night for worrying about the plan. She gave him a weak smile back.

"Ready?" he asked.

She nodded. Walter cracked the whip and Daisy set off at a steady trot.

~~~

Lucky barked as the car drove off in a cloud of dust. He was glad it was gone. He didn't like the men, especially not the one who had whipped him. He sat down on the ground and licked his side. It hurt. The boy had been nice though. He hoped the boy would come back. He stood up and sniffed the handlebars of the bicycle. They smelt of the boy. He would remember that smell and know the boy for a friend if he saw him again.

He looked towards the house. The girls were in the house. Should he go back inside? He wanted to. But the girl he loved best had told him to go. Then he remembered something. He'd been digging in the garden earlier when the other girl had turned up. He'd been sure he was going to find something. If he found what he was looking for and took it inside then maybe the girl he loved best wouldn't tell him to go away again.

He returned to the hole he had begun and carried on digging. The soil was dry and powdery and flew into the air, sending a colony of ants running in all directions. But there was a smell here, a smell of something that didn't belong in the earth.

His paws scratched against something hard. He stuck his nose into the earth and sniffed. Then he dug some more, and yes, there was definitely something here. He put his mouth into the hole and pulled out a black stone. The stone was attached to another black stone, and then another one. There was a whole row of black stones. It
~~~

seemed special. He didn't know what it was but he hoped the girl would like it.

He trotted back to the house, the stones dangling from his mouth.

CHAPTER THIRTEEN

Dan rolled over in the boot of the car and a sharp pain shot through his right shoulder. The guy with the tattoo had wrenched his arm behind his back before shoving him into the car. Dan thought he might have torn a ligament. The last time he'd had a pain like that was when he'd suffered a rugby injury which had put him off rugby for life.

It was pitch black in the boot, cramped and unbearably hot. He lay with his legs bent, the top of the boot only inches from his face. With his good arm Dan tried to reach into his back pocket for his phone but it wasn't there. Those bastards must have nicked it. Now he was done for. He used his fingers to feel around in the darkness but couldn't find any way of opening the boot from the inside. In the end he lay on his back and tried to work out where they might be going.

He thought they had turned left out of the lane and he now had the sense that they were going downhill, so they must be heading towards the centre of town. But most of the time the car seemed to be barely moving and Dan guessed they had hit the traffic jam that he'd been stuck in earlier on the way back from the hospital. If only he could open the damn boot, he'd have a chance of jumping out and making a run for it. He tried once more to find a catch that would open the boot but found nothing. For now he had no choice but to lie still and try to stay calm. What was bothering him most right at that moment was that he was so thirsty. The cycle ride, the struggle and now being shut in a hot, confined space had left him drained. He was getting a throbbing headache. If he didn't get something to drink soon he'd pass out, and then he'd have no chance of escaping the clutches of these thugs.

The car lurched forward a few more feet and then braked again. At this rate it would take them forever to get where they were going.

~~~

It was hot in the basement and Rose had started to drift off. She was terribly thirsty and guessed Zoe must be feeling the same. If they didn't get out of here soon they'd end up in hospital suffering from dehydration, or worse. Rose tried not to think about what would happen to them if they couldn't get out. When was the building due to be demolished? She couldn't remember. But surely the builders would check the place over before sending in the wrecking ball? But what if the builders didn't come for weeks or months? They'd be dead by then. She felt like crying but didn't want to risk losing fluid from her body so she forced herself to hold back the tears. She jerked her head up at the sound of Lucky's paws clattering down the basement steps.

"Lucky, good boy," cried Zoe. Her voice sounded thick. "Come here."

The dog trotted over and stood in front of them, looking from one to the other. Now they were sitting on the floor, they were at the same height as him. He was probably wondering why neither of them gave him a pat.

"What have you got there?" asked Zoe. Lucky dropped
~~~

the object in front of his mistress and sat back, his pink tongue lolling from his mouth, clearly expecting some thanks for his gift.

"What is it?" asked Rose.

"It looks like a necklace," said Zoe. "It's quite a fancy one. Made out of black stones. He must have found it in the garden. He's been digging there for days."

Rose leaned over to get a closer look. "Oh!" she said.

"What is it?"

"I know that necklace."

"What, this old thing? It looks like it's been buried in the ground for years."

"Well maybe it has," said Rose, "but I still know it. It belonged to my great-great-grandmother's friend, Alice, the one I was telling you about. The lady who was locked up here. I've got a photograph of her wearing it on the sea-front."

"No kidding!" said Zoe. "So what was it doing in the garden?"

"I don't know." Rose bit her lip. If the necklace had ended up buried in the garden, what had happened to Alice? Was she buried there too?

"I hope we're not going to end up buried in the garden," said Zoe, as if she could read Rose's thoughts.

"Yeah, me too."

~~~

There was a knock at the dressing room door. Kitty put down her pot of rouge, pulled her robe tight around her waist, and went to see who was there. The show wasn't due to start for another forty-five minutes. Gentleman visitors usually called afterwards to ask her to dinner, although she'd put a stop to that since meeting Jackson. Not that he was here anymore. He'd vanished into thin air after that business in the church with Alice and the nasty man with the ginger whiskers. Kitty opened the door and
~~~

peered out into the dingy corridor beyond. It was Alfie.

"Please Miss, sorry to bother you, but I've got a letter for you."

"Who is it from?" she asked.

"Dunno Miss. But it's got a foreign stamp, see?" He pointed to the stamp in the top right hand corner which was indeed, foreign. "Will that be all Miss?"

"Yes, thank you Alfie," said Kitty, clutching the letter. She closed the door and took the letter back to her dressing table.

The envelope was slightly crumpled and the ink smudged as if the letter had travelled many miles to reach her, here in Scarborough. She opened it carefully and pulled out a folded sheet of paper.

Amsterdam,
1st September, 1899

My Dearest Kitty,

By now you must think me a vile rascal for deserting you. However, if you have it in your heart to forgive me, please know that I fled from Scarborough in extreme circumstances. But I now realise this was the cowardly thing to do. Kitty, I am on my way back to you now and am asking you to marry me.

If you are willing, we can set sail for Amsterdam and start a new life away from the dangers that await me in my own country.

I will wait for you tomorrow by the harbour. I hope that you will join me. If you do not, then I will leave Scarborough and never bother you again. But no other woman will capture my heart in the way you have taken it prisoner.

With deepest affection, your ever loving,
Jackson.

Kitty had to read the letter twice more to fully take it in. He hadn't abandoned her after all, well only temporarily and because of circumstances beyond his control. If the man Kitty had seen in the church was Jackson's employer, then it was no wonder Jackson had fled. But here was her chance to escape the life of the stage, her chance to travel and see something of the world, her chance to marry a man who, even if he was a bit of a dark horse, was someone she loved.

She looked at her painted face in the mirror. She was still an attractive woman, but for how much longer? It was the end of the summer season and audiences were dwindling. Soon the theatre would close for the winter and Kitty would be faced with the prospect of living on her savings until the next season, assuming that the theatre manager still wanted her. Younger performers were coming on the scene all the time and Kitty knew that one day she'd be relegated to the dust heap of faded artistes, mocked for being old-fashioned, mimicked cruelly by a new generation of stars.

There was a sharp knock at the door and Kitty jumped.

"Ten minutes to curtain up," called the stage manager.

"Thank you," Kitty called back. She tucked the letter into her corset, finished applying her make-up and put on her dress. Tonight she would sing *The boy I love is up in the gallery* one last time, and tomorrow she would go to the harbour and take her chances with this enigmatic man that fate had thrown into her path.

~~~

"Come here, Lucky," said Zoe.

The dog put his face up close to hers and licked her nose. He was looking sorry for himself, thought Rose, probably wondering why Zoe hadn't hugged him for bringing her the necklace.

"Listen, Lucky." Zoe spoke earnestly to the dog. "My hands are tied. I can't move."

Lucky cocked his head to one side but showed no sign of understanding.

This is ridiculous, thought Rose. *If this was a movie she'd give*
~~~

the dog instructions to go and fetch the local constable and he'd do it.

"My hands," persisted Zoe. She tilted her head backwards to show the dog where to look. "Behind me, Lucky."

Lucky took a cautious step to the side and peered behind Zoe's back.

"I'm stuck!" wailed Zoe, getting more desperate now. She jiggled her arms around, making the metal bed-frame shake. Lucky sniffed at her wrists. And then, as if he actually understood her predicament, he started gnawing at the leather with his teeth.

"Good dog!" said Zoe. "Keep going."

Rose thought she might be dreaming and any minute now she'd wake up and find the dog gone. But it seemed that Lucky really was trying to chew his way through the leather strap that held Zoe prisoner. If they got out of here alive Rose was going to buy that dog the biggest bone she could find.

It seemed to take forever but then suddenly Zoe wrenched her arms free of the strap and shook her wrists in the air. Lucky barked and Zoe hugged him tight.

"That dog is amazing," said Rose as Zoe undid the straps around Rose's wrists.

"Yes, he is rather special, isn't he?"

Free of her bonds, Rose staggered to her feet and dusted herself down. "We have to call for help," she said. "Those men took Dan. But they took my mobile phone. Can I use yours?"

"Sorry," said Zoe. "I don't have one."

"You don't…?" Rose was speechless. Who didn't have a mobile phone in this day and age? "Then I have to get into town." She ran up the basement steps, Zoe and Lucky close behind.

Outside, they could see the tyre tracks left by the car in the dust. Lying on its side on the ground, was Dan's bike. Rose grabbed the handle-bars and pulled the bike into an upright position. It was a road racing bike with dropped handle-bars, and bigger than she would have liked, but it was all she had. It would be quicker than walking.

"I'm going to get help for Dan," she said. "But I won't tell the police about this place. I promise."

"It's all right," said Zoe. "Tell them whatever you want. I can't stay here forever. It's time I moved on."

"I'll let you know what happens," said Rose. She hugged Zoe, then knelt down and hugged Lucky.

"Good luck," called Zoe, as Rose climbed onto the bike and wobbled down the path.

~~~

Nurse Cooper came into the dormitory this morning, her usual red-faced, cross self. We were making our beds and Dorothy was singing at the top of her voice, an out-of-tune rendition of *Come into the Garden, Maud,* which I had once heard sung in London by Marie Lloyd. Despite all the wrong notes, I found it strangely comforting to listen to.

"Pack it in," shouted Nurse Cooper. Dorothy ignored her and carried on singing.

"I said shut it, ye mad cow!" Nurse Cooper stormed over to Dorothy and raised her hand as if to hit her.

I darted towards them, placing myself between Dorothy and Nurse Cooper. "Leave her alone," I said. "She's not doing any harm." The room fell silent and the other women stared in shock that someone had dared stand up to Nurse Cooper.

"And who d'ye think you are, Miss Hoity-Toity?" asked Nurse Cooper, her face redder than ever. "Reckon I'll just take these things back downstairs and tell Dr Collins you ain't ready to leave 'ere. 'Ow about that then? I've a good mind to tell 'im you've gone completely bonkers and should be put into solitary confinement." She held her face close to mine and her eyes gleamed with malicious intent. It was then that I noticed she was carrying the black dress
~~~

I was wearing when Henry had first brought me here. Mary's dress. She also had my jet necklace which I had thought never to see again.

"What's the matter? Cat got yer tongue?"

I shook my head.

"Ge' yer togs on." She threw the clothes at my feet. "You're leaving 'ere. And good riddance. The posh'uns are always more trouble than they're worth."

"Leaving?" I asked, not sure that I had heard her right.

"You 'eard me," she said. "Or 'ave you really gone and lost yer wits?"

That brought me to my senses. I did not know how my release had been secured, but I was not about to lose this opportunity.

"I will dress straight away," I said. "Thank you for coming to tell me." She snorted at that and walked away. The other women in the dormitory stared at me as if I was some kind of alien being. I suppose they were not used to one of their number being told she could leave. Even Dorothy lost her tongue for a few moments.

~~~

"Come on Lucky." Zoe led the dog back towards the house, the place that she had come to regard as her home. But it was time to move on. She looked up at the huge, stone walls and felt a pang of regret. She had felt safe here. Some people, she knew, would be creeped out by the idea of living in a deserted Victorian lunatic asylum. They would have all sorts of nightmares, imagining the ghosts of the former residents haunting the abandoned corridors. But in Zoe's experience it wasn't the dead you needed to fear but the living, as the last hour had proved only too well.

Zoe wished Rose well in her search for Dan, but it was inevitable now that enquiries would be made that would bring the police to the asylum and Zoe had no desire to be
~~~

found.

She went up to the room she had slept in and rolled up her sleeping bag. She stuffed it into her rucksack along with the blue blanket that Rose had brought earlier that afternoon. There was barely room for both items, but Zoe didn't want to leave the blanket behind. It meant more to her than just physical warmth. It was proof that there was generosity and kindness in the world, and sometimes she was in danger of forgetting that. Then she packed the camping stove and the few tins of food she had left.

She didn't know where she would go. Maybe further up the coast, towards Whitby.

She heaved her rucksack onto her back and took one last look at the room to make sure she hadn't left anything behind. Then she remembered. In their haste to get out of the basement they had left the necklace lying on the floor. She didn't feel much like going back down there, but the necklace looked like it might be valuable. She shouldn't just leave it lying around. Leaving her rucksack at the top of the basement steps and keeping Lucky close by her side, Zoe descended to the basement once more. The necklace was still there, lying in a heap on the floor by the bedstead. Zoe picked it up and ran the stones through her fingers. It was tempting to keep the necklace, maybe try and sell it later, but she couldn't do that. Rose had said the necklace belonged to her great-great-grandmother's friend. She should return the necklace to Rose. But where to find her? Then Zoe remembered something about Tollergate. Hadn't Rose said that was where she was staying? Tollergate was only a small street with a handful of houses on it. It shouldn't be that difficult to knock on a few doors and find out which one Rose was in. Yes, that was what she would do. Her last act, before leaving Scarborough for good.

Zoe turned towards the stairs, and that was when she felt it. A vibration underfoot, like a rumbling deep within the earth. The pile of metal-framed beds creaked. One of the windows cracked.

What the…?

Zoe ran up the steps and grabbed her rucksack. Something was wrong with the building, or the ground on which it stood. It was definitely time to get moving.

"Ready, Lucky?"

The dog barked and wagged his tail in reply. He'd follow her anywhere. And right now, that was anywhere out of here.

~~~

Henry climbed into the carriage that was waiting for him outside the Grand Hotel and commanded the driver to take him to Highcliff Asylum. By now Dr Collins should have received his note saying that he would be taking Alice away this morning and to make sure she was ready. He trusted that the short time she had spent in the asylum would be enough to subdue her wayward spirit and teach her a lesson. In Henry's opinion women were like horses. You just had to break them in and after that they would become docile and provide you with years of domestic servitude. Besides, he'd had enough of this windswept corner of the north of England where the locals spoke in harsh, clipped accents and the seagulls shat on his top hat. He'd ruined two hats already and he didn't want to ruin a third.

If Henry had been given to self-introspection, he would have admitted that failing to kill his opponent in the duel had badly wounded his pride. He couldn't understand why the shot had gone wide, wounding the man's arm but nothing more. It was true that he hadn't fired a shot in years: his London life didn't allow for such pleasurable pursuits, but he had always thought his skill with a pistol was innate, something as intrinsic to himself as the colour of his hair or his taste in fine wine. Never mind, the painter had proved to be an even worse shot than himself
~~~

and Henry felt that he, Henry, had acquitted himself the better of the two.

As the carriage climbed the hill to the asylum Henry calculated the latest date he could make Alice his wife. She would be twenty-one in ten days' time at which point she would inherit an immense fortune from her late uncle, a man who had traded in tea and silk from the Far East. It was imperative that they should marry before her birthday because then, according to the wording of her uncle's will, the inheritance would be split evenly between husband and wife. The carriage pulled into the grounds of the asylum and Henry determined to set the wedding date seven days from now. But he was not going to take her back to London where she might escape his clutches once more. Oh no! Henry had secured two fares on a ship sailing for the Continent. He would take her to Amsterdam and marry her there. It would be less fuss than a fancy London do after all.

Henry climbed down from the carriage and walked up the steps to the front door of the asylum. Inside, his fortune awaited him.

~~~

Rose cycled down the lane, the bike tyres bumping over the rough ground. Twice she wobbled and almost fell off, but she clung on, holding the top of the handlebars. If she'd been riding her own bike it wouldn't have been such a problem, but on Dan's bike her feet only just reached the pedals and she couldn't reach the gear system without bending down low and endangering her balance. At the end of the lane she waited for a stream of cars to go past and then turned onto the main road. There was no footpath to cycle on so she had to take her chances with the other vehicles. She held on tight as cars sped past her, some of them so close she could have touched them with an outstretched arm.
~~~

As soon as a footpath became available, she moved off the road and cycled on the path instead. There were no pedestrians this far out of the town so she figured she'd be all right for now. As she approached the outskirts of the town she realised she was actually going faster than the cars which had ground to a halt in a massive traffic jam. The number of pedestrians on the pavement increased the closer she got to the town centre. She slowed her pace. Soon she'd have to get off and walk. And then she saw them.

The Jaguar was stuck in the traffic. In front of the Jaguar was a white delivery van, its windows rolled down and loud music blaring out. Behind the Jag was a family hatchback with three children arguing in the back seat and the parents in the front looking tired and fed up. Rose jumped off the bike and held back, not wanting the men to see her in the wing mirror. The traffic crawled forwards. At this pace she could keep pace with them just by walking.

At the roundabout outside Peasholm Park the car suddenly turned left without indicating and, free of the traffic, started moving towards the headland. Desperate not to lose them, Rose jumped on the bike and pedalled as fast as she could. There was a wide prom to cycle on here, but the tide was coming in and the prom was crowded with families leaving the beach. Once she almost collided with a small boy on a scooter, the father hurling insults at her. Rose ignored him and pressed on. If she didn't keep up she'd be in danger of losing sight of the Jaguar.

She did lose sight of it as it disappeared round the headland. She pushed down hard on the pedals. Her thighs would kill her tomorrow, but for now she was going to use every last ounce of energy she had. She rounded the headland and looked for the car but couldn't see it anywhere. She banged the top of the handlebars in frustration. Then suddenly she saw it, turning towards the harbour. She skidded to a halt. The car was driving towards the lighthouse at the end of the jetty. It would have to stop soon or it would end up in the water. Rose got off the bike and followed.

~~~

She should have known it would be Henry coming for her.

For a short while, as Alice put on Mary's black dress and fastened the jet necklace around her neck, she had believed that Mary and George had come to her rescue. She had envisioned them waiting for her in Dr Collins' room. She had even imagined Dr Collins apologising to her for her incarceration and saying that it had all been a dreadful mistake. But of course, those thoughts had been nothing but foolish fancy and maybe even proved that she was mentally deficient after all.

When Nurse Cooper led her into Dr Collins' room, Henry was standing there, a look of triumph on his face. Alice let out a startled cry. She threw herself at Dr Collins, clutching hold of his lapels. "Please, Doctor, I would rather stay here than go with that man. Tell Nurse Cooper to take me back to the ward. I beg you."

"Miss Hawthorne," said Dr Collins. "Please, control yourself. This is most unseemly behaviour." He gently took hold of her hands and placed them into Henry's large, sweaty palms. "Your husband-to-be will take care of you now. You are formally discharged from this establishment."

"Thank you Doctor," said Henry. He held Alice's hands tightly. "I appreciate everything you have done for me and my future wife. Now we must hurry." He led her towards the door. Alice tried to pull away from him. "Walk," he hissed into her ear, "or I'll put you in a far worse place than this."

As Henry led her away from the asylum, Alice looked back at the house, almost with longing. It was a frightful
~~~

place, without a doubt. Nurse Cooper was a bully; the food was inedible; Dr Collins was obsessed with his theories and researches and many, if not all, of the patients were suffering from delusions and manias with little hope of ever being cured. But she had escaped from one prison to find herself at the mercy of a man who would treat her no better than a slave. She had to get away from Henry, even if it meant going back inside the asylum.

Their route took them past a row of rose bushes, big, mature shrubs, heavy with late summer blooms. Without a thought to how much it would hurt, Alice stretched out a hand and grabbed the nearest stem, deliberately dragging her hand over the thorns, allowing the sharp spikes to tear at the delicate skin.

"Oh, I am bleeding," she cried, holding up her hand where beads of bright red blood were forming like rubies across the palm of her hand. The wound stung, but it was a good feeling, giving her a sense of release.

"What is it now woman?" growled Henry. He grabbed hold of her wrist and examined her hand.

"I think I should go back inside and get this wound attended to." She tried to keep her voice steady. "Else it may become infected."

"What utter nonsense. It's nothing more than a scratch." He flung her wrist aside in disgust. But then his eyes came to rest on the jet necklace around her neck. "What is this piece of frippery?"

Alice's hand closed over the necklace. "It is nothing. Leave it." In her haste, she had forgotten to hide it under her dress and now she cursed her foolishness.

"I don't believe you! *He* gave it to you didn't he? That painter fellow you were going around with, like a common whore!"

"No, please."

"Give me that!" He wrenched the necklace from her neck, the clasp popping undone, and tossed it aside. It disappeared into a pile of horse muck that the gardeners had recently spread around the base of the roses. "Now get into the carriage. We are leaving."

~~~

The car engine was turned off. They had arrived at their destination, although Dan didn't know where that was. He listened for any familiar sounds, trying to get his bearings.

Seagulls.

The screeching and squawking was unmistakable, even from within the boot of the car. There was only one place Dan knew where the gulls made this sort of racket. Down by the harbour, when the fishing boats came in, laden with crates of pilchards and shrimp.

Dan held his breath, waiting to see what would happen next. If they left him in the boot of the car the heat would rise to intolerable levels and he would be dead before he knew it. To his relief, the boot of the car was pulled open. Dan blinked in the blinding sun.

"You're coming with us, mate," said the guy with the tattoo. The other man, the one that resembled a bulldog, showed Dan that he had a gun hidden inside his jacket pocket. "And don't try any funny business."

As his eyes adjusted to the bright light Dan realised that the car was parked by the lighthouse, at the far end of the jetty, the boot angled so as to be well away from prying eyes. There was no one nearby to come to his rescue.

The men hauled him out of the boot and walked either side of him towards a fancy-looking yacht. Dan recognised it as the one he'd seen the men on before. As they pushed him up the gangplank, Dan caught a glimpse of the name painted on the side of the boat. *Scarborough Fair.*

~~~

Walter stopped the cart behind a large laurel bush, out

of sight of the asylum. Then Mary, Ellie and George made their way on foot to the edge of the garden and waited for the crocodile line of patients to appear.

After an anxious few minutes the front door opened wide and a rag-tag line of forlorn individuals, some stooped and shuffling, some walking as if in a daze, exited the building. They were accompanied by male and female nurses who watched their every step. Mary counted the patients off one by one, desperately hoping that Alice would be the next to appear. But the last patient came out, an old man with skeletal features and a pronounced limp, and the door closed. Mary examined the line of patients once more as they made their way along the path, circling the rose beds and lavender bushes. Had she missed Alice? Surely not. She would have known her immediately if she had been there, but she wasn't in the group.

"She's not there," said Mary. "We're going to have to go inside." The walkers were now at the far end of the garden. Mary, George and Ellie moved quickly towards the door and George pulled the bell rope with his good arm. After what felt like an interminable wait, the door opened and Mary was dismayed to see Nurse Cooper standing there. She had hoped for a more docile nurse, not this dragon of a woman. However, if she had to deal with Nurse Cooper, then deal with her she would.

"What is it?" asked Nurse Cooper. She stood in the doorway like a Titan, arms crossed in front of her. The sleeves of her dress were rolled up to the elbows and the muscles in her forearms bulged unattractively.

"We have come to see Miss Alice Hawthorne," said Mary in her best voice, the one she normally reserved for vicars and upper-crust ladies who were apt to look down on people with a working class accent. "This is her brother, Mr Geoffrey Hawthorne." She indicated George, who inclined his head to Nurse Cooper.

"She ain't in 'ere no more," said Nurse Cooper.

"Do you mean to say she has left the asylum?" asked

Mary. She was becoming proud of her ability to decipher the local tongue.

"Aye."

Mary blinked at Nurse Cooper in disbelief. "But how did she leave? Was she on her own?"

Nurse Cooper snorted in derision. "Course she weren't. I wouldn't've let 'er go missen, but this man came for 'er 'alf an 'our ago. The one what brought 'er 'ere. Now, I ain't got time ter stand round gossipin'." And with that she closed the door in their faces.

Mary couldn't believe their bad luck. If Alice really had left the asylum, and there was no reason to doubt Nurse Cooper, then there was only one person who could have removed her and that was Henry Blackwood. How she would dearly love to see that man disappear. Nurse Cooper had said that Alice had left half an hour ago which meant they couldn't have gone far. But the question was where? Mary's guess was that Alice and Henry would be headed for the railway station. He'd want to take her back to London.

"Come on," said Mary to George and Ellie. "If we hurry we might catch them yet."

~~~

Rose deposited the bicycle round the back of some public toilets. She didn't have the key to the security lock that was attached to the crossbar so she'd have to hope the bike didn't get nicked.

The Jaguar was parked right at the far end of the jetty, by the lighthouse, well away from the tourists who were milling around looking at the boats. She'd seen the two Geordies escorting Dan, no doubt at gun point, onto the yacht. It was a big vessel with a long, pointed prow, like the sort of boat you'd see cruising round the Mediterranean, a luxury floating home on which to host cocktail parties for the rich and famous. Rose didn't have
~~~

to wonder how Max could afford such a boat, given what she'd seen stored in the basement at the asylum.

Rose had just enough change in her pocket to buy herself a bottle of Coke from a booth. She gulped the liquid down and tossed the bottle into a nearby bin. Then she walked towards the lighthouse, and hid behind a pile of empty crates that reeked of fish. Max was standing on the jetty, talking to a fisherman. The fisherman, a big, ruddy-faced chap dressed in oilskins and wellington boots, had a deep, resounding voice and Rose overheard him saying something about high tides and a full moon. It sounded as if Max was planning to set sail and was getting advice from one of the locals.

Then the two Geordies appeared on the deck of the yacht. They walked down the gangplank, jumped onto the jetty and went to join Max and the fisherman. Dan wasn't with them so he must still be on the boat and she didn't think they'd invited him to the captain's cabin and served him a plate of caviar. The garrulous old fisherman was still holding forth about strong currents and powerful tides. This was her chance. She darted across the jetty, ran up the gangplank and jumped on board. There was no one to stop her. All she had to do now was find Dan, and do it quickly before the men came back.

The top deck was deserted. She pulled open a door and headed down below, calling his name as she went.

She found herself in a long, narrow corridor with cabin doors on either side. Her heart hammering in her chest, she tried the first door to her left. It opened onto a luxurious cabin with sofas, a flat-screen television, abstract works of art on the walls and a well-stocked wine rack in one corner. Not surprisingly, Dan wasn't there. The next door led to the kitchen; another to a Swedish-style sauna; then a bedroom. There was still no sign of Dan and Rose was starting to feel desperate. The men would be back soon. Time was running out.

"Dan!" she called. "Are you down here? Can you hear

me?"

There was a thump from behind the door at the far end. Rose ran over and hammered on the door. "Dan, is that you?" There was a muffled groan from inside, as if he was gagged or something. Rose tried the door handle but the door was locked. She examined the lock. It was a Yale and the catch only just reached across. Her mother always said Yale locks were not sufficient on their own, that you needed a dead lock too. Well, she was going to find out if her mother was right after all.

"Stay back," cried Rose. She flung herself at the door. It flew open and she fell into the room. It was a tiny, windowless cabin with bunk beds against one wall. Dan was sitting on the floor, his mouth gagged with a dirty cloth and his hands tied behind his back with the sort of thick rope sailors used to moor their boats to the pillars on the jetty. Rose untied the gag and then started work on the rope. The knot was expertly tied and her fingers fumbled with the rope until she worked out how to undo it.

"How did you find me?" spluttered Dan.

"Long story. Tell you later. We have to get out of here."

She pulled him into the corridor. At that moment there was a loud rumbling from the engine and the boat vibrated into life.

"We're too late," said Dan. "The boat's sailing."

~~~

Kitty paid the driver handsomely.

"Thank you, ma'am." The coachman doffed his cap to her and lifted her case down. "I 'ope you 'ave a pleasant crossing and that the seas aren't too rough."

"I hope so too," said Kitty.

She climbed down from the carriage and looked around at the passengers and sailors thronging the quayside.
~~~

Then she saw him.

He was standing apart from the other people, his bowler hat pulled down low over his brow as if he didn't want anyone to recognise him. She picked up her case and walked briskly towards him.

At the sound of her footsteps he looked up and his face broke into a smile.

"Kitty," he said. "You came."

"Of course, Jackson."

"Shall we?" He held out his arm to her and looked towards the boat.

Kitty looked up at the tall mast. It wasn't too late to change her mind. The theatre manager had said he was sorry to see her go. If she went back now she was sure he'd let her have her old job back. And what did she really know of Jackson? But he'd kept his word, hadn't he? He'd come back for her when most men she'd known would have just fled. She looked across the harbour at the town of Scarborough. It was picture-postcard perfect, with the ruined castle on the headland, St Mary's Church up on the hill, the sweep of golden sand, the windows of the Grand Hotel glinting in the afternoon sun. She would miss it, but it was time to move on.

She slipped her arm through Jackson's and together they made their way up the gangplank. *Fortune favours the brave,* thought Kitty as she took the first steps towards her new life.

~~~

It took Zoe and Lucky a good hour to walk from the asylum to Tollergate in the centre of town. They would have made faster progress if Zoe hadn't been carrying her rucksack, but there was nowhere safe to leave it and she didn't want to have to go back to the asylum for it. Rose was right. It wasn't safe there anymore. She wished now she'd let Rose call the police when they'd had the chance,
~~~

but there was no point dwelling on past mistakes. All that mattered now was that she find Rose, make sure she was all right and give her back the necklace. She'd worry about herself later.

She paused at the top of Tollergate and looked down the steep, cobbled street. The houses were all on one side, to her left, a row of quaint terraced cottages, some of them painted in pretty pastel shades. She looked with longing at the painted doors and Georgian windows and thought how wonderful it would be to live in one of those little houses, just her and Lucky, and her mum. But houses like this, small as they might be, were out of her league. The best she could hope for was a poky council flat on some rundown estate on the outskirts of town.

"So which house do you think Rose lives in?" she asked the dog. Lucky looked up at her with his trusting brown eyes. "I guess we'll just have to start knocking on doors, then."

There was no answer at the first two houses. The owners must be away or out at work. Half-way down the street a door opened and a man in a suit stepped out. He climbed into a small hatchback that was parked half on the pavement and half on the cobbled road and drove off. The car, a lurid shade of purple, was painted with the name, logo and telephone number of one of the local estate agents. Zoe remembered that Rose had said she was staying with her grandmother but that her grandmother had died, so it would make sense if they were trying to sell the house. Just then a woman stepped out onto the pavement and stood looking anxiously up and down the street.

"That's her," said Zoe to Lucky. "That's Rose's mum." The resemblance to Rose was unmistakable. Although this woman was so much older, she had Rose's colouring and the same shaped face. It was like looking into the future, seeing how Rose herself would look in thirty years' time. Zoe hurried down the street. "Excuse me," she called.

The woman stiffened, took one look at Zoe and turned to go back inside. Zoe recognised that look, she'd seen it so many times before. It was the look people gave her when she walked down a crowded street with Lucky at her heels. A small dose of pity mixed with a much larger dose of mistrust. Whenever she approached people they shrank away from her because they thought she was going to ask them for money. They judged her hair, her clothes, her dog. Some of them called her a scrounger.

"No, wait please," called Zoe. "I don't want anything. But are you Rose's mother?"

"Yes," said the woman, suspiciously. "What do you want?"

"I have something to give back to Rose."

"How do you know Rose? And where is she?"

"Isn't she back yet?" asked Zoe. That wasn't a good sign. She'd thought Rose would go straight to the police. Zoe hoped Rose hadn't tried anything stupid.

"She's been gone all afternoon," said Rose's mother, her voice tight. "She only went out to take some sheets and a blanket to the charity shop." Her eyes darted to the blue blanket that was poking out of the top of Zoe's rucksack. "Who are you?"

"I'm Zoe and Rose is a friend of mine."

Rose's mother looked as if she didn't believe a word of it.

"I have something for you." Zoe reached a hand into her trouser pocket and pulled out the jet necklace. "I believe this belonged to a woman who was a friend of Rose's great-great-grandmother. Alice?"

"I don't understand," said Rose's mother, taking the necklace from Zoe's fingers. "Where did you find this? And *where* is Rose?" There was a noticeable edge of panic in her voice now.

"I don't know where she is," admitted Zoe. "I last saw her over an hour ago. It's a long story, but I think she might be in danger. We need to call the police."

Rose's mother paled in fright. "The police? What's going on?"

"I'll explain everything," said Zoe. "But right now I need to use your telephone."

"You'd better come inside then." The woman looked doubtfully at Lucky.

"He's very friendly," said Zoe. "And very well behaved."

Rose's mother stood aside and let Zoe and Lucky into the house.

~~~

Henry forced Alice into the waiting carriage and climbed in after her, slamming the door behind him. He rapped his cane on the carriage roof, the coachman cracked his whip and the pair of horses bolted forward. Alice cowered in the corner of the carriage, afraid of Henry's temper. He sat opposite her, mopping his brow with a silk handkerchief. Neither of them spoke.

Her time in the asylum had taught Alice to be resourceful and look after herself. She had spent many hours alone with her thoughts, thinking about her life and how she wanted to live it. She had come to the conclusion that if she couldn't marry the man she loved, then she would rather not marry at all and now, as the carriage jolted down the hill, she vowed that she would certainly never marry Henry Blackwood, even if he marched her up the aisle himself. She would simply refuse. If asked the question, *Do you take this man to be your lawful wedded husband?* she would reply, "No, I do not." Then she would throw herself on the mercy of the priest. She would make a fool of him in the house of God and that would serve him right.

Alice peered out of the window to see where they were going. She had expected they would go directly to the railway station and would return to London by train that
~~~

afternoon, so she was surprised to find the carriage drawing to a halt by the harbour. The screech of the seagulls, that she had come to love, pierced her heart.

Henry flung open the carriage door and jumped down. Alice hesitated. "Come on, woman," he growled, "or do I have to drag you out of there myself?"

Alice climbed down from the carriage and Henry took her by the arm. "Where are we going?" she asked.

Henry motioned towards a sailing ship, a fine vessel with three tall masts, that was moored in the harbour. "I thought a little trip would do us both good. Help us get reacquainted with one another." He started to lead her towards the waiting boat.

~~~

"Get back," said Dan. "They mustn't see us." He pushed Rose back inside the cabin and closed the door.

"What are we going to do?" asked Rose. It felt as if they were already moving at a rate of knots. If they jumped off now they could almost certainly still swim to shore but they were below deck and there was little hope of going up top without being seen. Every second that passed was taking them further and further away from land.

"I wish there was a porthole," said Rose. "It's so claustrophobic in here."

The boat lifted with the swell of a wave and then plunged downward. They must have left the relative safety of the harbour and were already out on the open sea.

"Whoa!" Rose grabbed hold of the side of the bunk bed to stop herself falling over. The Coke she had drunk so hastily was swilling around in her stomach, threatening to make a reappearance. She didn't know if she had sea legs or not, but she suspected she was going to find out.

Dan thrust his head under the tap of the tiny basin in the corner of the room and gulped down mouthfuls of water as if he hadn't drunk anything for days.
~~~

"That's better," he said when he'd finished. His face and hair were wet and he towelled them dry on his T-shirt.

Rose sank down onto the lower bunk. It was hot and airless in the cabin and the throb of the engine combined with the lurching movement of the boat was making her feel queasy. Beads of sweat broke out on her forehead and upper lip. She shut her eyes and moaned as the yacht plunged into another trough.

Dan sat next to her, taking her hand in his. "Try and relax," he said. "You have to let yourself go with the boat and not try to fight against it. Breathe deeply."

"I think I'm going to puke."

"Pretend you're on a ride at the fair."

Rose closed her eyes and imagined herself at the fairground with its flashing lights and pumping music. She inhaled sharply through her nose, exhaled through her mouth and tried to relax. Gradually the queasiness subsided. It was choppy on the sea, but no worse than being on the Kamikaze swing at the fair.

"Feeling better?" he asked.

She nodded and opened her eyes. "Listen, we have to get out of here. Those men are drug smugglers. They're storing the stuff at the asylum."

Dan nodded. "I know. And they were getting my dad to…" He didn't finish his sentence. The cabin door banged open and the two Geordies walked in.

~~~

Jackson had never felt more content in his life. Kitty slipped her arm through his and they strolled the deck, feeling the wind in their hair and the gentle rise and fall of the boat under their feet. They discussed their plans for the future, how they would set up a shop in London and earn a decent living selling ladies' fashions. Kitty had a good eye for what women liked to wear and Jackson trusted she would make a smart business woman. Above
~~~

all, there would be no more Henry Blackwood; no more running sordid errands for that man, procuring whores and opium for him; no more haranguing creditors. No more spying on innocent young females… Jackson stopped suddenly and drew in a sharp breath.

"What is it?" asked Kitty. They had walked the length of the boat and just turned towards the stern.

"Over there," said Jackson, clenching his jaw.

Kitty squinted into the sun. "Oh!" She clutched his arm tighter.

A woman in a black dress was standing as still as a statue, her hands clasping the railing, staring fixedly at the receding coastline. Beside her, looking immensely pleased with himself, was a man with ginger hair and whiskers. He brought a pipe to his fat lips, inhaled deeply, and blew the smoke out with the air of a man on whom fortune has smiled favourably. He had not yet noticed the arrival of Kitty and Jackson who were still some ten yards off.

"It's them isn't it?" said Kitty, leaning close to whisper in Jackson's ear. "Alice and Henry. I'd recognise him anywhere. I saw him drag her away from the church. She looks thinner, though. That stay in the asylum hasn't done her any good."

Jackson made a snap decision. "Stay here," he said, releasing Kitty's arm. "I don't believe Alice is here by choice and Henry's not going to get away with this. I'm going to sort this out once and for all."

"Wait," said Kitty. She tried to hold him back but Jackson was already striding towards the man he detested.

"Henry Blackwood!" shouted Jackson.

Henry turned at the sound of his name and for a fleeting moment a look of surprise registered on his flabby face. Then the surprise turned to disdain. "Well, well, well," he said, pointing the pipe at Jackson. "What hell-hole have you crept out of? You failed in your duty to me and yet you dare to show your face."

Jackson didn't bother to reply but resorted to familiar

tactics, punching Henry squarely in the jaw. The pipe flew out of Henry's hand and skidded across the deck. Alice spun around from the railing and moved to the side out of harm's way.

"What the devil?" spluttered Henry when he had recovered his balance. "What the hell do you think you're playing at man?"

Jackson grabbed Henry by the lapels of his coat. "You're a gambler and a womaniser and a cheat, and you don't deserve this young lady." He nodded at Alice who stared at him, open-mouthed.

"How dare you, you stinking scoundrel," shouted Henry. "If it weren't for me you'd still be crawling in the gutter. I saved you from a life of crime and poverty."

Jackson landed a second blow, this time to Henry's chest and Henry responded with an upper cut to Jackson's jaw. Jackson staggered backwards for a moment before charging at Henry, throwing him down onto the deck.

Kitty watched with a mixture of alarm and excitement fluttering in her breast. From what she knew of Henry Blackwood, he deserved everything he was getting, and more. She had no doubt that Jackson would prevail. But what about Alice? Now was Kitty's chance to show the female solidarity she had failed to show in St Mary's church. She turned away from the fight to see something that made her heart skip a beat. Alice was lifting her skirts and climbing onto the railings at the back of the boat. She held onto a pole with one hand and leaned out precariously with the other.

"Alice!" screeched Kitty. "Stop!"

Her strident singer's voice carried over the wind and the waves. Jackson paused mid punch and, scrambling to his feet, turned his attention to Alice. "Take my hand," he shouted to her. "Don't do anything stupid!" She ignored him.

"What the blazes do you think you're playing at woman?" fumed Henry. He was slower than Jackson to stand up and swayed like a drunkard, blood running from his nose and spittle flying from the corners of his mouth. "Get down from there at once! Stop making an exhibition of yourself."

"No," called Alice. "I won't climb down until you promise to set me free. I do not wish to marry you. If you refuse to let me go then I will set myself free by throwing myself into the water. You will never get your hands on me or my fortune."

Henry stormed forwards and grabbed hold of her ankles. "Have you completely lost your wits woman? I should have left you to rot in that asylum. I command you to get down at once and stop this theatrical nonsense."

"Never!" Alice kicked her right foot free of Henry's grasp and leaned out even further towards the sea.

"Careful!" cried Kitty.

"Damn and blast!" shouted Henry. He grabbed hold of the railings and started to manoeuvre himself with considerable difficulty onto the top rail. He reached out a hand towards Alice.

Alice looked at the man she was supposed to marry as he balanced precariously on the rail like a grotesque circus act. She looked at Jackson and Kitty standing on the deck, pleading with their eyes for her not to do anything foolish. Then she looked down at the water churned up in the wake of the boat, a silvery white line curving back towards the shore. In an instant she made up her mind. She let go of the pole and jumped lightly back onto the deck. Jackson caught her in his arms

"Thank God," murmured Kitty, leading Alice safely away from the edge.

Jackson turned back to Henry who was still standing on the railing as if paralysed by fear. He reached into his breast pocket and withdrew the knife that he always kept for emergencies. The blade glittered in the sunlight, cold and dangerous.

"What's it to be?" asked Jackson. "There doesn't have

to be any bloodshed if you simply agree to let Alice go."

Henry glanced uneasily at the knife. He looked as if he was about to speak, but then the boat rose on the swell of a wave and a second later plunged into the ensuing trough. Henry wobbled, made a strangled noise that was somewhere between a curse and a scream, and fell, with a splash, into the water.

Kitty and Alice ran to join Jackson at the railing and all three of them leaned over the edge. The boat was picking up speed and they were already some distance from Henry whose black top hat could be seen bobbing on the water. Every now and then a hand appeared from beneath the surface.

"What should we do?" asked Kitty. "Call for help?"

Alice looked calmly at the sight of the drowning figure. "No," she said. "He deserved his fate."

~~~

"I don't fookin' believe this," said the guy with the tattoo, looking from Rose to Dan and back to Rose. "How the hell did she get here?"

The fat guy scoffed. "Ye didna tie 'er oop tightly enough, man."

"Ah, shut yer gob!"

Tattoo-face threw his cigarette stub onto the floor, ground it out with his boot and marched into the room. He pulled his gun from his jacket. "Now, don't try anything funny like," he snarled at Dan, pulling him to his feet and stabbing the barrel of the gun into the centre of Dan's back.

"No!" shouted Rose.

"Don't worry sweetheart," said the fat man. "Ye didna think we'd leave ye here didya?" He also pulled out his gun and grabbed Rose's upper arm with his free hand.

"Now walk," hissed tattoo-face, shoving Dan towards the door. The men led them up to the deck.
~~~

Rose felt her insides turning to jelly. Why hadn't she tried to contact the police? She could have asked for help when she bought the bottle of Coke. *Idiot*, she berated herself. She'd done nothing to help Dan and now both their lives were in danger. She had visions of them being made to walk the plank. It was the sort of punishment that somebody like Max would no doubt find amusing. She tried to see how far they had sailed. The coastline was still in sight, but it was way too far to swim to shore. They were not moving now and the yacht was bobbing about in the water like a cork. A gusty wind had got up and dark clouds were rolling in from the North Sea like an invading army. Rose could see the outline of Highcliff House, perched on the edge of the cliff, silhouetted against the setting sun. What wouldn't she give to be back there now, even in that rat-infested basement? She wondered what Zoe and Lucky were doing. Had they fled? But where would they go?

The men marched them to the prow of the boat where Max was standing, leaning against the handrail, smoking a cigar. He turned to face them, a look of amused admiration on his face.

"I must congratulate you both," he said. "It seems that whatever I do to keep you tied up, you manage to break free. You should consider careers as escape artists. You could join a circus."

"Where are you taking us?" demanded Dan.

"Well, that depends," said Max. "I have a few choices." He took a long drag on his cigar and blew the smoke out across the sea. "I could take you to Amsterdam with me, or I could throw you overboard now. We're about three quarters of a mile from the coast. How good is your swimming?" He laughed. "Or I could have you shot. Feed you to the fish. Why don't you choose?"

Rose felt the fear inside her turning to hatred. He was playing with them, tormenting them. The guy had to be some kind of psychopath. The barrel of the gun pressed painfully into her back and the man holding her tightened his grip on her arm.

Max took a step towards them, but as he did the black clouds blotted out the remains of the sun. There was a sudden drop in air temperature followed immediately by a wind that caused the sea to churn. The yacht lurched to the side, throwing them all off balance. In that moment Dan spun around and swung his free arm at tattoo-face, knocking the gun from his grasp. Rose felt the grip on her arm loosen for a send and she ducked down. She heard an ear-splitting crack. She screamed. *Oh my God, the fat guy shot Dan!* Then something sharp hit her on the back of the head. It came again and again, like tiny daggers trying to penetrate her skull. It took her a moment to realise that she was being bombarded by hailstones. Huge, sharp lumps of ice were raining down out of the sky and the crack she had heard was not gunshot, but thunder. The sea heaved and boiled, tossing the boat around like a plastic toy. She was aware of Dan, a short distance away, grappling with tattoo-face who was trying to reach for his gun. Behind her, the fat guy was struggling to maintain his balance and Rose saw her chance. She reached out with both hands and grabbed his ankle, yanking it as hard as she could. He fell backwards, hitting his head on the deck with a sickening thud. The gun slid from his fingers and skidded towards the stern as a huge wave lifted the bow of the boat high into the air.

There was a flash of lightning followed almost instantaneously by a crack of thunder. The hailstones intensified, battering Rose on the top of her head and bouncing off the deck like marbles. The fat guy lay motionless, but Dan was still putting up a fight with tattoo-face. Rose started to crawl along the tilting deck towards them. Suddenly a boot stamped down on her hand and excruciating pain shot through her fingers.

"Not so fast, little lady!" She looked up to see Max towering above her, a gun aimed at her head. He grabbed hold of her upper arm and hauled her to her feet. The hailstones had drenched her to the skin and she was shaking uncontrollably. Her hand felt as if it had shattered into a thousand splinters.

"Get over there!" Twisting her arm behind her back, Max pushed her to the railing. *This is it,* thought Rose, staring down into the seething water. *He's going to shoot me and throw me overboard.* She felt the barrel of the gun against the back of her head. She thought of her mother, alone in the cottage. She thought of her grandmother. She could almost smell the lavender soap. She thought of Dan and Zoe and Lucky. Her own luck had run out, that was for sure. And yet she was still staring at the water, feeling the heave and tilt of the yacht. *What's he waiting for? Why hasn't he pulled the trigger yet?*

But something was holding him back. Rose dared to lift her gaze towards the land. The storm had reached the coast and a flash of lightning suddenly illuminated Highcliff House, standing alone and vulnerable on the edge of the cliff. The lightning was followed by a rumbling that was more than just thunder. It seemed to be coming from the ground itself, from deep within the bowels of the earth. And then the cliff upon which the asylum had stood for over a hundred years started to slide, imperceptibly at first, but then gaining in momentum. The earth groaned and the cliff tumbled into the sea, as weak and insubstantial as a sandcastle. Highcliff House abandoned itself to the waves and was lost forever.

Behind her, Max let out a cry of despair. *He's just lost his supply of cocaine,* thought Rose with a feeling of triumph. The thought made her bold. She swivelled round, hoping to throw him off balance, but then a giant shock wave hit the yacht. The boat lurched to the side, water sloshed over the hull and Rose felt her feet lose contact with the deck. She tried to grab hold of the railing but it slipped from her fingers. For a second she was flying through the air. Then she hit the water and the drag of the wave pulled her under. Everything went black.

CHAPTER FOURTEEN

The blackness was comforting, like velvet. Rose could stay there forever. But someone was calling her name and she became aware of the touch of a hand on her arm.

Rose, Rose, try and wake up darling.

She fluttered her eyelids open and immediately shut them again. The overhead light was unbearably bright. But the voice inside her head became even more excited.

Rose, you're awake. Oh, thank God!

She opened her eyes again, more cautiously this time. White-painted walls, overhead fluorescent lights, a familiar smell. She turned her head to the side and saw her mother, sitting there, dabbing her eyes with a handkerchief. Standing behind her mother was Zoe. Rose didn't recognise her at first because she'd undone her braids and was wearing her hair loose around her shoulders. It suited her better.

"Where am I?" asked Rose. Her voice came out in a tiny croak. She didn't feel like she had the energy to sit up.

"You're safe in hospital," said her mother.

"I'll go and find a doctor," said Zoe. "Tell them she's woken up."

"Thank you," said Andrea. She turned back to Rose.

There were tears in her eyes. "Oh Rose, I'm so glad you're awake. I was worried that…" Her voice trailed off and she suppressed a sob.

"What happened Mum? How did I get here? I know I was on a boat, and then…there was a storm. Everything went black."

"It's all right, sweetheart." Her mother patted her hand. "The boat capsized in the storm. Although what on earth you were doing on board…" She checked herself and said in a calmer tone, "A fisherman who knew about the boat setting sail alerted the coastguard who sent out the lifeboat." Andrea blew her nose. She was obviously quite choked up about the whole thing. "I'll be making the biggest donation to that lifeboat team," she added. "You could have drowned!"

I could have been shot, thought Rose, remembering Max and the gun, but she didn't say anything to her mother, fearing an hysterical outburst. Instead she said, "Did they…did they rescue anyone else from the sea?"

"I think there was one other," said Andrea. "I don't know who."

"There were five people on the boat," said Rose. *But only one other was worth rescuing.*

The door opened and Zoe returned with the doctor. "Good afternoon, Rose," said a woman in a white coat. "I'm Doctor Chandler and I'm in charge of your care. How are you feeling?"

"Um, OK, I think," said Rose. Every muscle in her body ached, her head throbbed and her right hand felt like a dead weight. But other than that she seemed to be all right. She was alive, at least.

"It will be a little while before you're fully recovered," said Doctor Chandler. She lifted Rose's wrist to check her pulse and then listened to her breathing through a stethoscope. "We'll keep you here for a day or two to check for signs of concussion, but after that you should be fine to go home."

Andrea had been smiling at her all the time the doctor was speaking, but at the words *go home* she looked away and a shadow passed across her face.

The doctor made some notes on a clipboard at the end of the bed. "Can I ask you something?" said Rose.

"Of course," said Doctor Chandler.

"The other person who was rescued. Do you know…?"

Doctor Chandler came and stood next to Rose. "A young man was rescued," she said. "Dan. The other…"

"Don't worry about the others," said Rose. Right then she didn't want to know. Dan was safe, that was all that mattered. She yawned.

"You should get some more sleep now," said the doctor. "Your body needs to recover."

Rose closed her eyes and drifted into a dreamless sleep.

~~~

It had been a bumper catch. The boat that came ashore that morning had caught as much fish as they normally caught in a week. And they were big fish too, as though they'd had extra food to feed on.

Walter carried the crates off the boat and stacked them on the quayside. Overhead the seagulls screeched and swooped, attracted by the smell of fresh fish. When he had brought the last crate ashore, he decided to take a walk along the beach. There was something he wanted to think about, or rather someone.

Mary.

Ever since he'd rescued her that day, he had thought of little else. She was like a breath of fresh air come into his dull existence. She had brightened their lives despite the tragic circumstances which had brought her to them. Ellie loved her like a sister, and he loved her like a man loves a woman. She had stayed in Scarborough looking for her friend Alice, but Alice had eluded them. Walter feared that
~~~

with nothing to keep her here, Mary would return home, and he didn't want that to happen. Not if she would agree to marry him. He would ask her this afternoon.

He was about to turn around and head for home when something caught his eye. Something black lying further up the beach. A piece of driftwood? Probably. He decided to check it out. Driftwood could be useful, once it had dried.

He quickened his pace and walked towards the thing lying on the sand. The closer he got the less it looked to him like driftwood. In fact, it looked like…

He started to run.

His legs wouldn't move fast enough. He could see clearly now. It was the body of a man.

He was lying face down in the sand, his ginger hair tangled with seaweed.

He turned the body over and blank eyes stared back at him. Dead.

~~~

Rose and Dan linked hands and walked across the sands, barefoot. It was the end of the season and the holidaymakers had dwindled to a trickle. September was fast approaching and a new school term, but for now they were determined to enjoy this last gasp of summer.

They'd both been out of hospital just over a week and were taking things slowly. Rose had two broken fingers from when Max had stamped on her hand. They were splinted together and wrapped in a white bandage. She had sustained a cut to her right temple which had been stitched. The stitches were due to come out in a few days but Rose feared she'd be left with a permanent mark. Dan had not fared much better. He'd swallowed so much water he'd almost drowned and he now had a scar on his cheek, but Rose thought it just made him look more rugged.

"What's going to happen to the amusement arcade?"
~~~

asked Rose.

"It's going up for sale," said Dan. "The estate agents were thrilled to get their hands on it. They think it will fetch quite a good price. But we're not going to be rich. Most of the money will go on dad's lawyer's fees.

"When does his case come up?"

"In a couple of months. He could go to prison." Dan's voice cracked when he spoke.

"I'm sorry," said Rose.

"The lawyer, Baker-Howard, thinks the judge might be lenient if Dad can prove that Max was blackmailing him into delivering the drugs. Max had lent him money to keep the business going and when Dad couldn't pay it back he forced him to get involved in the drugs smuggling business instead."

Rose shuddered at the mention of Max. The bodies of the Geordies had washed up the day after the boat capsized, but Max's whereabouts were a mystery. He had vanished into thin air. *Or sunk to the bottom of the sea with any luck,* thought Rose. The local papers were full of stories about how he had used the yacht to smuggle drugs into the country from Amsterdam and then laundered the money through the fairground.

"What will you and your mum do?" she asked.

"We're selling the house. Mum's decided we'd be better off living somewhere more modest. She's training to become a massage and beauty therapist at the spa where she used to go herself." Dan fell silent. He stopped walking and turned to look at Rose. "When are you going back to London?" His voice sounded flat. "I'm going to miss you."

"Well, that's the thing," said Rose, grinning. She had been bursting to tell him her news ever since they'd set out, but had wanted to ask him about his dad first. "Whilst we were in hospital, Mum heard that her job had fallen through."

"Is that good news?" asked Dan, looking confused.

"Why are you smiling like that?"

"Well," said Rose. "Mum has decided that we're going to stay on in Scarborough. We're going to keep Gran's house and live there. We can earn a lot of money from renting out the house in London and Mum has already found some work as a legal secretary in a local firm."

Dan stared at her in disbelief. "That's fantastic!" He lifted her off the sand and swung her round in the air. Then he put her down gently, holding her close. Their lips met in a kiss as the waves lapped around their feet.

~~~

Mary was scrubbing the kitchen floor when Ellie rushed in, breathless.

"This just came for you," she said, holding out a rather crumpled letter.

Mary stood up and took the letter from Ellie's trembling hands.

"It has a foreign stamp on it," said Ellie. "Look." She pointed at the unfamiliar stamp in the corner. The letter was addressed to Mary Brewer, care of Mrs Goodley at the Grand Hotel, Scarborough. Mary recognised the handwriting immediately. A momentary faintness came over her and she reached for the nearest chair and sank onto it. Then she tore the letter open, pulled out the piece of paper that was inside and started to read.

Amsterdam,
10th September, 1899

Dearest Mary,

I hope this letter reaches you. I am sending it to Mrs Goodley at the Grand Hotel in the hope that she will know where to find you. I want you to know that I am safe and well in Amsterdam, being looked after by Jackson and Kitty. They were married a few days ago
~~~

and are both very happy.

How I came to be here is a long story, and one that I will tell you in person when I next see you. If George is still waiting for me, please tell him that I will be travelling back to England shortly and that if he still wishes to marry me then I still wish to marry him.

Mary, you have been a good friend to me, the best I've ever had. I enjoyed our trip to Scarborough more than anything, even though it ended so badly. But I do not want to dwell on past misfortunes. I believe that we make our own luck in this world and from now on I intend to do just that.

I hope to see you again soon. Until then, be happy in all that you do and I wish you all the very best for the future.

Your loving friend,

Alice

ACKNOWLEDGEMENTS

My heartfelt thanks to my proofreader Josie who helped weed out the typos. And special thanks, as always, to Steve for his critical input and unwavering support.

ABOUT THE AUTHOR

Margarita Morris was born in Harrogate, North Yorkshire. She studied Modern Languages at Jesus College, Oxford and worked in computing for eleven years. She lives in Oxfordshire with her husband and two sons.

OTHER BOOKS BY MARGARITA

SCARBOROUGH BALL

A party should be fun.
Not a matter of life and death.

ORANGES FOR CHRISTMAS

Berlin 1961. The War is over.
But the fight for freedom has only just begun.

THE SLEEPING ANGEL

Something is astir in Highgate Cemetery.
The dead want justice and so do the living.

FIND MARGARITA ONLINE

Website:
http://margaritamorris.com

Facebook:
https://www.facebook.com/margaritamorrisauthor

Twitter:
https://twitter.com/MargaritaMorris

Made in the USA
Columbia, SC
19 March 2019